Happily Ever After

Jenn Faulk

DEDICATION

To Connor. Sometimes little brothers get to be the biggest heroes.

CONTENTS

For I am sure that neither death nor life, nor angels nor rulers, nor things present nor things to come, nor powers, nor height nor depth, nor anything else in all creation, will be able to separate us from the love of God in Christ Jesus our Lord.
Romans 8: 38, 39

YOUTH CAMP

It had been the most amazing week of her life. Thus far, at least.

At seventeen, Cammie Evans was a girl with a profound calling. She'd given Jesus her heart at six, had given Him every choice since then, and had, just that week at her last summer of youth camp ever, given Him the future.

She'd gone forward one night after a foreign missions presentation, committing the rest of her life to service overseas.

It hadn't been the first time she'd heard about going to the nations. She'd grown up in one of the biggest churches in the convention, New Life-Dallas, where missionary speakers were familiar faces, the stories they told were thrilling, and the plea at the end of their services was one she could very nearly recite from memory.

She'd heard it before. It hadn't ever spoken to her quite like it did that week at youth camp, though.

For the first time ever, Cammie had heard something different in what was a standard foreign missions presentation. People in a small country she'd never heard of dying without Jesus. The fields being ready for harvest but the workers being few. The authority of Christ, as He called His people to go and make disciples, His command clear as delivered there in the hot summer heat, where teenagers were distracted, sponsors were exhausted, and Cammie's heart burned within her.

Because she heard it. *Really* heard it.

The words were personal, the instructions were implicit, and the call was clear. She believed it, she was moved by it, and she gave her life to it.

Foreign missions. Her whole life given overseas. It was thrilling, embracing this as a reality.

And what made it even more thrilling was the cute guy from Cabin #3 who was similarly called to missions right after the very same presentation. How well had that worked out, right? Cammie had been ecstatic about it, seeing the same excitement in his eyes as they'd both gone forward... noting the smile he'd given her so many times since then. They'd spent every evening after the service talking about what God was doing in their lives and marveling that He was doing the same thing in them both.

Jeremy Fulton. Missionary in the making. Sigh.

Cammie could see it now. They would end up together, of course. Promises made during the short week at camp would lead to something substantial, something real, just a few weeks from then, a lifetime ahead...

Meeting up on weekends home from college. Or even better, going to college together! Seminary, barely scraping by together. Appointment with the mission board. A house in a jungle somewhere. An apartment in a bustling city. Somewhere, together, married and happy. And babies. Loads of babies. Born quickly, one right after another, the whole family a missionary team.

Her happily ever after.

Oh, Lord, let it be. Cammie prayed it again and again, even as she made her way to Jeremy that night.

She had plans to meet him between rec time and dinner, and as she let her mind go wild with all the possibilities that were surely waiting for them just beyond youth camp, she didn't hear the squeaky voice until it was right over her shoulder.

"Cammie! Hey, Cammie, wait up!"

She turned to see who was there and barely refrained from rolling her eyes.

David Connor.

Ugh.

He'd been like her shadow all week. She knew him from church, where his father was the senior pastor. Of the thousands of church members there at youth camp that David could have picked to annoy most regularly, though, he picked Cammie. She was good friends with his sisters, and while he'd been annoying and a nuisance of grand proportions for the majority of her life, he'd gone a step beyond normal those past few months and that past week in particular.

He'd probably finally hit puberty and had a crush on her. Was probably already imagining them together.

Ugh. As if.

Sure enough, as soon as he had her attention, he crossed his scrawny arms over his sweaty t-shirt and said, "What's up, Cammie?" with a bizarre head nod, the annoying twang of his voice even worse than normal.

Oh, good grief. Was this his impression of smooth? Jeremy Fulton was worlds beyond this. Because Jeremy Fulton loved the Lord, because he had a heart for the world, and because he was a whole foot taller than David Connor and not a fraction as smelly.

"David, why are you that sweaty?," she asked, looking down at him and visibly crinkling her nose when she saw the massive sweat stains barely hidden underneath his pitiful biceps.

"Oh, you know," he said, trying to make his voice sound deeper… and failing. "From playing some basketball with the guys. Got recruited to play with the older guys. Those dudes are in eleventh grade, Cammie."

"And what grade are you in?," she asked, knowing the answer but wanting to hear him say it on the off-chance that he would be shamed by his age and would stop trying to act older than he was.

"Going into tenth," he said, not shamed in the slightest. "I'm fifteen. Going to get my license this year. Can take you out on a date, you know… well, if you've got a license. Because I can't legally drive without another driver in the car until my birthday."

"Oh, no," she barely managed, momentarily stunned by this. David Connor. Assuming that she would want to go on a date with him. Not in this universe, not any time in all of eternity --

"No license, huh?," he sighed. "Well, we can wait until I'm sixteen --"

"Oh, no, I've got a license," she said, correcting him on this point.

"Cool," he said, smiling, his voice squeaking as he was obviously getting very excited, thinking that a license meant she would be seen in public with him. "So, I can pick you up, take you out just as soon as –"

"Oh, no, you little weirdo," she said, intent on straightening him out. "We're not going out. Like, ever, David. In fact, we won't even be seeing each other after this week. I'm leaving for college."

He looked disappointed at this. "Really?"

"Yeah. Really."

"But it's only the first week of August," he protested, frowning.

"Moving into the dorm early," she muttered. She looked around again for Jeremy. Any moment now, he'd be out here, looking for her, ready to promise her the future she'd been hoping for, ready to be the guy she'd been dreaming of, ready to be her happily ever after –

"Why do you keep looking around, Cammie?"

She kept looking, tossing discarded words David's direction. "I'm looking for someone. And it's none of your business."

"Who are you looking for?"

The little doofus just wouldn't take a hint.

"Good grief, David," she sighed. "Don't you have somewhere to be?"

"No," he said, smiling. "Got someone else to take care of clean up duty in the cabin for me. Paid him twenty bucks."

She glanced at him. "Why would you do that? Do you hate clean up duty that much?"

"No, I did it so I could walk you to dinner. Maybe sit with you in worship later tonight."

A mental image of David with his scrawny arm around her popped into her mind.

No way.

"I already have someone who I'm going to sit with."

"Charity? Hope?" His sisters, her best friends. But no.

"No. Jeremy Fulton," she said.

He looked confused. "Why would you want to sit with him?"

She gave him a knowing look. "Because."

This seemed to wound him. "Oh."

And just when she was sure he'd been silenced (at last), he added, with a shrug, "Well, tomorrow morning we can sit together then, huh?"

She shook her head at his persistence. "No, David. Go away, David. Good bye, David."

"Cammie," he said, almost desperate now, "Jeremy's really not a serious guy, you know."

She frowned at this, at even the suggestion that her future could be anything less than perfect. "What?"

"Well," he said, "I mean, I get that you like him probably. Most of the girls here do."

They did. Cammie had noticed that, how he'd spent most of the camp with a swarm of girls around him.

But she was different. He felt something real for her, of course.

David kept right on talking. "He's just not all that serious about Jesus. You know?"

"Plenty serious," Cammie said. "Called to missions, just this week. Just like me."

David's eyes grew round at this. "Really? Is that why you went down to the front during the invitation on Monday night?"

"Yeah," she said. "And that's why Jeremy did, too. Called to foreign missions. So he's got it together, you know —"

"Really?," David asked. "You're called to missions?"

"That's what I said," she offered, glancing around again.

"Wow," David said. "That's wonderful, Cammie. I can see you doing that. You'll be perfect for it."

And Cammie gave him another look, puzzled by these affirming words that sounded eerily like wisdom, coming from her best friends' smelly kid brother.

"Uh... thanks," she murmured.

David nodded. "It's great about you, of course. But Jeremy Fulton..." He shook his head and raised his eyebrows. "Just because he's going into missions doesn't mean you should spend all of your time with him, you know."

"I'm not spending all of my time with him," she said irritably. "And if I am? So what? Maybe God intends it, you know." She smiled at the thought. "Intends for him and me to fall madly in love with one another."

"That can't be," David said, shaking his head.

"Oh? And why not?"

"Because."

"Because why, David?," she asked, getting a headache the longer the little snot kept talking.

"Because God already told me that you're going to marry me."

She frowned at this. He simply smiled.

Oh, the very thought. Horrific.

"Shut up."

"Okay, so maybe He didn't –"

"Goodbye, David."

And she left him standing there with his mouth hanging open.

THE STATES

Ten Years Later

Cammie

"And that was that," Camille sighed, finishing the last bite on her plate, then pushing it to the center of the table.

She was amazed she'd been able to eat so quickly, given how much she'd been talking.

Her sister, Chelsea, however, wasn't even halfway done with her own meal. But that had more to do with the baby she'd been nursing practically since they sat down. She only just now had Avery back on her shoulder, coaxing a burp from her as her own meal grew cold in front of her.

"And that was that?," Chelsea sighed, the question in her voice.

"Yeah," Camille nodded. "Hey, give her to me so you can eat." She reached out for the tiny little bundle, her heart clenching at the sweet smell of the baby shampoo as Avery turned towards her. As she nestled her niece close to her shoulder, she smiled at how the baby put her tiny fist on her aunt's chest, content to hear her heartbeat.

Such sweetness. It made the conversation even more bittersweet.

"Oh, Cammie, I really thought this one might work out," Chelsea said sadly, picking up her fork and going back to her food. "He seemed so serious."

He had seemed that way. He really had. She'd thought just last week that he was as serious as she was about calling, about going, about being sent... but only a few dates in, it had become apparent that he wasn't very serious at all. She was sure that he probably had a very fruitful and meaningful ministry here in the US, but as far as calling went to go to the nations, he had no desire to go anywhere.

Most men didn't.

She understood it... in part, at least. When she finished college, she'd gone directly to the mission field for a one year term in Brazil. She'd been single, of course, but she remembered not being bothered much by this because the rest of her life was still in front of her. Plenty of time for romance, for marriage, for babies. At the end of her term, she'd come back, spent six months in transition, hoping that she'd meet someone at the seminary as she prepared for the next term...

... and nothing. She signed on for two years in Russia and was gone before the US had become normal to her again. She'd been single, of course, but she remembered counting two years as not very long at all. She would be back stateside, still with plenty of time for marriage and a family, and her whole life ahead of her.

And nothing. Another trip back to the US, another transition, another two year term.

She'd been single, of course.

That last two year stint in Japan had convinced her of a few things. That calling was better than romance, most definitely. That she really didn't need a man. That she could live the rest of her life without children.

She'd met a man, though. Of all things during this transition, she'd met a man. He said the right things, lived the right way, and was immersed in the right kind of ministry in the US. She'd begun to think that God was finally giving her what she'd been too ashamed to pray for all those years on the different mission fields.

Love. A husband. A family.

And she could have had it, she knew. But Jason had no call overseas, so she would have had to forfeit her own calling, her own passion, to meet his.

It wasn't worth it... was it?

She sighed and smiled at Chelsea. "It's okay. I can just love on your children. When I'm home, that is."

"You're not home enough," Chelsea began. "And it —"

"Hey, Chelsea." Camille glanced up at the cute guy holding two dessert samplers out to their table. "Thought I'd bring these by since you're almost finished."

Chelsea smiled at him. "Thank you, Grant. Do you remember my sister, Camille?"

"Sure do," he said. "How's Japan?"

"Wonderful," she said, sincerely meaning this. She'd hoped to be sent back to Tokyo, had considered going career status for a seven year term, but had backed out at the last minute. Seven years was a long time. And signing up single in a career capacity felt like giving up any last dream she had of ever meeting anyone. "Back for just a while. Then, onto what's next."

"Well, I hope you enjoy your time in the US," he said. "Chelsea, it's all on the house."

And before Chelsea could thank him for his generosity, he was making his way back to the kitchen.

"Why," Camille said, watching him leave as she kissed her niece's head, "didn't you ever fix me up with him?"

Chelsea frowned. "I tried, Cammie," she said. "Do you not remember?"

She did... vaguely. She'd resisted her sister's attempts to fix her up with this successful, godly guy, her husband's best friend, because he clearly wasn't going overseas.

Maybe she was being too picky, huh? Maybe it was...

"Too late now," Chelsea sighed. "He's married."

"Ugh," Camille groaned. "Who isn't?"

"You know," Chelsea noted, "there's nothing to say that God can't bring you someone on the mission field, Cammie. That as you're being obedient to what He's called you to that He won't bring someone right to you. Or bring you right to someone."

"It doesn't matter anyway," Camille murmured. "Life is about more than men. I've lasted this long without a man, and —"

"You're only twenty-seven," Chelsea reminded her.

"Only," Camille sighed. "How many children did you have by the time you were my age, Chels?"

"Two," Chelsea said quietly. "And my husband was dying of cancer. And I had no job and no way to take care of my family. But you, you have nothing but a bright future ahead of you, with your degree, with your exciting career –"

"And you have it all," Camille noted, looking back down at the infant. "God worked it out. You got a job, you remarried, you started having even more babies."

Chelsea watched her for a moment. "Different callings for all of us, I guess." Then, more quietly, "But saying yes to God doesn't mean you say no to everything else. Maybe Jason was just –"

"Not the right guy," Camille confirmed. "Even if he had been called... he just wasn't right. I need to just do what God has for me to do and not worry about things that don't really matter."

Chelsea nodded quietly at this. "Where is your new position? How long are you going this time?"

"Three years," Camille said, struggling for a smile. She'd be thirty when she returned. "Another temporary position....then maybe I'll finally go career, huh?"

"Is it Japan?," Chelsea asked, studying her sister.

"Oh, no, they assigned me to something totally different," Camille shook her head. "They're sending me to some place in Africa. A country called Namibia."

David

David Connor shut the vents off in the car not even two minutes into the drive.

Why were Americans always using so much AC, anyway? The buildings were like ice boxes, and the cars they drove were freezing.

He hadn't remembered this about home. Three years overseas hadn't erased memories and the very foundational elements of his heart, mind, and soul, but they'd done a number on how he remembered common, every day things. He'd already nearly had a wreck, so unaccustomed after just a few years to driving on the other side of the road.

This is why he was the passenger on this car ride. That and Paul Connor rarely let anyone else take the wheel in his presence.

"Cold, son?"

David glanced over at his father, noting the slight smile on the older man's face. "Older" almost felt like a subjective thing in this case. David could confirm, without any doubt, that he was Paul Connor's son. He'd tried to grow out a goatee his first semester away at college and had shaved it off immediately when, at parents' weekend, his mother, there in pearls, heels, and a dress so expensive that it could have paid the tuition for the semester (had he not been given a full ride based on his parentage alone), had put her hand to his face and murmured, "Mercy, David Paul... you're like the second coming of your father."

Yes. They would all be in need of divine mercy of the highest sort if there was a second coming of Paul Connor. David had been clean shaven ever since, but the resemblance was still there. But he looked more like Paul Connor's younger brother than his son, given the way the election committee had obviously taken care of the gray in Paul's hair and beard. Distinguished was a good look for traditional convention presidents, but Paul wasn't going to be their traditional guy.

He was going to be the guy to change it all.

David was glad he would be overseas and wouldn't have to witness any of it. His sister, Hope, had filled him in on the details the night before as they'd sat around the kitchen in the home they'd grown up in, eating cereal at 3am while David had shivered just slightly, still jet lagged and freezing.

Air conditioning. Sixty degrees below everywhere he went. Why had it not bothered him before?

"Yeah," he said, finally answering Paul's question. "I'm going to come down with pneumonia with the constant changes from heat to cold."

"No time to be sick," Paul declared.

David knew that. Had always known it. A childhood spent as a VIP to the church's pastor, a lifetime spent as an accessory to the high profile pastoral couple, and now... well, now an important man by his own right.

David Connor. Missionary for the board. The youngest ever appointed in a career capacity. He'd come home for the first time in three years to share wisdom from the field at a regional recruitment meeting focusing on high school students. He'd gone to one just like it years ago when he was finishing up his senior year of high school and looking towards college, and every choice he'd made since had been towards the mission field, towards youth ministry, and towards reaching a new generation for Christ, wherever he was sent.

He could well remember being the age of the students who would be there that weekend, largely thanks to the students he worked with overseas even now, who were a constant reminder of what his teenage years had been like, how he'd never been spectacular in any sense of the word, how Christ had shown Himself to be constant and true even in light of this, and how God had shown Himself to be able to work through even the least of these.

Even David Connor, son of the most powerful man in the convention, but just another guy half a world away, speaking simple truths about life and faith, watching as God did the work of changing eternities.

"Busy weekend ahead," David noted, thinking of the schedule he'd been emailed weeks ago, along with flight information, which had him arriving in Dallas two days early, at the special request of Paul Connor.

David had been glad for it, though, even if his father was still just as intimidating as he'd grown to be during those years of change at New Life-Dallas. His children had been teenagers when the church membership had multiplied exponentially, and as they had spent those difficult years watching one drama after another unfold at church because of their father's strong-fisted leadership, they'd seen life at home change as well.

David could well remember the evening dinners, as a family, that his mother had insisted on, no matter what changed in their lives. Paul Connor would come in the door on time, drop his briefcase and his phone on the couch, and visibly pause there for a moment, leaving the church and all of its troubles there, then come to the table. Charity would talk all of their ears off about cheerleading and drill team. Hope would offer the occasional odd commentary on whatever book they were studying in her English class. Phoebe would talk about the different things they had on the calendar, expertly steering clear of the church obligations, making a life for them all apart from the church.

Paul would watch them all with an amused grin, his face visibly older from the stress of his life in the office, which always seemed to come back home with him, no matter how hard he tried to leave it and no matter how hard the women in the family tried to pretend like he had. When the ladies were just getting started on *really* talking, he'd turn to his son and say, "What about you, David Paul? What have you got going on?"

And David would look up from the perfect gourmet meal his mother had prepared, shrug, and say, very simply and very honestly, "Just Bible study. And discipleship group. And youth praise band. I practically live at New Life, Dad."

All three women would look back at him, at this mention of church, then glance back at Paul, waiting to see him pick up the mantle of the pastorate, along with all of its stresses.

But he would always smile and say, "Lord help us, David Paul. We all do, don't we?"

The talk at the dinner table would always move to spiritual matters, as Paul took his role as shepherd to his family seriously, as he taught them Scripture and its place in their lives. He was there for each of the girls in the way that best befit them. To Charity, encouragement for the gifts she was given and nudging towards the role she was likely to play one day. A wife and a mother, given her affinity for and popularity with the opposite sex (David could very nearly hear Phoebe draw in a concerned breath and mutter a prayer at this) and her natural way with children. To Hope, straight up honesty about what she was made to do. Ministry, full-time, in some capacity, and wasn't it a shame that she wasn't a boy because even at seventeen she could exposit the Scriptures like a well seasoned theologian. (Although she was an odd duck socially speaking and had Phoebe regularly, yes, drawing in a concerned breath and muttering up a prayer at social functions.)

And to David Paul, the prized only son...

Well, David would end up doing something, surely. The awkward, immature boy hadn't been fit for much except being there for every single event the youth ministry of the church put on, soaking in more than anyone would have suspected a boy his age could, and finding his significance not in what he could do for the Lord but in what the Lord had done for him.

There was the real prize. A genuine faith, born of a genuine heart.

Paul Connor had finally seen this in his son, just as David was coming of age, was growing into his own man with his own calling, and he'd taken him under his wing, just as David had expressed a calling to ministry.

But it ended up being a calling to the foreign mission field, not to the pastorate. What a surprise for them all.

David would never forget Paul's words to this, there in the pastor's office, when he'd told him what was ahead.

What a waste.

Not that Paul hated the nations or despised Christ's call to them. But he'd obviously grown to see something of significance in his son, after so many years of wishing it and believing it wasn't going to happen, only to have his hopes for a future ministry dynasty at New Life-Dallas all but dashed to pieces.

Paul's work, apart from his hopes for his son, had only gotten harder for him, harder for them all, in those last few years David had still been stateside. He'd come home from college to find that the church was stable again, that the leadership was moving forward with all the changes had brought, and that life was good at New Life-Dallas.

The difficulty had become the convention.

A man couldn't do what Paul Connor had done at New Life-Dallas without creating a stir seen and heard of, far and wide. As David was preparing for a future on the mission field, the convention was preparing Paul for a campaign, backed by the sizable and influential New Life-Dallas and the Texas arm of the convention.

He was going to be the next president of the convention. It would be a mess, electing him, because he was so conservative, theologically speaking. David could well imagine the infighting and politics that would be involved in the election, especially with his father at the helm, almost encouraging it with his smug grin.

As Paul had once told him, "The convention is shifting to the left. It needs a jerk to the right. And I, David Paul? Am that jerk."

He was right about that. But David would be back overseas and wouldn't have to witness any of the drama involved.

"Busy weekend," Paul repeated even then, as he pulled into a parking space at last, looking over at David. "Your mother and I wanted to come and hear you give the keynote address on Saturday night. But the convention's booked us for something."

David nodded at this, touched despite himself that they'd wanted to hear him speak. Not such a waste after all, if they were that proud of him. "Well, you've heard the stories already. Still get my newsletter from the field."

"We do," Paul said. "Your mother ferries it around to every Sunday school class in the building. You've got thousands of people at New Life who love you as their own, David Paul." He watched his son for a long moment. "Which is part of what I wanted to talk to you about today. Let's go get some grub."

And before David could ask what he meant, Paul was out of the car and making his way into the steakhouse. David hurried to keep up with him.

"Thought we were just going to eat," he said. "Catch up a little."

"Never go out and eat just to catch up," Paul said. "Eating's for big meetings, you know. Especially over steaks. For getting things done. Getting things decided. Hope and I solve half the world's problems every time we meet up for steak."

David could well imagine it, thinking of Paul Connor and his feminine progeny banging their fists on the table and loudly putting everything in its place.

"What problems are we solving today?," David asked.

Paul smiled at this, striding into the restaurant. "Mine, David. You're going to solve mine. And you should probably tell that to our guests."

"Guests? Aren't we eating alone?"

"No," Paul said, stepping up to a table already occupied by two older men who stood as they saw him. "David, you remember Hollis McGregor and Stan Ellis."

He did. They'd been deacons at New Life-Dallas since the day Jesus had resurrected from the dead. Or at least it felt like they'd been around that long.

"I remember," he said, holding out his hand. "Good to see you gentlemen."

"Welcome back from Africa," Stan said, smiling, returning his handshake. "Your mother keeps us all well informed about all the wonderful work you're doing there."

"What's the name of that country again?," Hollis asked. "Nambibia? Or was it Nambia?"

"It's Namibia," David said, looking to his father again. "Southwest corner of Africa."

"Youth ministry, gentlemen," Paul said, smiling with a twinkle in his eyes. "My David is the only missionary there, working with an entire city full of teenagers, all by himself."

"Pioneer missionary, then?," Stan asked as all four men sat at the table. "First one on the ground, so to speak?"

"Well," David said, wondering at his father's earlier words about how he was here to solve problems, imagining what kind of problems those could be with the world's two oldest deacons present here, "I'm actually not the first. There was a couple there before me. For decades, actually. They retired before I went onto the field."

"Back in the States, then?," Stan asked. "This couple?"

David nodded. "I'm guessing. I've never been in touch with them."

Paul raised an eyebrow at this, still smiling. "That's odd. Isn't it?"

For a few seconds, David thought back to his introduction to the field so long ago, how his national friend, Piet, had mentioned these former missionaries in passing very briefly, and how his American girlfriend, Kait, had told him how she, too, had once worked for the board. She'd come to Namibia to help them retire, to close out the board's trusts there, and had just never moved on herself.

David was the only one from the board there now, building on a foundation set decades before by missionaries he'd never once been encouraged to call or communicate with regarding all that they could've taught him.

He hadn't thought it odd until now.

"They just moved on," he said to his father. "No sense in having me bother them when they're just trying to enjoy retirement."

"Something's not quite right there," Paul said simply, putting on a frown for this. "There should be some connection between the past and the present there, if the board really cared about the future of the ministry in Namibia." And even in his disapproval, David saw some delight in this, that there was indeed something not quite right in it all.

Of course.

Because even if Paul could appreciate the efforts on the foreign mission field, the calling overseas was still a waste for his own son, who could better be used for his purposes here at home.

And David suddenly figured out just why he was probably meeting with the deacons today.

Before he could speak to it, there were drinks to order, meals to order, and pleasantries to make. Inquiries about the rest of the family, all of them come into town for a couple of days to see David, of course.

Charity and her husband, John, pastoring a church out in west Texas, back in DFW with David's nephew with them, Charity expecting his soon-to-arrive niece in another few months.

Hope, still living at home and finishing up another post-graduate degree at the seminary, all while helping her father in the endeavors he had at church and giving her time to a job at an inner-city missions organization.

Phoebe and Paul, ever the same, just busier now with New Life-Dallas and the convention keeping them that way.

"And you, David," Hollis said, smiling at him, just as the food was delivered quickly (VIPs and all) and the blessing was said over it. "Well-seasoned now in the youth ministry. Hard experience won in that small church you served at in college. And now on the mission field. I would have thought the son of our future convention president would have pulled some strings to get more comfortable experience, quite honestly. But you're a self-made man, and we appreciate that about you."

Self-made man. Poor man, actually. David had found a small church during college where the membership was old enough to not know why the name Connor meant anything in the world of big churches and conventional matters. They'd let him come in to work for free as their "youth intern," and he'd taken the non-existent student ministry from a middle-aged couple who taught Sunday school for the occasional teenager who'd come to church to a huge ministry to over one hundred students. He'd gone into the schools in his free time, giving guitar lessons as an after-school elective, and he'd formed friendships, mentoring relationships, and made himself available. Students got to know him, looked up to him, and heard the words of life he shared. Before that little church could make the connection that this Connor was related to another Connor who had done for a dying church in Dallas what others had said was hopeless... well, David had become a legitimate pastor, shepherding a flock of young people who brought their friends, who became disciples then disciplers, and who went to college with hearts for ministry, just like David himself had done.

When graduation came, he left a booming program that had forever changed that small church for the better.

And Christ had forever changed him.

They'd never paid David a dime, but he couldn't have cared less. He was paid in lives changed, in seeing the fruit of seeds sown, and knowing that God had His hand on his life.

When he began looking for opportunities on the mission field where he could do likewise, he'd been contacted by a woman on the field in Africa with former ties to the board. Kait, of course.

She told him about a place he could come to, where teens were waiting even that very moment to know Christ, where he could set his own course, and where lives could be changed for generations, altering an entire nation. Though she needn't have worked so hard to convince him, she put her all into it, giving him information about the field, setting up correspondence between him and Piet, who had his own ministry as a medic traveling the country, and getting David back in touch with the board, where they offered him the position as a career missionary.

Where he still made next to nothing. Because, as Kait said, that was just part of the deal with the board and their interest in Namibia.

No matter, though. It had all been done on his own. Not because he was a Connor, not because of his father.

A self-made man.

"Yes, sir," David said, nodding at this. "I love what I do."

"That's what we were hoping to hear," Stan said, glancing over at Paul. "We have a proposition for you, David."

And here it was. David readied himself.

"A proposition?," he asked. "Is New Life-Dallas wanting to send a team out to Namibia to help? Because I could sure use it."

Not likely. He'd said it in jest, to affirm his fidelity to his current situation, but it caught the two deacons off guard.

Paul simply smiled at his son, knowing just what David was up to.

"Well," Hollis said, "not really. It's just that --"

"We've got a problem, David," Paul said, his man-to-man voice out. "A big ol' problem at New Life."

David refrained from saying "again?" and went with the more appropriate response of, "What seems to be the problem?"

"The in-fighting is done," Stan said simply. "Was over a long time ago. When your father brought the church back to a more conservative stance, he stood strong and the in-fighting stopped." He glanced over at Hollis.

"But now," Hollis said, "with his increased duties with the convention and all that we know is ahead, there's room for people to come in and undo what's been done, you see."

David looked between the men, thinking, above all, that this all seemed so secondary to the main thing -- sharing the Gospel, discipling others, reaching the nations.

"And?," he asked, feeling bolder and bolder by the minute, simply because he didn't care about the politics or what was so clearly bothering these men.

"There could be issues," Stan said delicately. "People coming up and threatening all that your father worked so hard for. All that you certainly suffered through as his son, walking with him during all of that."

David thought of Paul, dropping his briefcase on the couch, and pausing for a long moment to leave his work at work... never succeeding.

He could see that. It had made a difference in their lives. But what did that have to do with him now?

"Let's just cut through the crap, gentlemen," Paul drawled, taking delicacy out and tossing it away like garbage. Classic Paul Connor. "David, Jay hates my guts now. I said some things about the inerrancy of Scripture. And he hates Scripture. And now? He'd like to turn half the church against me, if he could."

Jay. Jay Middleton. He was the long time student minister at New Life-Dallas. So long, in fact, that he'd been David's student minister. Charity and Hope's as well. He was in his fifties, had a family, teenage sons of his own now, and a long tenure at the church.

"Jay hates Scripture?," David asked, having a hard time believing this.

"Not all of it," Paul conceded. "But there are parts he'd like to ignore. Explain away. Tell everyone that they're not as important as other parts. But you know where that thinking gets you."

If all of Scripture wasn't true then none of it was. If Jesus couldn't be trusted with even one of His words, then none of His Words could be trusted, including those He'd said about who He was and what He'd come to do. The Gospel hinged on the inerrancy of Scripture, and if you didn't have that, you didn't have anything.

David knew that from all he'd been taught as a child, from all he himself had taught to others.

"That's a problem," he affirmed.

"Yes," Stan cut in. "And so we're looking to make some changes. Termination for Jay, likely, if we can find the right man to bring in to replace him. Someone the church will affirm unanimously, so that there won't be conflict when Jay is forced out."

David thought, with significant discomfort, of his student minister, a man who, despite his more liberal leanings, still had the good of the Gospel in his heart, who probably had no idea of what was going on here today.

"Dad," he said, looking over at Paul, "I get your concerns. But you just can't do that to a man who's faithfully served for so long. And served so well. Blindsiding him like that. It —"

"But I can do that," Paul said, shrugging. "And I will. The inerrancy of Scripture is a big deal, son. That, and he would have my own job if he could manage it."

"But why would --"

"David," Hollis interrupted. "Don't worry about Jay. He'll find something else. The main thing we want you to think about now is our offer."

"Offer?," David asked, his mind rushing. Then, stillness. And comprehension. "Oh, no..."

"The job is yours," Stan said. "Jay's salary, all of his benefits, with the added prestige of being named not solely the student minister of the largest church in Texas but also the associate pastor of that church. Second only to your father. Who, of course, would pass the pastorate on to you one day."

Paul smiled at his son.

David very nearly cringed.

"Really?," he asked. "This seems like a bad idea."

"The church loves you," Stan said. "There would be no argument as far as you're concerned. This kind of position would never normally go to a man your age with your limited experience. But you're David Paul Connor. And with you on staff..."

He looked to the other men, waiting for them to say it.

"Well, just go on," David said, knowing just exactly where this was going.

"David," Hollis spoke up, "with you on staff, there's going to be a shift in power at the church. Towards our purposes, of course, with keeping your father on in full force at the church, even with the convention responsibilities that will be on him as well. It'll be impossible, in other words, to vote your father out on anything with you standing there as the next in command."

"You're assuming I'd vote with him," David said, shooting Paul a look.

And at this? Paul laughed out loud. "Grew up finally, didn't you, David? Took three years in Africa, but I think you're finally the right man for the job."

"Yeah, I don't think so, Dad," he said, putting his napkin down on the table. "I thank you for your time, gentlemen, but I don't think I'm hungry anymore."

And with that, David committed a faux pas that would have shamed his mother plenty and left the table without being excused.

He was all the way to the lobby when his father finally caught up with him.

Paul Connor was laughing.

"That's the way to do it," he said. "Leave the negotiations like you're never coming back. Jay's salary package sucks. Make them offer you more."

David shook his head. "I don't know why it surprises me that you think that, Dad," he said, "but I'm still very nearly speechless. And I'm not leaving the work in Namibia."

"And it doesn't surprise me at all that you'd say that," Paul said, smiling at him, then sighing. "Can you blame me, though, for wanting my son by my side, ready to take over the pastorate one day?"

A vision of himself at the New Life-Dallas pulpit raced through David's mind.

"It's just not me," he said.

"You love Scripture, and you have a heart for the Lord," Paul murmured. "Don't limit yourself in what God might make you into for His purposes, David Paul."

David took in a breath at this, praying that he wouldn't become his father one day. Surely not...

"But you, in Namibia?," Paul shrugged. "Still good for what's going on. We can still make it work."

"What?," David asked, befuddled by this. "What do you mean --"

"I mean I support what you're doing," Paul said, still leaving many more things unsaid, likely. "And you'll forgive me for pushing my limits in this. We just miss you around here. That's all."

And that wasn't all, of course. But David accepted it.

"I know, Dad," he said.

"Come back and have lunch," he said. "No more talk of New Life and all that. Promise."

David watched him for a long moment, wondering if this was really it.

He'd be back in Namibia in a few days. What did it matter?

"Okay," he said softly, allowing himself to be led back to his father's table.

Cammie

The man on the elevator was sweaty.

It had been a full morning for Camille as she'd led a breakout session on short-term opportunities for a group of about two hundred teenagers. She'd talked about the different continents where she'd served, talked about the kind of work she'd done, and talked about how there were opportunities, even now, for them as teenagers to go and do summer trips, semester trips during college, and beyond.

Of the two hundred students there, three-fourths were guys. But she'd directed most of her message to the small percentage of girls there, knowing the ratios for the mission field, knowing that they were the ones who would likely end up going. Reality was that women went and men didn't, because men, who held the great majority of the church jobs stateside, were always given greater ministry opportunities closer to home. And clearly because men? Just weren't as spiritual as women.

Okay, so maybe she was a little unfairly biased about this.

She felt her unfair bias affirmed when most of the men present kept looking at her chest and her legs as she stood before them in a perfectly modest outfit, nearly none of her words likely even making it to their heads. Their big heads on their shoulders, that is.

She'd seen it before. Every place she went abroad she went to work with youth, and in every place, it had been the same. Boys. Always boys, wanting to hear what the pretty foreign woman had to say. And while she'd seen some lives changed in her work, even amongst those boys, it had been the girls who'd come with them whose lives she'd invested in most deeply, as was appropriate, of course. And it had been the girls who had been changed, who had found significance in Christ, who had become who He was calling them to be.

Her love for youth ministry had shifted to a love for girls' ministry, a calling to reach and disciple young women for the wonderful calling God had for them.

She'd been thinking about the young ladies she'd talked to after the session when she got on the elevator, hoping to make it up to her room in time to change clothes to something more casual for the time she'd be manning one of the missions tables during break time. She'd been looking through the list of names she'd gotten to pass along to the board when the sweaty man stepped onto the elevator behind her.

Seriously. He was disgusting.

Camille watched him from the corner of her eyes, wondering at how he'd managed to get himself so gross and disgusting, even as he rolled his neck from side to side, stretching... and humming a hymn underneath his breath in a deep, rich voice. As he continued on, unaware of the audience he had, she caught herself looking at the shape of his shoulders, the muscles in his arms, the way his tight abs constricted as he raised up part of his shirt to wipe the sweat from his face, still humming that hymn.

Not so gross and disgusting after all.

She snapped her eyes forward again. She was leaving for a new assignment in two weeks. Checking out random men on the elevator wasn't helpful. And how stupid was this anyway? She was as bad as those hormonal boys who kept looking at her chest even as she tried to share truths with them about the great purposes of God.

She moved away slightly and vowed to keep her eyes on the prize, so to speak. No sweaty, smelly men.

Except now the random man was looking at her. She glanced over at him. Then directed her eyes forward again. Another glance over at him.

Sure enough, he was grinning at her. Wow. Nice smile. Amazing eyes. And –

Not helpful, Camille.

The gorgeous stranger took a breath. "Well," he said slowly, his voice deep and full, an obvious twang to the way he drew out the word slowly. "Cammie."

She blinked at the name. She hadn't gone by Cammie since high school. "It's Camille," she said. A pause as he continued watching her, smiling. "I'm sorry… do we know each other?"

"Yeah," he nodded, grinning. "We do."

She waited for an explanation. He offered none, seeming to enjoy himself in this as he crossed his very built arms over his sweaty t-shirt. "What's up, Cammie?"

"Okay, so clearly you know me," she said a little impatiently. "But I don't think I've ever even met you."

"Oh, yeah, you have," he said, laughing. "But you don't recognize me. There's some sweet justice for you."

"What?" There was something familiar about him. She just couldn't place it…

"Imagine me a foot shorter. Seventy pounds lighter. Youth camp…" He raised his eyebrows at this.

She thought back to youth camp and could vaguely remember some idiot boy she'd had a crush on and had followed around the whole time, only to find him kissing some other girl their last night there…

Wow. Life was totally and completely unfair if *that* jerk had grown up to look *this* good.

"I followed you around youth camp," the gorgeous stranger kept on, waiting for her to recognize him.

Well. He wasn't that idiot boy, then. She'd been the one following that jerk around.

Had someone followed *her* that summer, though?

She looked at the stranger blankly.

"Wow, Cammie," he continued on. "How many of us followed you around that summer?"

She opened her mouth to respond to this... then shut it without offering an excuse.

"David Connor," he said with just a trace of disbelief. "I'm David Connor."

She could see him, short and pitiful looking in his basketball shorts and his ratty shirt, finding her crying just outside the worship center on the last night of camp. She could see him saying, *Aww, Cammie, I'm sorry. But you deserve better than that putz.* She could see him telling her really dumb jokes to make her laugh, until the worship service let out and she went back to her cabin, reaching out to mess up his hair as she passed by him, just like she'd done a thousand other times when they were kids.

David Connor. Glory. *This* was *David Connor.*

And just as the dots connected in her head, the elevator dinged.

"David," she barely managed.

"Cammie," he said.

"Camille," she offered weakly, surprised to find herself very flustered as he watched her.

"Camille," he nodded. A quick glance to her left hand. "Still Camille Evans, right?"

"Oh," she swallowed. "Yeah. Camille Evans." A pause. "And you're still David Connor?"

Oh, good grief, Cammie. Really?

He grinned at this and held up his left hand. No ring. "Yep. Still David Connor."

"Well," she said, beyond mortified, stepping off the elevator. "Good seeing you."

He took a step out with her. "You, too."

She began walking briskly to her room... and paused once she realized he was following her. He stopped when she stopped. She turned to face him, and he smiled at her.

"Hey... David," she muttered.

"Hey... Camille."

"Are you following me?"

He tried to suppress a grin. "Uh, no. Just trying to get back to my own room so that I can shower. But yeah, I can see why you'd think that since I spent most of my childhood following you around."

And how. As far as annoying little brothers went, David was the worst. Charity and Hope had called Camille their third twin, which had made David every bit her little brother as theirs.

Except he wasn't so little anymore. And he wasn't, she noted as her eyes trailed over him again, her brother.

Praise God.

Good grief. What was she even thinking?

"You just came from rec time, then, huh?," she asked, trying to think of anything but how good he looked all these years later.

Time had been very kind to David Connor.

"Yeah," he said. "Those teenagers are really showing me my age out there. I'm worn out."

"Oh, please," she said. "You're only... what? Twenty-two?"

"Twenty-five."

"So young," she sighed. "I remember twenty-five."

"As well you should," David said. "Since it was only a couple of years ago."

She frowned slightly at this. "And just how would you know that?"

"Charity and Hope," he said. "You all three celebrated birthdays together. Late August. And I've had to listen to them bemoan every single year since twenty-one."

"Hmm," Camille murmured, thinking of how long it had been since she'd celebrated much of anything with the twins. They'd gone on to college, all at different universities, then she'd gone off into the world. She'd missed them. "Are Charity and Hope here this week?"

He grinned. "No. Why would they be?"

"Well, if you're here with the rec team from your dad's church, maybe they came, too. A family affair and all."

A shadow fell over his face. "I guess I can see why you'd think that. That I'm working for my dad and all." And he continued walking down the hall.

She fell into step behind him, searching for her own room number, wondering at the change in his demeanor. And before she could question it too much, he stopped in front of the door on their right... which was across from her room on the left.

They both turned to each other to say goodbye, saw where they were each headed, and looked back at one another.

"Well," David said, grinning. "Looks like we're right across the hall from each other."

"Yeah," she said. "Guess that means I'll... probably see you again at some point this week."

He grinned even more. "Oh, yeah. I'll be seeing you again."

David

He closed the door behind him and exhaled deeply.

Cammie Evans.

Well, *Camille* now. And while Cammie Evans had been the star of every teenage dream he'd ever had with her sophisticated and classy seventeen year old style, he was quite certain that twenty-seven year old *Camille* was even more interesting.

She looked amazing. All these years later, and she still looked so amazing. And what was more, her attendance here this week suggested that she'd gone onto the mission field like she'd said she intended to do, all those years after youth camp.

This made her even more interesting.

He threw down his key and began kicking off his shoes. Even as he smiled, thinking of Camille and the way she'd looked him over with admiring surprise, he glanced at his watch and calculated the time. Middle of the night in Namibia. Oh, well.

Piet picked up on the third ring. "Neeeeee, man..."

"Goeie more to you, too, Piet," David answered. "Though it's not morning here."

"I was still asleep," he mumbled.

"Has Kait not called already and given you a long list of chores?," he said, thinking of the bossy American, standing there in Piet's cottage, her arms crossed over her chest, her red hair pinned up, even her frown demanding as she said *well, there are things to be done, you know.*

Piet was in love with her. David couldn't figure out why.

"She's not," Piet yawned. "She's been helping my mother get things ready for a new arrival."

"New arrival?," David asked. Then, with realization, "Did we finally get clearance for a short-term worker?"

They'd put in for someone six months ago, with little hope of having the request filled. The work had been successful enough that David found himself unable to do it all alone, especially as Kait and Piet were oftentimes consumed with their own work, sharing Christ at the medical clinics they did throughout the country. Kait had said there might be a chance that the board would send a short-term worker, even though it had been enough of a miracle that they'd sent David himself, given the size of Namibia and its small population.

Seems like there had been another miracle, though. Another worker. A helper for David. A new guy.

"Ja," Piet answered, glee in his voice. "Finally. The board is sending another one of you."

"Who is it?," David asked. "Did you get a name? I could look him up while I'm here."

"Kait did not get a name," he said. "Only said it will be another two weeks. You'll be back before the new guy arrives."

David barely refrained from pumping his fist in the air at this. Help. Someone to help. He could already start seeing all the work they could do, all that could be expanded, how many more teenagers could be reached, all because the new guy was coming.

"That's the best news I've heard all week," he said, thinking of how he'd turned down the job of a lifetime because it wasn't Namibia. Not *his* job of a lifetime but what any other man in his position would have coveted and gone for in a heartbeat.

This news felt like confirmation that God saw what he was doing, where his heart was, and that He was affirming the decision.

"It's good news," Piet confirmed.

"The best," David answered, grinning. "I can't wait to see what God's going to do in Namibia."

Cammie

David Connor.

Cammie had taken some time for herself in between the different duties assigned to her that afternoon, and she'd spent the majority of that "herself time" trying her best to forget that she'd seen David Connor.

He looked different, obviously. He seemed to know it as well, as his confidence as they'd said goodbye had suggested.

He'd always been like that, though. Even as a goofy, irritating kid, he'd always had more self-confidence than was warranted. Camille had never seen it as cocky, though. She'd seen it as joy, as genuine confidence in who he was in Christ.

She'd never thought much about it, honestly. Until, of course, she'd run into him on the elevator and spent the rest of the afternoon thinking through who he'd been as a kid, who she'd been, who they were now, and chiding herself for thinking anything either way.

Enough of that. She was tucking every single thought of David Connor and the past into a corner of her mind where she wouldn't be tempted to retrieve it. Why? Because she was going to the main session that night to hear from a career missionary. This? This was what she lived for, not for random meetings with a childhood annoyance who looked really hot, and --

Tuck it away, Cammie, she scolded herself, closing her eyes as the worship set concluded in the huge auditorium, just as all over the room teenagers were taking their seats, preparing to hear from the mission field, from the missionary.

No more thoughts of David Connor, she silently vowed as the conference director began speaking, heralding all the resume points of the missionary who was about to speak. She kept muttering prayers in her heart, hardly listening as he continued on with his introduction. Just as she finished, telling herself again to not think about David Connor, she directed her eyes to the stage set up in the front of the room...

...just as David Connor took to the pulpit.

For several seconds, Camille wondered if she'd wandered into the wrong room. Sure, the entire assembly from the conference was here, in large numbers, in full attendance, but wasn't there supposed to be a missionary speaking? David Connor was just from New Life-Dallas.

"Thanks for that great introduction," David said, grinning, looking over his shoulder at the man from the convention who had just spent a good five minutes heralding the praises of some foreign missionary.

Three years into life in Africa. Youth ministry. Hundreds of teenagers, won to Christ. Discipleship groups. Teens going home to the rural parts of their nation, sharing Christ with older generations. A whole culture coming to Jesus. A missionary on his own, all by himself, seeing it happen.

David Connor? Surely not.

David seemed to be having a hard time believing it as well as he continued smiling at the convention man. "And it was a great introduction," he said. "Though hearing it, I have to wonder if you were really talking about me."

You and me both, David, Camille thought.

"Because," David said, looking out at the sea of teenagers gathered before him, "I'm just the weird, nerdy kid from my church's youth group, who never really fit in anywhere or was anything special."

That was the truth. Camille could see him even now, a junior high kid going from youth event to youth event, always just a little out of place, still smiling and grinning, though.

Just as he was now, even as teenagers laughed a little at his description. "But Jesus saw something special in me," he said. "And He sees it in you, too. Each and every one of you."

For the next thirty minutes, Camille sat, stunned by the stories he told.

He began with Scripture, and she could hear the strong, conservative, unyielding theology of his father with every word... but softer, more compassionate, gentler, coming from him. Words about Jesus, about the absolute sovereignty, holiness, and power of Christ, about how He sought the least of these, beautifully expressed and delivered in David's soothing drawl, so different from the squeaky voice Camille had known better than she wanted to back then.

And then, he asked them. What then? If Christ says this, what difference does it make?

And he told them about where he was, never specifying the country, never naming the nation, but speaking in generalities, about people, about their hearts, about the longings everyone has on the most human level, for Christ. No matter where you went or what the story was, every person, at the basest level, was the same.

In need of significance. In need of redemption. In need of Christ.

No one knew it better than Camille, who had been so many different places and could affirm that beyond culture and circumstance, the human heart was the same, at its deepest level.

And as David spoke about seeing lives changed and an entire generation living for Christ somewhere on the African continent, Camille found herself wiping away tears. The stories. Wow, the stories. Lives being changed, a generation being moved to more, and a movement of God half a world away. It wasn't David's doing... but he was so much a part of it, as evidenced by the way he spoke about "his" students, that it was impossible to remove him from the situation and all that had gone on.

His heart, his passion, his calling... it all resonated with Camille, because it was so like her own. She connected with his stories and silently praised God that there was meaningful work being done in so many places, all over the world, by men and women set apart for His purposes.

As he prayed over the students there, she bowed her head, too, continuing to wipe at the tears that were all over her face now. It was an ugly cry, like Camille always cried when she heard about the nations, because what David had been sharing, what he'd built his life on, the sufficiency of Christ and His power to change lives? She was living the same reality.

And it cost something. Jesus was even more precious because it cost something to live for Him, the way she did, the way David did.

She only lifted her head long after his prayer was concluded and the convention man was again delivering announcements to the students.

And she sucked in a breath when, just down several seats from her and several rows in front of her, David Connor's eyes met hers.

And he grinned.

Well, he'd seen the ugly cry, then, as evidenced by the way he mimed wiping away tears as well. Had he been watching her the whole time? Little weirdo. Okay, so grown up and gorgeous weirdo.

Just as she was preparing to frown at him and mouth some choice words (just like she'd done on occasion as a teenager), he held up a finger, then pointed to where she sat.

Hey, Cammie, meet up with me after worship, okay? I mean, right where you're sitting and all. I'll come to you!

She could hear his squeaky voice even in the gesture.

Figuring she wouldn't get away from him since he knew where she was staying anyway (right across the hall from him, of course), she nodded and looked away again.

Ten minutes later, the hall had very nearly cleared out apart from the small group of students that were gathered around David, asking him questions. He was captivating them all with more stories, and Camille, with her hands in her lap, doodling in a notebook, was nonchalantly listening right along with them. She was amazed to find that she was disappointed when the last student left, wishing that she could hear even more about what God was doing on the other side of the world.

"Hey, Cammie."

Not the squeaky voice in her head. And not the boy he'd been, as she looked up at him, even as he was sliding into the seat next to her.

"I mean, Camille," he said, grinning as he corrected himself.

"Hey, David," she answered.

"Gotta tell you," he continued, still smiling, "that's the first time my preaching has ever brought someone to tears. Well, apart from my mother."

Camille thought of Phoebe, daintily wiping away tears at her son's words. No ugly crying on that perfect woman's part.

"Was it that poorly done?," he asked, laughing. "Was my handling of the Scripture so dismal that you were weeping on behalf of the Lord?"

"It wasn't that at all," she said, surprised that he'd jump to this conclusion. "I just... the stories. What you're doing. It's... I get it."

He watched her for a long silent moment, apparently taken aback by the sincerity in her words.

"So," he eventually said, "I'm not working at my dad's church."

"I got that," she said. "I mean, I didn't, when we ran into each other and I just assumed that's what you were doing."

"Most people do," he said, nodding and grinning again.

"You didn't correct me," she said, just a trace of annoyance in her voice. For his omission, for her assumption, for the crazy way her heart was pounding as he looked at her.

David Connor. Well, this was unexpected.

"Figured you'd figure it out on your own," he said, smiling.

"Yeah," she said. "David Paul Connor. Missionary to Africa. What in the world?"

"Who knew, right?," he said. "I can see why you thought what you did. But I've never worked at New Life. I've been on the field now for three years. Went straight out of college. Career appointment."

"How?," she couldn't keep from asking, thinking about how the board worked and how career appointment, with its greater benefits and better opportunities, only came after short-term assignments and their successful completion. "You're not old enough."

"They appointed me anyway," he said, shrugging. "How about you? I'm assuming since you're here that you went overseas, just like you said you would when we were teenagers."

He remembered that. How had he remembered that?

"Uh, yeah," she said. "With the board, obviously."

"Career as well?," he asked.

"No short-term. One appointment after the other. I've been hesitant to go career."

"Why is that?," he asked.

And she almost told him how she hadn't found the right place yet, how committing to one place, still unmarried and without prospects, felt like resigning herself to this forever.

But that sounded weak, honestly. And for some reason, she actually cared what he thought.

What in the world? Exactly.

"Just keeping my options open," she said instead.

He nodded, accepting what she offered and prying for no more.

"And just where did you come from to join us here in Dallas?," he asked, that familiar drawl back in his voice.

"Japan," she said, focusing on the last assignment. "Tokyo."

"Wow," he grinned. "I've always wanted to go to Japan. What kind of ministry do you do there?"

"Student ministry," she said, smiling as well, hesitantly, almost shyly. "Girls' ministry mainly. English teacher at a high school in the city, which led to opportunities."

He smiled at this. "That's why you get it, then."

She looked at him for a long moment, disturbed yet comforted by the look in his eyes. So familiar, yet so different...

"Yeah," she breathed. "I get it. And not just for the type of work. But the why behind it. Jesus. Being everything. Being worth giving up everything." A pause as she thought about this, at all she felt that she was trading in for Christ and His purpose for her. "I get it."

And neither one of them said anything for a long while, looking towards the empty pulpit together, the room silent.

"You grabbed dinner yet?," he asked, glancing over at her.

"Not yet," she said softly.

"Wanna have dinner with me?," he asked. Then, a little self-consciously, "I mean, I can catch you up on all that you've missed at New Life and in the exciting lives of Hope and Charity since you've been in Japan."

And she stopped herself from saying that she would have gladly had dinner with him without the reminiscing, simply for who he was right now and the words he'd spoken to her very heart right there from the pulpit --

No, wait. This was David Connor.

She very nearly shook her head to clear out these disturbing thoughts, even as she murmured, "Sure."

David

He'd been halfway through his sermon when he'd seen her.

Cammie Evans, sitting several rows back, watching him with rapt attention, tears streaming down her face.

He was more than comfortable preaching to a crowd of students, but when the audience extended beyond that, he often found himself nervous.

And she was Cammie Evans, after all.

Camille. Camille Evans.

He could picture her listening to his own father, back in high school, her attention just as focused but minus the tears, of course. He'd crowd himself into the pew with Hope and Charity, never because he wanted to sit with them especially but because Cammie was there, too. He'd listen to his father, of course, but he'd watch Cammie as well. She always listened, always took notes, and always nodded affirmation.

But tonight as he saw her, there were just tears.

It had very nearly thrown off the whole rhythm he'd been keeping.

Paul Connor, a commanding presence in the pulpit.

David Connor, making people weep with his incompetence.

But that hadn't been it, he assured himself as he walked to the restaurant there in the hotel with her. She'd said it was that she "got it," just like he did, he reminded himself as they were directed to a table, and he pulled her chair out for her. She knew what he was talking about because she was living it as well on the other side of the world, he affirmed, as they ordered their food and began eating, as she told him similar stories about Tokyo.

He was about to ask her about her long-term plans in Asia, when a student walked right up to their table there and said hello to Camille.

David could see that he'd come from a table full of other young men, all of them grinning over, watching their friend as he stared at Camille and smiled.

He was an older high school student, probably done with his last year and looking towards college. And looking at Camille with clear interest in his eyes, of course, even as she turned to him and smiled politely.

"Miss Evans," he said. "I was in your first session this afternoon... it is *Miss* Evans, isn't it?"

David frowned at this. Sure, he'd said nearly the same thing earlier, but this guy? Was a kid. (Though had he been David's own age, it still would have been annoying.)

"It is," Camille said kindly. "Did you enjoy the session?"

"It was great," the kid kept on, never even glancing at David. "I really liked what you said about semester missions opportunities." He paused. "In Japan. Where you serve. I'd really like to join you in your work there."

Good grief. David glanced over at Camille, wondering if she could see through this blatant flirtation.

She could if the patient, carefully unaffected expression on her face was any indication.

"That's wonderful," she said. "Of course, to do the semester program, you'll need to have at least eighteen hours of college credit already earned." Another pause. "Are you in college yet?"

"Not yet," he said. "I start next fall. I just turned eighteen." Another pointed look at Camille.

David could read a whole lot into that pointed look.

But Camille went on without acknowledging it, reaching down to grab her purse. "I've got a card for you, then," she said. "With a number for more information once you get those eighteen hours completed. Or if you have questions before then."

She was giving this kid her phone number? David was ready to open his mouth and protest this when she handed the now grinning kid the card.

"That's the number of one of my colleagues here stateside," she said. "His name is Chad. He'll be thrilled to hear that you're interested in the program, and he'll be happy to talk you through the process."

The young man regarded the card with a look of dejection. "Oh," he said. "Well, that's... great. Thanks, Miss Evans."

And with that, he turned and left.

David watched the young man walk away with a strange desire to hurl a spoon his direction, aimed right at the back of his head. Looking at Cammie like that, trying to put the moves on her when he was just a kid...

"Look at you, Camille," he said instead, keeping his spoon on the table and his tone light. "Inspiring a whole new generation of young men towards the mission field."

She raised an eyebrow at this and suppressed a smile. "Just trying to do my part," she said. "But that guy? Won't end up overseas. They never do."

David frowned at this. "What do you mean?"

"A kid like that," she said. "Look at him."

David did, even as the kid sat back down and his buddies laughed at him. He looked annoying. Irritating. Butt ugly, too.

"Yeah?"

"Good looking young man," she said. "Well spoken. Clearly thinks well of himself and has confidence. Likely the darling of his home church, right? If he expresses any legitimate calling to ministry beyond just wanting to get a good look at my cleavage --"

And at this mention, David had to force himself to not glance that way, consciously warning himself to keep his eyes on the prize, so to speak.

"--well," Cammie continued on, with thankfully no clue what he was thinking, "there are so many other options for him, none of which require moving to the other side of the world where the pay is horrible, the work is hard, and the benefits are non-existent."

"You make the mission field sound like an awful place," David said.

"Not an awful place," she said. "No matter where I've been, it's been wonderful. But it's been hard. Not that ministry in the States isn't equally hard in its own ways, I'm sure, but there's something different about being overseas, isn't there?"

David nodded at this, knowing the truth of it.

"But I've been called to it," she said, "so it's been infinitely better than I could ever have imagined."

David smiled, ready to tell her it was the same for him.

"But you," she cut him off. "You can't tell me you haven't gotten offers for a lot of other opportunities here in the States that were very attractive."

He had. Just the day before, actually. Student ministry, New Life-Dallas. He wouldn't tell her this, of course, but it was there in his mind as the glaring example of what she was saying.

"And if you wanted to, David," she said, looking up at him, "you could do something different, surely. Could get the keys to the kingdom, likely, given who you are."

She had no idea. His dad and those deacons had practically had the spare keys to the kingdom already copied and in his pocket before he could finish his steak.

"But I'm called overseas as well," he said, affirming this again for himself and to others, just like he'd spent the whole weekend doing. "Just like you."

She nodded. "But you have options," she said. "Much more than women in your position do. And you can see why the mission field is full of women, not men."

"Not where I'm at," he said. "I'm only the lonely out there."

She smiled. "Yeah, that was mentioned. Impressive. Blazing a trail all on your own. Being the big man and all."

"Not so much," he said, thinking of how often he'd found himself on his knees praying that God would do the work He'd called David to do on His behalf. Because that's what it was. Being called to witness a task that only God Himself could do, sometimes by David's very human efforts, much to his shock and all to His glory.

David tried to put this in words for her. "Just figuring it out as I go. Getting out of the way so that the real Big Man can do the job."

She watched him with something that looked like... admiration.

Glory. Admiration. From Camille Evans. In his mind, he could see his twelve year old self jumping up and down, cheering. Hey, even his twenty-five year old self was wanting to jump on the table and celebrate as well.

"Well said," Camille noted softly. "Wonderful things happening. All the time."

"Very nearly."

"Even still, though... it gets lonely probably. By your own admission as only the lonely and all, like you said."

And it did get lonely. There were the students. There was Piet. There was Kait. He was luckier than most, having so many people there surrounding him and being a part of the same work.

But it was still lonely.

"You get lonely out in Japan?," he asked.

"Oh, yeah," she sighed. "Not sure how you can be in a crowd of people all the time and still feel alone. But you can."

He knew this better than she could guess, probably.

"It costs something," she murmured. She looked up at him. "Makes it more of an offering, a sacrifice, going out and doing what we do when it costs something, doesn't it?"

"It does."

"But your work," she said, smiling. "You do it all on your own?"

"I have friends who help out," he said. "But as far as the board goes, it's just me. Well, for another couple of weeks, at least. We're getting a new guy on the field."

At this, her face brightened. "Are you? That's great news."

And it was, of course. As they talked about all that he hoped to do with more help on the field, about people they both knew from home, about the past, and about the future, David found himself wishing that he had more time here in the US to spend with her.

What for, though? She had a life in Japan, and he had a life in Namibia.

Even as they took the elevator back upstairs and walked to their rooms, he thought about how far apart the two destinations actually were.

"Well," he said, when they got to their doors, "it was great seeing you again, Camille."

"I'm sure we'll see each other a few more times this week," she said, smiling.

Oh, he wished they would.

"I'm leaving tomorrow morning," he said, deflated at the thought.

And was it his imagination, or did the mention of him being gone make her look a little disappointed as well?

"Really?," she asked. "You're not staying for the rest of the conference?"

"No," he said. "Gotta get back to work. Taking the first flight out tomorrow. 5am."

"That's early," she said, looking at her watch. "And I've kept you out way too late with all my talking."

He'd loved every minute, every word.

"It was great," he said. "No other way I'd have rather spent my last night in Texas."

And she blushed just slightly at this, even as she smiled at him.

So beautiful. Even all these years later.

"Well, then," she said, looking at him. "Good luck to you. With all of your work. And the new guy coming to help you out."

He nodded. "Thanks. You, too."

And before he could even ask her for her number or a way to get in touch with her... well, he watched her unlock her door and step inside, offering neither.

It was probably for the best.

NAMIBIA

Cammie

An international flight for Camille Evans always involved a lot of drugs.

Back when she'd felt the call to foreign missions, she'd never actually been on an airplane. Her first experience with flying had been to a training session in Virginia, and before she even left the ground in Dallas, there had been an issue with the plane. Once the small airline deemed it safe to fly, they took off with Camille nervously chewing her lip and looking out the window, wondering at every bump and sway, praying silently that they'd make it.

Then, there was smoke. Not a good smoke, though Camille didn't know it at first since she'd never been on a plane, of course. They'd landed in Little Rock to switch planes, and it was a miracle that Camille didn't declare Arkansas as good enough for a lifetime, refusing to ever fly again. The anxiety had only gotten worse with every flight, until she'd gone to a doctor, asking for a prescription. Magic happy pills.

It made flying possible, reaching the nations a reality.

And it made for crazy weird dreams.

Camille was nearly to Namibia when her sleep gave way to fanciful imaginings. Crazy stuff. Jumping off skyscrapers. Being lost in a jungle. Going to a wedding only to find herself standing alone as the last single woman on earth when the bride went to throw the bouquet.

Scary stuff.

Then, it just got weirder, as it transitioned from bizarre scenarios to real memories. Scenes that had really happened, so long ago.

She was sitting on one of the couches in the youth room at New Life-Dallas.

Well, that wasn't quite right. She was actually lying down on the couch because she was the only one there. The youth room was full of teenagers during services and on the odd weekends, the Wednesday night discipleship groups, and the events that Jay, her youth minister, was always putting together. It was hard to find a seat most times, let alone have enough space to stretch on out like she was.

But she was there when no one else was, long after her girls' Bible study had concluded. She'd been walking a group of junior high girls through the book of Ephesians that semester, and their meeting time just happened to coincide with the hospitality committee her mother led alongside Phoebe Connor, the pastor's wife. So, Camille always hitched a ride with her mother and always found herself stuck at the church, much later than she would have preferred.

That hospitality committee could go on for hours and hours.

She was resting her eyes, her mind running through a long list of tasks that she had ahead of her once she finally got home. Geometry homework, reading another chapter for English literature, calling Chelsea to double-check when she was supposed to babysit her niece and nephew, so that she and Kyle could go out to dinner to celebrate their anniversary.

Their anniversary. Their wedding anniversary. Their wedding hadn't been much to write home about, honestly. At least not to Camille's recollections, as she'd only been eleven back when her sister had gone to college and gotten married before the first semester's grades were turned in. Simple and ordinary, unassuming and subdued, Kyle and Chelsea saying their vows without ever looking at anyone else, so consumed with one another that they could have been all alone, honestly.

Her wedding was so NOT going to be like that.

No, she was going to do it right. She smiled even as she imagined it. A big wedding. Huge, in fact. Right at New Life-Dallas. With so many people there, the whole church decorated just right, and the perfect groom, waiting at the front for her after she'd walked down the aisle, his lips ready to say --

"Hey, Cammie, why are you smiling like that?"

Her eyes popped open to find fourteen year old David Connor standing over her, watching her curiously. When her gaze met his, he grinned.

"What?," she asked, wondering why he was up here at this hour.

Probably hitched a ride with his mother as well.

He shifted the guitar he was wearing. "I wanted to know why you were smiling. Good dreams?"

"Not dreaming," she said, sitting up and smoothing down her hair. "Just thinking through all I still have to do tonight when I get home. If I ever get home. Which you know all about, since you're stuck up here doing the same."

"Oh, no," he said. "I'm not stuck. Well, I mean, I'm here until my mother finally finishes her meeting. But I've been keeping busy." With that, he sat next to her and balanced the guitar in his lap.

"Busy," she said, nodding at the guitar. "You're learning to play?"

"Sure am," he smiled. "Only a week into lessons, and listen to this." He strummed a chord... that didn't sound quite right. "Awesome, huh?"

"Mmmhmm," she murmured, glancing at her watch. "How long did you practice that?"

"Oh, just the last thirty minutes," he said. "Went to do that when your girls' group let out. Which is when my group let out."

"You're in a group, too?," she asked, thinking about how there weren't any groups other than hers scheduled for the middle of the week like this.

"Well, not a group," he said. "Just me and Jay, talking about Scripture."

Cammie narrowed her eyes at this, surprised to hear that David did this. "Really?"

"Oh, yeah," David said, studying his fingers, going for another chord apparently. "We meet every week. Just like you meet up with your group. Hey, listen to this." Another chord. Poorly done.

And followed by a huge smile over at her.

"David," she gasped, grabbing his face with one hand, pushing his cheeks in, and very nearly making him drop the guitar as he jumped at her touch.

Well, that was weird. But not as weird as the sight of his teeth, finally free from their braces.

"When did that happen?!," she exclaimed.

"When did what happen, Cammie?," he managed, even as she still squeezed his face.

"Your braces are gone!," she said, letting go of him and smiling.

He rubbed his face just a little, looking at her and smiling himself. "This morning," he said. "The orthodontist yanked them all off. My mouth is still sore."

"That probably didn't help, then," she said. "Me grabbing you like that. I was just so surprised! You look different without them!"

"Yeah," he said, looking back down at his guitar, trying for yet another chord. "Mom got me out of school and took me over there. We weren't even expecting that they'd come off today, but they said it was time. Hurts so bad I had to drink a milkshake for lunch. And I feel all slimy now."

"Maybe because your nose is running," she said, nodding at his face.

"Oh, my bad," he said, turning his head to wipe his nose on his shirt. "Hey, listen to this, Cammie."

Another chord.

"Wow," she said, unimpressed. "All of... what? Three chords?"

"I'll be able to join the youth praise band in no time at all," he said, grinning. "Will be able to play some backup for you while you sing."

"High hopes," she said.

"I can't wait," he said. "You have such a great voice."

"Thanks, David," she said, surprised by this compliment. She'd only been singing with the youth praise band for a few months. Not even long enough for anyone to even notice.

Except for David, obviously.

"And I'm sure you'll be... just great," she offered. "Once you learn some more chords."

"Totally what's going to happen," he grinned, studying the guitar in his hands. "Always have lots of time to practice when I'm up here. Mom can talk and talk and talk at her meeting. Won't get home until late tonight."

"I know," Cammie sighed, leaning back on the couch again. "I guess Charity and Hope didn't come up with you?"

"Nah," he said, shaking his head. "They're still at home. Dad tried to get them to lead groups like you're leading, but Charity has cheerleading. And Hope? Well, she scares off the junior high girls."

Cammie smiled at this, thinking of her high-strung friend. "She's a little different, isn't she?"

"Just a little weird," he confirmed. "But you're great. The girls in your group are always talking about you. I think they want to *be* you, Cammie."

Just like Cammie had wanted to be her sister for a while, back when Chelsea had walked with her through Scripture. Just like Cammie had wanted to be like the older girls in youth, back when she'd been in junior high, and they'd been so good to befriend her.

Foundations had been laid that would last a lifetime, surely. All because of young women who had taught her Scriptural truths.

Cammie was glad to be able to do the same, even if it was just one night a week.

"Maybe that's just the way it is when you teach someone, huh?," she said. "You probably want to be just like Jay, right?"

David kept strumming the guitar, a wondering look on his face. "Nah, not really."

"Your dad, then? I mean, he must teach you things about Jesus all the time."

David very nearly laughed at this, glancing over at her. "He does. But, glory, *no*. I don't want to be just like my dad."

Cammie wondered at this briefly, at the commanding presence their pastor had, of the way he could move an entire auditorium of people, of the way he spoke the truth so unapologetically... so harshly at times.

David likely didn't have it in him to ever speak with such authority. Goofy, little kid.

"Who do you want to be like, then?," she asked, glancing at her watch and willing the time to pass more quickly so that she could get on with her life.

"I just want to be like Jesus," he said.

And before she could say anything, Camille, half a lifetime and half a world away, felt her eyes fly open as the plane hit a patch of turbulence.

The pills were wearing off. The dreams were still strange, of course, but even now they were just remembrances of what had happened, not fabricated imaginings.

But David Connor...

61

She felt a little embarrassed that her subconscious had produced any kind of recollection of him. Of course, a lot of her memories involved him, given how much a part of his sisters' lives she'd been back then and how often they'd been together.

Dreaming about him, though, had never been an issue. Not until they'd been at that missions event in Dallas two weeks ago.

Yes, she'd said goodnight to him at her door, after hearing him say so many wonderful things about his life's work, after wishing him well, and after chiding herself for wishing that he wasn't leaving so soon. She'd gone into her room, resisting the urge to go back out, knock on his door, and force her contact information on him, as though he wanted to get in touch with her.

As if she wanted him to get in touch with her.

She'd berated herself for thinking this way about her friends' weird little brother, reasoning that she was being silly, even as she slipped into bed and turned off the lights.

Then, she dreamt of him.

Oh, wow. And it was a crazy weird dream, too. Side by side with David, working with him, discipling teenagers with him, leading worship next to him... and afterwards, leaning over and laying a giant smooch on him, kissing smelly, sweaty, squeaky David Connor, right on the lips, very nearly knocking him right over in her exuberance.

That kiss? That dream kiss? Was good. *Really* good. And it might have led to more had she not woken right up at the right time.

Whoa. And she hadn't even been on her magic happy pills when her mind created that one. It was *all* Camille, that dream was.

As the plane continued its descent, she shook her head free of the thoughts, finally feeling some clarity. Not about David Connor and all the crazy thinking she'd done regarding him but about moving on, moving towards what was next.

She was coming out of the fog and, she noted, as she looked out the window, coming up on a small city. David Connor could be anywhere on this huge continent, and so, she put him out of her mind.

"It looks like we'll be landing ahead of schedule," the pilot's voice rang out over the intercom. "Cloudless, sunny day below for a smooth landing. Welcome to Windhoek."

Thirty minutes later, Camille was through passport control.

With her bags in her hands, her makeup refreshed, and her hair redone, she made her way out into the arrival lounge, ready for the next assignment.

It was always an anxious thing, anticipating the first few moments of the next thing. No matter how much she had already corresponded with those on the field or how well she felt she knew the job and the destination ahead, she always felt nervous taking those last few steps before the big welcome.

But this time was different. The nerves were still there but for good reason.

She looked around the small airport, wondering who she was supposed to meet, exactly. The personnel on the field had been oddly quiet, and Camille was left with no idea what she was even walking into in coming to this new place.

Was there a team on the ground already? Were they all based in one location? Was there training to be involved at the beginning?

She had no answers for any of it and literally no idea who she was supposed to be meeting. She bit her lip for a moment, still confidently walking forward to where a few groups of people were gathered, waiting for passengers. Her eyes fell on each group, skipping over their faces, wondering --

"Hey, are you... you're from the board, aren't you?"

Camille took in a breath at the voice, putting a smile on her face and readying herself for the introductions to begin.

But there was just one woman standing there. She'd been sent to a country with only one missionary. A woman. With bright orange hair, a tank top, shorts... and was that dirt on her face?

How odd.

The woman seemed to be thinking the same thing as she looked Cammie over, puzzlement in her eyes. "You've got to be from the board," she said simply. "I mean, I can spot you missionaries from miles away."

Well, this was even more odd.

"Yes, I'm from the board," Camille offered, holding her hand out. "I'm Camille Evans, your new worker. And you are?"

"You're a woman," the other woman said. Then, she smiled. And laughed out loud. "Oh, wow."

Camille bristled at this. "Well, yes. Do you mind telling me what's so funny?"

"Oh, nothing," she said. "I just got a weird sense of deja vu. And we just expected that... well, this changes plans." She took a breath. "Well, welcome, Camille. I'm Kaitlyn Smith. But you can call me Kait."

"Kait," Camille repeated, shaking her hand, vowing to move past the odd comments. "You're with the board as well, then?"

"Oh, no," Kait said, picking up Camille's second bag and leading them out of the airport. "I was. For years. But not anymore."

Then why was she here picking up mission personnel? And what did she mean, she was but not anymore?

"You're an American?," Camille asked. "I mean, your accent and all."

"I am," Kait grinned. "And Namibian, too. Permanent residence. Came here years ago then stayed. Applied for citizenship, and here we are. It's a total God thing, but that's another story for another time." She pointed the key bob in her hand towards a small car that chirped back at her. "You up for a drive?"

Camille tugged off the jacket she'd been wearing, surprised by the high temperatures as they moved out into the sunshine.

There were so many questions.

She asked what was sure to be the first of many.

"Why are you picking me up if you don't work for the board?" Better yet, how had she even known to look for someone?

"I'm doing a bad job of explaining it all," Kait smiled. "And I swear, I'll answer your questions. But we've got to get to Tsumeb."

"Tsumeb?"

"Up north," Kait said. "I'm here, on behalf of the board, to take you there. I'm legit. I swear."

This was good enough for now. Because what was the other alternative? Hanging out in the airport until she could confirm something with someone more official?

Kait seemed to know what she was thinking... and grinned.

"Legit," she said again. "I can recite the personnel manual for the board for you if you'd like, just to prove it."

Yeah, this wouldn't be necessary.

"Legit. Okay. So... Tsumeb, it is," Camille said. "I take it there won't be any training here in the capitol? With the rest of the team?"

"Training?," Kait said, smiling. "Uh... no. And there really isn't a team to speak of. But we'll get to all of that."

The more Kait spoke, the less confident Camille felt about what she'd walked into here. No training, no team, and an introduction to the country alongside a woman who had once been with the board but now wasn't... a woman who was now holding citizenship here with no explanations as to why.

"We've got quite a trip ahead of us," Kait said as they put the luggage in the car's trunk. She looked at Camille and smiled. "I'll explain more as we go. We've got all the time in the world."

David

The roof had nearly killed him. Very nearly.

Piet, too, though he wouldn't admit it as he breathlessly reclined right there on it, demanding a break.

It was too hot up north to be doing this. Ironically enough, it was summertime in Texas, wintertime in Namibia, and David was still certain that Namibia was hotter. How it could be winter and still be so scorching had him befuddled, honestly. It would be worse in another few months when it actually was summer, which is why they'd taken on the job now of re-roofing the house that had once been the property of the mission board.

It belonged to Piet now, who had made it into a stopping point for their trips up north. Piet's trips to run his clinics in Tsumeb and David's trips to visit his students when they were on holiday and school was out of session -- both types of trips made it certain that they were here a lot.

Enough that they'd finally gone ahead and done the work of re-roofing the house.

It had been a good reintroduction back to Namibia. David had left the overly air conditioned hotel just a few hours after saying goodnight to Cammie back in Dallas, hesitating more than a few minutes outside of her door.

It had been too early for her to be up. But he hadn't cared. He had still wanted to knock on her door, say goodbye to her, ask her if he could have a way to get in touch with her, see if there was any interest in her eyes...

Stupid, actually. Even if she wasn't going to be on another continent, she was still Camille Evans. *The* Camille Evans. That was reason enough that she wouldn't ever consider spending more than just a brief dinner with him, chatting about the past, not dreaming of any kind of future with him in it.

As if there could be any future at all, given where they were each headed, in opposite directions.

Just as well. That had been his thought as he'd turned away from her door and made his way down to the lobby, where Hope had been waiting for him, her car double parked, ready to take him to the airport and send him halfway around the world.

He'd thought about Cammie a few times on the long flights back. Okay, so he'd thought about her a lot. But he'd also thought about the new guy who would be arriving on the field soon. He'd been making plans for all that they could begin to do initially, before the school session even began in Swakopmund. He'd pick the new guy up at the airport, drive him straight up to Tsumeb, and introduce him around. Then, in Swakopmund, the work could really get going.

Plans changed, though, thanks to the roof.

David had been on enough summer missions teams from his dad's church that he knew a few things about roofing a house. He knew how long it would take and knew that he and Piet could get the job done by the end of the day if they just kept working. So, he'd reluctantly sent Kait on to pick up the new guy from the airport in Windhoek, which she'd done gladly, telling them both that watching them work was exhausting her.

It had exhausted Piet as well, if the way he was lying on the roof was any indication.

"Not much more to go," David said, kicking him softly in the side. "If you get your big butt up, we can have it finished in the next hour."

"Nee, man," Piet groaned. "It's so hot. I need to rest."

"No, you don't," he answered. "We gave up being there to welcome the new guy in. Don't make the time we gave up go to waste."

And with that, Piet heaved himself up, his bulky frame blocking at least some of the sunlight from David's eyes. "Ja," he droned. "Heard it before. Should have been there, Piet. All of us should have been there, Piet."

David grinned, thinking about the day he himself had arrived and how Kait and Piet had both been there. He'd know that neither one was still connected to the board, that neither one was there in any kind of official capacity, but that they were both so excited, as if they had more invested in David's arrival than their distance from the situation certainly dictated.

It was because they loved the students. They loved the work that had gone on when the former missionaries were here. They were still a part of it, even in a non-official capacity.

It had been a good welcome. They'd headed straight to the coast and gotten right to work. David hoped that even though the initial introductions would be different for the new guy, it would still be a good welcome, coming up north with Kait, right to where the work was happening.

"Well, we should have been there," David said, nodding at the roof. "But it's more important that we finish this. Let's get back to it."

"How did you learn how to do all of this anyway?," Piet grumbled, getting down beside him, placing shingles and preparing to secure them.

"Long summers, working in neighborhoods with my dad's church," he said. "We'd fix up houses for people who couldn't afford the repairs themselves. Got so good at it in high school that I had some men offer to put me on their construction crews once I graduated. Tried to talk me into that instead of college. Tried to talk me into making a career of it."

Piet glanced over at him. "You'd have been paid better."

"True enough," David acknowledged. "But it's God's grace to you that I wasn't. Otherwise you'd be doing this all by yourself."

"Ja," Piet grinned. "And clearing out the brush. It's crept up to the back door again. Will take us a few hours to get it done."

"I know all about that, too," David murmured, thinking about the jobs he'd been given those summers before he'd been old enough and strong enough to handle the roofs.

He remembered Jay, pointing the older boys towards the ladders, pointing him towards the weeds in the yard.

He had grumbled at this, of course. But only for a minute. Because out there in the yard in a really cute pair of cut-off jeans, a T-shirt, and a baseball cap with her ponytail hanging out the back was Cammie Evans.

Oh, how his heart raced every time he saw her... even when she was standing with Hope and Charity.

"Hey, Cammie," he yelled, running towards her and totally ignoring his sisters in the process.

"Hey, David," she said, straightening her hat and looking out at the yard. "How is it already ten thousand degrees out here at nine in the morning?"

"Dunno," he grinned, moving closer to her, very nearly breaking out in a sweat because she smelled so *good*, even out in that yard, and --

"Look at Matt, up on that roof," Charity murmured, grabbing Cammie's arm. "Gets any hotter, he's gonna take off his shirt. And then, it'll be *really* hot."

Cammie fought a grin at this as they both watched the older boy. David glanced over at him as well, even as he gave a head nod the girls' direction.

He really hoped that nod was for Charity and not Cammie. Though if Matt was smart, he'd be doing everything he could to get Cammie's attention because Cammie was --

"Hot, yeah. Well, I really hope he doesn't take off his shirt," Hope said. "He'll probably blind us all with his pasty white self if he does."

"What?," Charity asked, looking over at her twin. Fraternal twin. They didn't even look like sisters. Certainly didn't act like it either.

"He's pale," Hope said. "I mean, bless his heart. Do you remember back in third grade when we went to the lake over spring break, and he blistered up like a lobster?"

Cammie laughed out loud at this. David couldn't remember it, of course, because he hadn't been there. He had been in kindergarten. Always three steps behind Charity, Hope, and Cammie. It hadn't bothered him, then, but watching Cammie totally see through him now as if he wasn't even there had him feeling it differently.

"Well, holy moly," Charity said. "Maybe he should leave his shirt on, then."

"That's the problem, you know," Cammie said, smiling wistfully.

"That Matt's got a pasty white chest?," David said, trying to insert himself back in the conversation and feeling that pointing out Matt's flaws was an excellent way to do it.

All three girls looked at him as though they'd forgotten that he was there. Of course.

"No," Cammie said, shaking her head and watching him oddly. "The problem," and she turned to the twins, "is that we've grown up with these guys. We know too much about them, remember them in decidedly uncool contexts. It's hard to see any of them with any real potential because we know them all too well. I mean, who can think romantically about someone when you've known them their whole lives and --"

Her musings had been cut off by Jay, who came up to them with several unappealing yard tools in his hands. "You girls planning on working at all today?," he asked, just lumping David together with the womenfolk. (Which happened a lot and just came with having two older sisters.)

"I'm just here to look pretty, Jay," Charity said, grinning at him. Flirty, even with the youth pastor.

"Well, that won't do much to help this family," he said, ignoring her. "Hope, you and your sister take these hedge trimmers, and go over and cut back the bushes that are covering the windows."

"Can do," Hope said, taking the tools and dragging Charity with her.

"And you two," he said, looking at David and Cammie, holding out two pairs of work gloves and two garbage bags. "Weeding. Easy enough, right?"

David saw Cammie sigh then smile. "Where to?"

"The south side of the house," he said, nodding that way before leaving them.

"Let's see how bad it is," Cammie said, reaching over and messing up David's hair just like she always did. From the time he'd been four and she and her family had moved to the church, where she'd become good friends with his sisters, Cammie had been treating him like her little brother, too.

He didn't mind, though. Because attention was attention.

He hurried to keep up with her, and once they got to the south side of the house, he let out a long whistle.

"Well, we've got a lot of work to do," she said, pulling on her gloves and getting down on her knees.

He followed suit, looking at those cute shorts that she was wearing...

"Seems a shame, doesn't it?," he asked softly.

"Tell me about it," she said even more softly. "The single mom who lives here has been working so hard that she doesn't have time to do any of this. And she doesn't make enough to do anything but cover her bills, much less pay anyone to help her out. My dad's coming up later to help out with some plumbing problems. Said the pipes are all rusted out."

David hadn't been thinking of the work at all, honestly. He'd been thinking that it was a shame that she'd be getting her pretty clothes all messed up. But there Cammie went, talking about the real reason they were here, the good they were doing, the way they were loving Christ. Calling him back to what he knew to be true, making him so thankful that he was here to do something, helping him --

"What's that look for, you little weirdo?," she asked, already looking back down at the work she was doing, pulling weeds right out of the ground.

"Nothing," he said, joining her, vowing silently to work even harder so that he would lighten her load as the day passed them by. "Just a lot of work, huh?"

"Good work," she said, smiling up at him. "Any work done with the right heart is good work, isn't it? Especially when it's done for Jesus."

David thought about her words as he and Piet continued sweating in the oppressive Namibian heat, thinking about all the good that would come from them both having this place up north, smiling even as he thought about it. It was good work, being here, giving his life to this, to all that Christ had called him to.

Thanks for that, Cammie.

"What are you smiling about, David?," Piet asked.

And David grinned and said, "Just glad to be back home."

Cammie

So, there was just one missionary on this team.

Except not really. Because Kait, who hadn't stopped talking from Windhoek to the outskirts of Tsumeb, was also part of the team. Kinda. Sorta.

Not really.

Camille still wasn't firm on all the details, and she had a feeling that Kait wasn't saying everything there was to say. And there was a guy named Piet who she kept mentioning who was also part of the board's team. Kinda. Sorta. Not really.

It was all very confusing.

But there was a missionary! On the field!

"And with you," Kait said, looking over at Camille with a smile, "we're up to two mission board personnel members in Namibia. Which, believe me, is a miracle."

Again, Camille didn't know what this meant. But her attention was less on the conversation now and more on the sight before her.

She could see a small house in the clearing. And two men... two, shirtless men, high fiving one another as they walked along the roof, one of them doing a celebratory jig of some sort.

Maybe the magic happy pills hadn't worn off completely.

"Praise God," Kait muttered under her breath. "Nearly thirty years since that roof has been done. Well past time. Though Piet likely only thought to do it because it gave him an excuse to take his shirt off."

Camille raised her eyebrows at this and looked more closely, even as she and Kait climbed out of the car. The two men finally heard them and yelled out greetings before leaping right off the roof.

The bigger of the two came towards them grinning, obstructing their view of the second man. "Kaity," he said, in a rather wonderful accent, "hoe gaan dit?"

"Nee, man," she sighed, rolling her eyes at him. "I'm not speaking another word to you until you put on a shirt. New personnel from the States, and her first impression of you is like this."

He grinned even more at this and held his hand out to Camille. "Her?," he laughed. "She's the new guy? Hmm."

Camille attempted a smile under his surprised scrutiny, irritated yet again to have the fact that she was a woman made into such a big deal.

Oh, well. More of the same, no matter what continent she found herself on.

"Well, welcome to Namibia, then," Piet said, genuinely smiling. "I'm Pieter Botha."

She put her hand in his, pushing her irritation aside. "Camille Evans."

And at this, the man behind Piet came into view, shock on his face.

Camille's eyes met his and widened.

David Connor.

David Connor!

For a long moment, they stood there, wordless at the sight of one another.

"Well," Kait said as they stared. "Maybe you need to put on a shirt, too, David. If we actually want Camille to be able to do any work –"

"David," Camille said, dumbfounded. Then, she put her hand out a second too late. He held it in his and smiled his wonderful smile at her. "David," she repeated dumbly.

"Yeah," he said, grinning. "Are you the new guy?"

"It would appear so," she murmured.

And he smiled even more. "Wow."

"Wow," she repeated, wondering at how... well, how he was here. A little piece of home, right here.

He seemed to be having similar thoughts.

"Praise God, then," David laughed out loud. "And welcome to Namibia, Camille."

They continued watching one another for a long moment, holding hands still.

"Okay," Kait said, exchanging a glance with Piet. "Camille, David is –"

"Your career missionary," she said, a breathless laugh escaping her as all the pieces fell into place, the details from his speech now connecting to this place. "I know all about it. Well, I know more than I thought I did. About the ministry, at least. The students."

"How?," Piet asked.

"We grew up together," David said, glancing over at them. "At church."

"And everywhere else," Camille added, strangely thrilled that his hand was still in hers. "David's like my little brother."

Well, that wasn't quite right.

She hadn't meant it... well, not entirely. He certainly wasn't her brother. Not at all. Not now, at least. Not after that great evening back in Dallas, spent talking to him, hearing his heart.

Wait, though. This was still David Connor. And feeling attracted to him didn't erase years of him being like family, did it?

Before she could clarify things either way, David let go of her hand and gave her a strange, resigned smile. He reached down to the two shirts on the ground, tossing one to Piet and pulling the other over his head.

"Wait," Kait said, oblivious to all that continued racing through Camille's mind. "Are you telling us that Camille grew up at New Life-Dallas?"

"I did," Camille answered, looking away from David at last.

"Paul Connor was your pastor?," Piet asked.

"Yeah," she said, flustered as David continued watching her. "From the time I was a very little girl. Then through high school. I was like a member of the Connor family --"

"Yeah, I'm like her little brother," David cut in with a tight grin.

Camille nodded at this absently.

"Excellent," Kait said, smiling over at Piet.

Piet grinned back at her. "That it is, Kaity."

"Hmm," she murmured, taking a deep breath. "Piet, you should take me inside and show me what still needs to be done apart from the roof."

"Will do," he said, and they headed that way together, bumping fists as they went.

"What was that about?," Camille asked, looking after them.

"Oh, who knows," David sighed. "There's enough sexual tension between those two to keep me thankful that I don't know all their inside jokes."

Camille raised her eyebrows at this. "Oh… are they…?"

"Oh, yeah," he said. "Together. For like, forever. Not married. Taking things slow, he says. Painfully, wretchedly slow. Been watching them try to keep it platonic for three years now."

"You've been here three years!," she exclaimed, turning to him, forgetting all about Kait and Piet and their drama. "All the stories! Everything you've seen! This is the place you were talking about!"

"You didn't even suspect that I would be here?," he asked, grinning.

"Well, you didn't specify in your speech, and it's a big continent, you know," she answered. "A *huge* continent, David. I never even thought it was a possibility that we'd…" She was at a loss again, looking at him, thinking about him…

"End up in the same place," he finished for her. "Yeah, especially since you're supposed to be in Japan." He looked around. "Doesn't look like Tokyo to me."

"New assignment," she said. "I didn't have a chance to mention it. I was too busy telling you stories about where I'd been, hearing about what you were doing, and…"

"And here we are," he concluded.

"Yeah, here we are," she said softly. "This is crazy, David."

"Crazy good," he said. "I need help. And God sent you."

For a long moment, they simply watched one another. Camille thought about what God might be doing here, wondering what exactly she wanted as he continued smiling at her.

"You were supposed to be a guy," he said.

Well, he recognized that she wasn't a guy. Which was a good thing, obviously... but still irritating.

"Yeah, I figured that out," she answered. "When Kait... whoever she is, kept going on and on about the fact that I wasn't."

"What do you mean 'whoever she is'?," David asked, smiling.

"She said she worked for the board," Camille said, not elaborating because Kait, in all the talking she'd done across Namibia, hadn't elaborated.

"She did work for the board," David answered.

"And now she lives here?"

"She does live here," he nodded.

"And?"

"And what?," he laughed.

Men. They never asked enough questions.

"Why did she quit? Did she quit? Why is she still here? What happened to the last missionaries?" Camille had days of questions prepared. But there seemed to be a whole lot that David didn't even consider worth asking.

Sure enough, he shrugged. "They retired. She quit to stay here. Because of Piet. Because of the work. I don't ask much more because it doesn't matter. What matters is what's going on here now."

Well, she'd have to be content with this.

"And what's going on here now," she said, looking over at the house, "is construction work?"

"For today, yes," he said. "We just finished up. Which is why Piet was dancing on the roof."

She'd seen that. "Yeah."

"The schools are on holiday," he said. "The teens will all come back to the coast, to Swakopmund, next week."

"That's where you're based, then?," she asked.

"Yes, and where you'll be based as well." He smiled. "It's so good to see you."

"You, too," she said, unable to stop from smiling back. "Though I have to wonder if it's a hallucination from all the pills I took on the plane."

"Pills?," he asked, raising his eyebrows.

"I have to be drugged to fly anywhere," she said dismissively. "I'm a horrible traveler."

"That's really ironic," he said. "Given all the places you've been."

"That it is," she said. "Makes it even more of a God thing that I'm able to do anything for Him at all overseas, given how pathetic I am when it comes to not losing my marbles on an airplane."

He grinned at this. "But you're good on travel via the roads, right?"

"Oh, yeah, I'm a great car traveler."

"Then, we'll be able to go out tomorrow," he said. "Up through Tsumeb, all over, visiting students who will be at the coast soon enough. I'd like to introduce you around."

She smiled at this. "I'd love that."

David

It had been enough of an affirmation to David when God had opened the door for them to get another worker in Namibia. It had very nearly felt like God giving him a big thumbs up, confirming that he was right where he needed to be.

And now? Now, that he knew it was Camille Evans that God had sent? David could very nearly imagine the Lord giving him a giant wink along with that big thumbs up.

Praise You, Jesus, David thought, grinning, even as they gathered around the living room of the mission house thirty minutes later, with Kait filling Camille in on more details and Piet shooting David questioning glances.

They'd been expecting a guy, obviously. They'd already planned on the new guy living with David in the cottage that had belonged to Piet's uncle and aunt, back before they relocated to the States. It had been a great home for David, and there was room for someone else. He'd been looking forward to the company, quite honestly.

For an irrational moment, as the women kept chatting about all things Namibia, David thought about how great the company would be if Camille was living in the cottage with him.

Which she couldn't, of course.

Didn't stop him from grinning like a fool, though, just imagining it.

"Why are you grinning like that, you domkop?," Piet said, laughing outright at him.

"Domkop?," Camille asked, glancing over at them.

She was so pretty. Prettier than she'd been even two weeks ago when she'd been wiping away tears during his presentation. How was it possible that she'd grown more beautiful in only --

"It means idiot," Kait said. "Or dumb head. First word I learned when I got here."

"And that," Camille said, "was a while ago, right?"

"Ja," Piet answered. "About six months before David came here, actually."

"And you were working for the board?," Camille asked.

David finally stopped staring at her and figured he should jump into the conversation. "She was," he said. "Personnel."

"Oh," Camille smiled. "I know a guy in personnel. Mark Jackson."

"Mark!," Piet laughed out loud. "That is a name I have not heard in a while!"

Kait smiled over at him. "Mark and I worked together. Did you ever meet him, Camille?"

"I did," she said. "He came to Brazil when I was there. Worked out some issues with some misallocated funds with career missionaries. He wasn't a very popular guy after that."

"I don't imagine so," Kait grinned. "I'm the female version of Mark. The angel of missionary death, so to speak. Or I was, David." She looked over at him. "Not anymore, so don't worry."

David had never heard as many details. He'd never cared to ask. The only important thing was the work he was doing now, and the past history?

Well, who cared?

Camille did, obviously.

"David mentioned that the last missionaries retired before he came," she said. "You were here when that happened."

"I was," Kait said, glancing over at Piet. "And I turned in my resignation with the board just as soon as I got them back to the States."

"Why?," Camille asked. "I mean, not to pry, but..."

But she was going to go ahead and pry. David looked at Kait, curious about the answer.

"I wanted to stay and see the work here continue," she said, very simply.

"And she was madly in love with me," Piet added, grinning at her, just as she grinned back at him.

David barely refrained from rolling his eyes. This? The two of them like this? Had gotten old approximately ten minutes after he'd arrived in Namibia three years ago. He loved his work, of course, but signing onto an assignment on the field, a seven year commitment in his career capacity, had felt like signing himself up for loneliness and the guarantee that there would be no woman in his life for a long, long while.

And so seeing these two, always flirting, was... well, it was annoying.

Camille didn't seem to think so, as she smiled.

"In love? Really?," she said, and David swore he could hear dreaminess in her voice.

"He thinks so," Kait muttered. "But I wasn't sure. He was just nice to look at. He's still nice to look at."

"Baie dankie, Kaity," Piet said, still grinning.

"Yeah, shut up," Kait said. "You keep interrupting the story."

"That's the whole story, though," Piet said. "You stayed because you love me, David came, and here we are, three years later."

"But that's not the whole story," Camille said, brushing a strand of hair out of her eyes, her fingers just resting on her cheek for a moment. Wow. David would have given anything to know how that felt, to touch her like that.

"Is it not?," Piet asked.

Camille continued on, unaware of how David watched her, obviously. "Kait told me that she has permanent residence. That it was a God thing."

"I'm surprised you remember that," Kait smiled. "Jet lag, and you're already ten times more observant than David."

David barely caught this because he was still staring at Camille. He heard his name and blinked. "Yeah."

Kait frowned at him. "See?," she said to Camille. "Just like I said."

"But the permanent residence thing was a God thing," Piet said. "Kait only had a short while on her visa, you see. And it's not easy to get a visa here. We had to jump through many hoops to get David's. And yours now, of course, though it was easier with David already here to secure that."

"Yeah, the government isn't too liberal with their visas," Kait clarified. "You have to really make it worth their while, make them see that you can benefit Namibia. David's done a lot for the youth here, so it's made the board more favorable in their eyes."

At this, Camille glanced over at him and smiled very faintly.

That smile. It made him feel like he'd grown ten feet taller.

"Well, I didn't do much," he said, self consciously.

"Not as much as Kaity," Piet agreed.

"Yes, Kaity," Kait said, her hand to her chest and her attention completely turned from David now, "went above and beyond to get a visa."

"Yes, Camille, the simple solution would have been for Kaity to marry me and get citizenship that way, instead of just a visa. I was certainly willing to make that happen," Piet said. "Am still willing to make that happen."

"Yeah, yeah," Kait said dismissively. "But a woman has to stand on her own, just in case. Make her own way in the world and all, you know."

"Stand on her own," David said sarcastically, knowing this part of the story. "By creating a job for herself with Piet's government job."

"Hey, he needed help," Kait said defensively. Then, to Camille, "Medical clinics up north, so much paperwork, administrative details, totally my thing. I got him to raise a stink at the government office about how he needed an assistant, as I was learning Afrikaans so that I would be the perfect applicant -- job experience, past career experience, and language skills. Moved in with Piet's mother and told her to not speak another word of English to me until I was speaking Afrikaans just as well as she does."

"Ja, insisted that I do the same for three whole months," Piet grinned. "Then, she got angry with us for doing it."

"It was so annoying," Kait groaned. "Like being in a foreign film without subtitles."

"She'd screech at us, *I don't understand!* Didn't make us switch to English, though," he said. "There were a few times that she was mad enough that she wouldn't even kiss me goodnight. Told me once," and here, he used a very good American accent, "*I hate you, Piet! And your language is STUPID!*"

"Nearly punched you in the throat a few times," she muttered.

"But it paid off," Piet laughed. "Camille, she walked into the interview for the job the government finally created, speaking better than I do."

"Baie dankie, P Dawg," Kait grinned.

David laughed at the name, but Cammie was still caught up on the obvious improbability.

"And you're still not married?," she asked. "Three years later?"

Piet looked at Kait rather pointedly.

"Nope," she said, unaware of the looks being exchanged all around her. "They granted me permanent residence when they gave me the job, which is unheard of. So, there was no need to get married to keep me here. I had permission to stay."

"But you..." And Camille shut her mouth, not finishing her thought. David could see all the questions still racing through her mind.

He remembered that about her, always asking questions in small group Bible study, always wanting to know more than the other students there, always digging deeper, always wanting to go farther and farther.

It had been endearing to him. Still was, as it made him look at Kait and Piet and wonder at some things he'd never thought of before.

"You're probably starving, huh, Camille?," Kait asked, something that sounded a little like uncertainty in her voice as she looked back at Piet... who still watched her with expectation. "We should have your welcome dinner."

"Oh, well, I'm okay," Camille said. "No need to make a big fuss or anything."

"No, we want to," Piet said, standing, finally looking away from Kait. "If not for you, then for poor David, who still has an entire kilometer of brush to clear out from the back part of the property tonight."

"Hooray," David muttered. "Will I have some help?"

"Ja, you always do," Piet answered.

"But dinner first," Kait said.

"Well, let me help," Camille said, making a move to get up.

"You sit here," Piet said, grinning, "and Kait and I will serve you both. A welcome meal, from the Namibians and all."

"Thank you," Camille murmured, as she and David watched them both go into the kitchen, right across the hall.

Camille watched them, all the unanswered questions still in her eyes.

"So, that's part of the story," David whispered, scooting over closer to her so that she'd be able to hear his lowered voice.

"Hmm," she said, turning and giving him that beautiful, incredible smile again. Had she *always* been this beautiful?

"I didn't mean to be nosy," she said, biting her lip. "Was I too nosy?"

"Nah, you're good," he said. "I've asked some of the same questions."

"About why she's still here and how the last missionaries left?," Camille asked.

Nope. He hadn't even thought about that, honestly.

"No, more about why Piet puts up with her," he said, barely concealing the laugh that came with this.

Camille smiled wider at his words. "Is she hard to get along with?," she whispered.

"She's just really intense," he said. "Always seems like she's scheming. And then, you know, she's been here for three years and won't marry the guy."

Camille shook her head at this. "I can't imagine," she said. "I mean, obviously, they care about each other. Three years is a long time to be with someone and not..."

David wondered at this. "Not what?"

"Well, give your heart completely, of course," she said, looking at him. "When clearly, he's wanting her to. If it were me and I felt about him the way she does, I would've married him right away, promised him forever without any hesitation at all. Life is too short to waste time. And you just get older and older..." She stopped talking and looked back at the kitchen.

He got that. In a removed way, since he'd never felt anything deep in any sense for any woman, apart from the infatuation he'd always felt as a teenager for...

... well, for the woman sitting right here with him.

This was almost as distracting as the thoughts of her moving in to be his roommate. Almost, but not quite.

"I don't know what her issues are specifically," David murmured, shifting his attention away from the way Camille smelled (wonderful, actually) and the way it felt as some of her hair just barely brushed his shoulder (amazing, actually), "but she's got some hang ups about marriage, obviously. Although with all the time they spend together and how interwoven their lives are, it's like they're married anyway. Well, as married as two people can be living in separate houses with separate bank accounts. And his mother always there as their constant chaperone."

Camille watched them, even as Kait raised a bite to Piet's mouth, and he took it, kissing her fingers, as she smiled at him and turned around to keep preparing something on the stove.

More of the same from them. But seeing them this time made him look at Camille... made him think again about how beautiful she was, about how it would feel to kiss her fingers just like that.

"Piet is okay with waiting," David spoke softly, glancing away again, chiding himself for thinking such crazy things. "Loves her enough that he's said he'll wait forever if he has to."

And they watched Kait and Piet continue to fix dinner, as the night sounds in Tsumeb could be heard just outside.

"Something genuine and true is worth waiting for, I guess," Camille murmured.

David simply nodded, wondering at the truth of this.

Cammie

Jet lag. She never got used to that.

She left Kait snoring in the tiny bedroom they'd shared in the Tsumeb house and got cleaned up in the bathroom before sunrise. With a quick glance to her hair and her clothes, she snuck through the living room where the boys had spent the night and made her way into the kitchen.

Where David was already sitting at the table with a cup of coffee and his Bible.

"Hey," he said as their eyes met. "Early riser, huh?"

"Yeah," she nodded. "And even worse now thanks to the jet lag."

"Coffee?," he asked, standing to his feet.

"Yes, please," she said. "But I can get it. I don't want to interrupt you."

"Just finishing up," he said, pouring the cup for her. "Milk, sugar?"

"Yes, both, please," she said, watching him as he moved around the kitchen. He smiled as he opened the sugar.

"You know, they say you can gauge a missionary's seniority by how he reacts to bugs in the sugar."

"Oh?," she murmured.

"Yeah," he said, stirring the coffee. "The first year on the field, he'll throw out all the sugar. The second year, he'll scoop out the sugar around the bugs. And by the third year, he'll just plop the bugs right into the coffee along with the sugar, not bothered in the least." He held out her coffee cup. "There you go."

She peered at it cautiously. "Are there bugs in there?"

"Oh, no," he said. "Just a little missionary humor."

She nodded at this, taking the mug from him. "Thanks."

He watched her for a minute, smiling. "Wow. Camille Evans."

They were both still very, very surprised, obviously.

"David Connor," she said, hiding her own smile with her mug.

"And it's still Connor," he said, holding his ring-less hand up to her with a laugh.

She frowned, blushing, embarrassed all over again. "You little...."

"Oh, Cammie," he said, still laughing, bending his head down slightly as he did so. "I'm just playing with you."

"David," she sighed.

"I said I was just playing," he insisted. "No need to take offense, and --"

"No, your forehead," she said, putting down her mug and reaching out to hold his head in her hands, marveling again as she moved close to him that David Connor had gotten so tall and big and... handsome.

What an unhelpful thought.

"What about my forehead?," David murmured, as she continued holding him.

"Well, you're bleeding," she said, focusing on something besides his gorgeous eyes.

"Oh, that," he said dismissively, as she let go of him. "Poked myself right in the head with some of that brush we cleared out last night. Got it to stop bleeding after I showered. Or at least I thought I did."

"Do you have any bandages?," she asked, moving over to the cabinets, already searching. "Or maybe a --"

And she turned to find David looking at her... well, looking at her backside, actually, then glancing up quickly to her face, his own face reddening as he did so.

Surely not.

"Uh, yeah," he said, not meeting her eyes. "First aid kit underneath the sink. I'm always knocking myself in the head with something, so we're always prepared."

"I remember that about you," she said, smiling, moving to get the kit out. "You knocked yourself out completely once during a Disciple Now weekend. I think you were... a seventh grader?"

She could remember it. In the dumbest move ever, Jay had the junior high boys play dodgeball against the senior high girls. Charity, Hope, and Cammie had all been aiming right for David, and before he could even throw the ball he'd been holding, he'd been hit in rapid succession -- one, two, three -- and had fallen backwards right onto a chair some other idiot thirteen year old boy was using as a totally illegal shield.

By the time he hit the floor, he was out cold.

The game had been called off before it had even started, with David lying flat on his back, unmoving.

While Hope and Charity had huddled around him, hysterical and close to tears because they honestly thought that they had just killed their weird little brother, one of their friends went to go find Jay. Cammie had knelt down beside David, put her hand to his face, and said to him, just as frantic as his sisters, "David Paul Connor, don't you *dare* die on us!"

She'd gone into lifesaving mode at that point, checking his breathing, illogically wondering if she should try to give him CPR anyway because he was lying there so still and horrifically pale. Just as she began to lower her lips to his (which wouldn't have helped at all since the fool was already breathing), David's eyes had popped open, and he had said, with her lips just inches from his, "Oh, praise Jesus!"

Little weirdo.

Still just a little weirdo, apparently, as he smiled at his own private memory of the incident.

"That was a great day," he said, laughing. "Had to go to the ER. My dad was convinced I was concussed because I told the doctor that Cammie Evans was just about to kiss me. Made me want to go hit my head again and not come to so quickly."

"Ha, ha, ha," she murmured, her cheeks blushed to hear him kid her this way. With an antiseptic wipe and a bandage in her hands, she turned to face him. "Come here."

He did, still grinning.

"Why don't you tell me what our plans are from here while I clean this up?," she said.

"Plans," he said as she put her hand to his forehead. "For the immediate future. With the work."

"That's right," she said, feeling a little rush of excitement as he put his hands to the counter behind her, his arms very nearly around her.

He probably wasn't even aware of what he was doing, as he winced at the sting of the wipe that she was carefully blotting on his forehead.

"Can I tell you, again, that you surprised us?," he said, his eyes closed as she worked. "We were supposed to be getting another man on the field. Not a woman."

"You mentioned that," she answered. "Everyone here has mentioned that, in fact."

"I know. Just wanted to affirm again, that plans have changed slightly."

In a good way, she hoped. She wanted to be effective here, needed, wanted...

"Well, I told you already," she said, praying that it would be so, "that the odds were better that the board would send a woman."

"Because you outnumber the men," he said. "Got it. But still. We were surprised. But honestly?" And here he lowered his voice. "I'm glad for it."

She could feel her heart race just a little, wondering at the reasons why David would be glad that she was here. Silly thoughts, of course, but... wow, he looked really great...

"Oh?," she asked, opening up the bandage, watching his face as she continued cleaning up.

"Yeah," he murmured, "because no matter what I do, I can't be there for the girls like they need someone to be. Because I'm a guy. A single, young guy."

She understood this. "Girls' ministry is my heart," she said.

"I remember," he nodded. "And today? You'll get to meet a lot of them."

"Today?," she asked, putting the bandage in place and securing it down with a soft touch, as he finally opened his eyes to look at her.

And he finally seemed to notice how close they were standing. With a blush that reminded her so much of the David Connor she had known her whole life, he backed up with a little laugh.

"Yeah, today," he said, his eyes shining as he watched her.

"I can't wait, David," she breathed, grinning.

David

Four hours later, Camille was officially part of the group.

They'd gone to a neighborhood familiar to David after many holiday seasons spent up here, visiting his students and their families. In one long mile row of homes, there were at least fifty teenagers, over half of them girls, who were part of his youth church in Swakopmund.

He had expected Camille to be overwhelmed by how many there were, at how energetic this culture was after being in conservative Japan, and how crazy busy the afternoon would get.

But she'd taken to it all with comfortable ease. Amazing, actually, how she'd handled the great majority of the introductions on her own, jumping right into the business of getting everyone's names down, starting her own conversations apart from David's leading, and finding commonalities with each young lady there.

The girls, who had been big fans of his these past three years barely gave him a second glance as they took to Camille and began chatting with her.

Well, then. Perhaps this would work out better than he could have imagined.

It had been an afternoon of soccer for the boys. Because it was always some kind of sport. Back in Swakopmund, he'd constructed a makeshift basketball court right by his cottage, and they'd play that seven days a week. It didn't always seem spiritual, these things he'd find himself doing in building relationships and living life alongside people, but days like this led to opportunities to lead students to Christ and to teach them how to walk with Him. Unspiritual things, still important for the work they were doing.

Camille seemed to get it entirely as she was... well, what was she doing?

David squinted even as he wiped the sweat off his face with his shirt, calling out to the boys that he'd be back in a minute, telling them to carry on. He made his way over to where all the girls were sitting, staring at their feet and laughing as Camille told them a story.

"So, I listened to her and went out and spent a whole month's salary from my part-time job on these dumb shoes called Tramps because I just knew that having a pair would make me popular with her and her friends, would make the boys like me... and all they did was give me blisters so huge that I couldn't even walk without a limp for days. So, I had to wear flip flops to class. In the winter. I became an expert on the art of the pedicure."

He stared at her, at all of them, as they laughed and talked and she went on without noticing him. One set of toes after another, all painted, as they passed bottles of nail polish along. All eyes on Camille, riveted by what she was saying.

"Camille," Laina, a sixteen year old active in David's Bible study group back in Swakopmund, said as she smiled at the newcomer, "were you popular after that?"

"No," Camille grinned. "But that's okay. Because changing who you are to please someone else," she said conversationally, "is totally not what God wants for your life. I learned that the hard way, through aching feet. When I was myself, just being me, I made some of the best friends I've ever had. I was who God wanted me to be, and that was enough."

She looked up finally and saw him standing there. "Hey, David, why are you so sweaty?," she asked, and he had a vague recollection of another time she'd asked him this.

Did she remember asking that question, too?

"Because I'm a sweaty guy," he said.

"Well, you do always seem to be that," she grinned.

She did. He could see his sweaty, fifteen year old self there in her eyes. And yet, she was still smiling.

"Where'd you get the fingernail polish?," he asked after a long silent pause which had all of the girls looking at him oddly.

"I keep it in my purse," Camille answered. "Always be prepared, David." Then, back to the girls, "Did you know that David and I grew up together?"

"Back in Texas?," another girl, Elizabeth, asked.

"Yeah," Camille answered. "His sisters were my best friends. And he would never leave us alone. Spent all of his time following us around like a sad little puppy dog."

All the girls laughed out loud at this.

Cammie looked up and mouthed "sorry" to him, still smiling. He shrugged dismissively, fighting a grin himself.

"What was he like?," two girls asked at the same time then giggled at one another.

"Sweaty, like he is right now, actually. Annoying. A little weird, honestly."

The girls were loving this.

"Brother David," Katrina, one of the girls sitting nearest Camille, said, laughing up at him, "you've told us this before, but it's still funny to hear someone else say it was true."

"And you were honest about it, David," Camille laughed, glancing up at him.

"Well, yeah," he said. "No need to lie about being some cool guy when I'm still not all that cool."

"But you probably didn't tell them the most important thing," she said.

He couldn't imagine what she could be thinking.

"What's that?"

"*Brother* David," she said, smiling at the name, "was a weird little kid. But can I tell you, in all the time I've known him, that his greatest ambition in life was just to be more and more like Jesus?"

David watched as all the girls' attention changed, focused to something more serious.

"And I'm sure he tells you that's the way it should be for you, too," she said, still painting toenails as she talked. "But I'm here to tell you that he lives what he says. And that God has honored even a weird kid's request to be more and more like Jesus. Gives me great hope that He can do just as much in my life, in all of our lives, after seeing what He's done in David's life."

He had no words for this. Not that Camille expected them, as the girls around her began chatting about so many things all at once, all vying for her attention. And even though she was too busy to notice, he still held up a hand to wave goodbye, going back to the soccer game, thinking on her words, amazed by what she was already doing.

Cammie

What a day.

What an *amazing* first day.

Every other assignment and place Camille had gone to had been a long adjustment. Training alongside a new team, reorienting herself to a new location, and beginning a new chapter, easing herself into it slowly.

Not here, though. On her first full day in Namibia, she found herself surrounded by teenage girls, all of them with questions for her, eager to share their hearts with her, so ready to jump into friendships with her.

No wonder, she had thought, watching as the boys were once again very into their game as David rejoined them. Absolutely none of the girls had an interest in that. Likely never had either.

"Is that what it's always like?," she asked Laina, even as the girl painted her toes for her.

"Is what like that, Camille?"

"That," she said, pointing over to where David's team was contesting a goal as the other team of boys was cheering their lead.

"Not always," Katrina spoke up. "Most of the time, yes. But back in Swakop, we do other things as well. There's Bible study. Worship. And the church."

Camille smiled at her. "All done with Brother David?"

"Yes," Elizabeth nodded. "It's been that way for three years now. We've all been there."

"How did you find out about it all?," Camille asked.

"Parties," Katrina said, grinning. "When we were grade seven students and came to Swakop at the beginning of the term, we heard about the parties David and his friends were throwing. Down on the beach."

"Longer than David has been here," Elizabeth spoke up. "My sister told me about Willem and Sophie, Daniel and Sara. That they would be on the beach at the beginning of each term. Do you know them, Camille?"

She didn't, of course. But she could imagine their connection to the board.

"No, I don't," she said. "But they had parties?"

"Not just parties," Katrina added. "That was part of it. And David has done the same. That's where I met him. He had packages ready for all of us, things to help us get through the school year. School supplies, you know. And then, he played some music for us."

"He has a lovely voice," Elizabeth smiled. "And the guitar! He plays so well. But you must know that already, Camille."

Camille thought about David sitting in the youth room, plucking out chords on a guitar, grinning like he'd done something spectacular. He'd eventually joined the youth praise band like he said he would, but she couldn't remember even hearing him as he did backup.

"Yes," she affirmed absently.

"And then, he spoke about Jesus," Laina said. "Very simply. Just told us about the Bible. Gave us Bibles. We'd heard it before, of course. But we'd not heard about Jesus like this, like David talked about Him, like He was a friend. David told us he'd be in Swakopmund for a good long while and that every week he'd have Bible studies, worship, and church."

Camille nodded, thinking about the schedule David had shared with her earlier. Days set aside for visiting the schools, teaching Life Skills classes, guitar lessons given some evenings, a discipleship group halfway through the week, mornings spent visiting hostels and eating with students, Friday night Bible study and game night, and Sunday morning services at an old warehouse he and Piet had gutted and converted to a makeshift sanctuary.

All of David's life was tailored around reaching and teaching these students about the Word of God.

"And you're believers now?," Camille asked. "I mean, you knew before, but --"

"Now, we are born again," Katrina answered, smiling. "Jesus is someone I know now, like a friend. Not just someone I can read about."

"We can talk to Him," Elizabeth said. "Can trust Him with our problems. Can know that He understands."

"And we can live for Him," Laina added, finishing up Camille's toes. "That's always what we can do, no matter where we go."

Camille watched the three girls for a long moment and looked out at the other girls gathered there, all of them passing around bottles of nail polish, laughing and talking amongst themselves.

"And it's happened for others as well?," she asked.

"Yes," Katrina said. "God is really moving in Swakopmund."

And Camille took a readying breath, so eager to be a part of what He was already clearly doing... and so awed that she would be a part of it alongside such an amazing man like David.

David

So, he felt a little convicted.

There Camille was, with an audience full of students, saying all of these wonderful things about him that were probably unwarranted. Sure, it felt good hearing them, but the last thing he needed was Camille idolizing him.

He was an important guy. He got that. And they all thought he was pretty special. He got that, too. But Camille? Wow. She was talking about him like he could walk on water.

Which was awesome, obviously, because this was *Camille Evans* and all.

But seriously. He was convicted.

Though it would likely rock her world to not have him as the center of her universe (well, maybe that was taking it too far), he knew he had to bring her back down to earth for her own good, for the good of the ministry.

Yes. He had to be honest about his own failings, about who he was. And he knew just the story to tell her to make her see it.

He was prepared to tell her that story as they worked on closing down the house and packing the truck so that they could head back to the coast. The food they'd left needed to be transported back to Swakopmund, and it was going to take a while to get it all moved. As they worked in the kitchen, he opened his mouth to tell her just exactly why she shouldn't idolize him and all.

But before he could say anything, she began talking.

"How are Charity and Hope?," she asked.

He took a second, putting his story on hold in his mind and smiling at her. "They're good. You don't keep in touch with them, I guess?"

"Haven't spoken to them in years," she said. She looked up at him. "Had a bit of a falling out with Charity our first year of college. Of course, we all went separate ways, but we kept up with each other. And she was... making some bad choices."

Yeah, David could just imagine, given the long line of boys that had been through their home when she was a teenager. College? There was no telling what that had been like.

"Anyway," Camille said, "I confronted her about it all. As her friend, you know? And she stopped talking to me. So did Hope."

Well, that sounded like Charity.

"Immature," he said. "When it probably would have done her good to listen to you. And I don't know the details, but if it's any consolation, I'm sure Hope lost touch not because she was angry but because Charity told her that's what they were going to do."

"She was bossy like that," Camille affirmed.

"Yeah," he said.

"But they're doing okay, right?"

He thought of the twins back in Texas, leading very different lives, still all up in one another's business all the time.

"They're doing great," he said. "Charity's married. To a pastor of all things."

Camille regarded him with mild shock. "Well, my goodness."

"That was pretty much my same reaction," he laughed. "John's been good for her. He was Hope's friend, so you can guess what kind of brainiac, good guy he is."

"I'm glad to hear that," she said softly. "That she's married and in ministry."

He heard just a twinge of sadness in her voice. Over the loss of a friend, life not working out the way she'd planned... he wasn't sure. But it was there.

"She's a stay at home mom," he continued. "My nephew, Aiden, is three, and my niece, Amelia, should be here sometime after the new year."

"I'll bet Charity's a great mom," Camille smiled. "She was always so good with the children we'd volunteer with at church."

David thought about Charity on this last visit, sitting in the floor in their parents' living room, singing Sesame Street songs along with Aiden as they drove plastic cars all over his mother's Persian rugs, always sure to include a huge crash at the conclusion of every tune. He thought about Aiden, who he'd never even met until that last trip back to the US, given that he'd been born only after David had taken the job in Namibia. But there had been no shyness at that introductory meeting, as the kid had launched himself into David's arms on first sight and shouted, "I know yeeeeewww!" before introductions could even be made, recognizing his uncle from the pictures Charity had shown him.

"Aiden is a really awesome kid," David said, grinning to think of how the small boy had eaten every meal that weekend perched in David's lap, sharing Cheetos with him and loudly talking about Africa like he knew it all. So like his mother. "So, she's doing something right."

Camille smiled at this. "And you're probably a really great uncle, huh?"

"As great as I can be from so far away," he grinned. "I told him I'd start talking to him on the computer. Which prompted a lot of questions about how I was going to crawl myself into John's laptop."

She laughed out loud at this.

"Do you have nieces and nephews?," he asked. "I mean, more than the two you had back when you were still in Dallas."

"I have those two still," she nodded. "Tanner and Maggie. And I have four more now as well. Livi, Ethan, Charlotte, and Avery."

David whistled low at this. "Whoa. That's a lot of babies."

"Well, after Kyle passed away, Chelsea remarried," she said. "A younger man." She looked up at him meaningfully.

"What?," he snorted. "Does being with a younger man increase fertility or something?"

She blushed at this. "I didn't mean that. It's just, you know, she's a lot older than most new moms and still having all these babies because her husband is younger, and if she was with a man her own age, I think they'd probably be done by now. I mean, they'd be worn out by now. Surely."

She stopped, blushing even more as David raised his eyebrows at her.

"Good grief, David, I didn't mean *that* --"

"Didn't mean what?," he laughed.

"I can tell what you're thinking!"

"Then, please enlighten me," he said, loving the innocence in how embarrassed she was over something she'd only thought she'd implied. "What was I thinking?"

"I mean, not like worn out, as in... well, you know. I don't mean to make Seth sound like --"

"A typical younger man," he shook his head, still grinning at her. "Lots of energy and all, I guess, and a healthy appetite for --"

"Stop it," she muttered, blushing deeply now, reaching out and hitting him lightly.

"I didn't mean it like that," he said, blushing himself, laughing. "I meant as in energy to keep up with a house full of toddlers. Which is what you meant, too, obviously."

"Whatever," she said. "We were talking about our sisters --"

"Not about younger men," David said again.

"David," she warned.

"Fine, fine," he laughed. Then, quieter, "We heard about Kyle. I mean, we were connected because of Chelsea. And my dad was connected as well because the church Kyle had been pastoring had been a New Life plant decades ago."

"I know," Cammie said, looking up at him. "Your parents were there for the funeral."

"I'm glad to hear that Chelsea is well," he said. "That she's okay after going through that. Remarried. Found happiness again."

She nodded. "And how about Hope? Is she married?"

David thought of Hope, wondering at what kind of man could coexist with her....

His mind was drawing a complete blank.

"No," he said. "Too busy earning degrees at the seminary and working her butt off at New Life. She started and runs a ministry to teenage, single mothers in inner-city Dallas."

"Wow," Camille breathed. "That's wonderful."

"She's just like she always was," he agreed. "Opinionated, uncensored, dogmatic. Makes my dad really, really proud."

He thought of Paul Connor, always an approving eye on Hope, his protege.

"And you," Camille noted. "You must make him even prouder."

Yeah. Not so much.

"Maybe," he conceded.

"What you do here, who you've become," she beamed at him. "Who wouldn't be proud?"

And there it was again, this appreciation.

She was thinking too highly of him. He had to bring her back down to earth.

"Funny that you mention Hope and Charity," he said, taking it from this angle.

"Oh?"

"Yeah, because I was thinking, back when you were telling those girls about how amazing I am and all... well, about a time when you were spending the night with the twins at our house," he said.

She watched him for a moment. "I didn't say amazing, did I?"

"Something like it," he said.

She smiled at this and narrowed her eyes just slightly. "Oh-kay... well, then, go on, big shot."

"Big shot?"

Was that sarcasm he heard?

"You were telling me about a time when I slept over. I did that a lot," she said, continuing to work alongside him.

"Yeah," he said, continuing on now that he'd started down this road. "But this was during the remodel. You remember when they took out the ceilings in the upstairs rooms and we just had the open beams?"

It had made their voices echo. His mom had come to tell the girls to keep it down when they'd get to giggling, telling them that they were keeping everyone awake.

"I do," she said. "We were really loud that night."

"Yeah," David nodded. "And I should know. My room was right next to Hope's."

"I remember," Camille nodded, looking up at him. "You and your dumb friends were just as loud as we were."

"Louder," he said. "Except when we climbed on my bookshelves and watched you girls get ready for bed. We were really quiet and sneaky when we did that."

Camille's hands stilled over the work. She turned to face him slowly. "What?"

"Don't worry," he said, feeling guilty all over again. "I was the only one who saw anything. And I got plenty of grief over it later, because my friends told me I should've gotten off the shelf earlier so they could see Charity. Because... well, you know."

Yeah. She knew, surely. Charity, at sixteen, had the body of a centerfold. It grossed him out, honestly, but his little dweeby friends couldn't hardly look at her back then without bursting into giggles.

"Gotta good eyeful of your sister, then, David?," Camille asked wryly.

"Oh, no," he sighed. "I couldn't take my eyes off you."

She stopped what she was doing and turned to him. "You little... what was I wearing?"

He closed his eyes for a minute, wondering if this had been a smart idea after all, sharing this story. "Oh, wow, I can still see it in my mind. My twelve year old mind was unredeemed, of course, but it had a wonderful photographic memory."

"How dare —"

"Pink," he said, barreling on despite the anger in her voice. "This really light pink color. With lace around... well, you know. Little red hearts all over the place. And the matching little...whew." He was sweating even now at the remembrance. He put his hand to his forehead and kept right on going, anticipating that she'd reach out and hit him at any moment. "I was so sheltered I didn't even know what you were supposed to do with a woman anyway, but my very bad pubescent boy mind concluded that I'd be perfectly content to just watch you dance around like that. And you did. All night long in my head. And for a few years after that."

"You little pervert!," she hissed at him.

"You're telling me," he said, hardly able to look at her now, remembering how she'd looked then, so beautiful, in a way he hadn't even been able to imagine before stepping on that bookshelf. And falling, of course. Making enough of a racket that his father had come up to see what the problem was, had rightly ascertained what David had been doing, and had a little talk with him later.

David would never forget that talk.

"I get it, son," Paul Connor had said, frowning at him. "I really do. Pretty girl. And it's easy just to have a peek because it's exciting, and you've had a crush on her for a while now--"

"No, sir, it's not like that," David had lied.

"Don't lie to me, boy," Paul had said.

David had merely nodded, already ashamed of what he'd done.

"I get it, David Paul," his father had said, his voice softer. "But you've not earned the right to look at Cammie Evans or any other woman like that until you've covenanted to God to love her, protect her, and honor her the rest of her life."

This had seemed more serious than the situation warranted, honestly. She hadn't been naked or anything.

"Get that look off your face," Paul had said. "It actually is that big of a deal. Christ says if you look at a woman with lust in your heart it's the same as having her like she's some cheap whore."

Well, good grief. He'd just been looking.

Paul kept on, discerning all of his son's thoughts, like always. "What, David Paul? Do you think Cammie Evans is a --"

"No," David had stuttered, not even wanting to hear those horrible words attached to the most perfect girl he'd ever known. "Of course not. She's perfect, Dad."

"Then don't you dare dishonor her like that," Paul said. "And don't dishonor Christ. You're made for better than that, David Paul."

Wow. Back in Tsumeb, he felt conviction all over again just remembering these harsh but true words from his father.

He cleared his throat, truly embarrassed now. "My dad found out what I had done, and he had Jay go through a purity study with me. And it worked. I haven't looked at another woman in that kind of getup since, knowing that it does nothing to honor Christ or benefit me. So, you're up there all by yourself, Camille, dancing around all alone."

Oh, wow. That sounded bad. Like he was, even now, fantasizing about her and --

She hit him on the arm. "You're an awful missionary, David!"

"Hey," he protested, "I'm not thinking anything now. That was years ago!"

"Younger men," she swore, pointing her finger right into his chest. "Okay, yeah, so that *was* what I was talking about earlier. I just didn't know *how* much younger I was talking about!"

He should have felt really bad. And he really did. But he also felt the urge to start laughing. An illogical response to the conviction, the embarrassment, the horror on her face, the hilarity of the whole situation... who knew? He bit his tongue and tried to control himself.

Camille was too horrified to notice his struggle.

"I remember you meeting with Jay! To talk about the Scriptures, you said! You didn't mention the catalyst that made it happen!," she continued. "Even then it was --"

"Well, it started out with that," he conceded. "Moral purity. Keeping my eye on the prize and not on other things, you know. But it moved on to deeper matters of faith. Those were some of the best days of my life, studying with him, beginning to have a heart for God's Word, beginning to have a heart for student ministry. I mean, forgive me for saying it, but seeing you in your underwear... well, you know, it's at least part of the reason I'm in ministry today."

Her eyes widened at this. "Camille Evans. Inspiring a whole new generation of young men towards the mission field."

He couldn't help himself anymore. He burst out laughing.

"That's funny!," he said. "I don't remember you being so funny, Cammie --"

"It's Camille," she said between clenched teeth. "And it's not funny. You were thinking of me in my underwear, back when you said that over dinner. You're probably thinking of me in my underwear even now, you little perv."

He wasn't. Praise God, he wasn't.

Because he was working really hard to not think of her that way...

"Oh, no," he said, finally getting his laughter under control. "I'm not. Honest. But that's what I've been trying to say. I've been trying my best to let God redeem my pitiful, lost, unredeemed soul since then and make me more like Jesus. But that's what I was. Who I am, really, without Christ." He nodded at this, glad to see that she would finally look at him again. "I just don't want you putting me on a pedestal."

She narrowed her eyes at him and opened her mouth to say something. Then, shut it. Then, said it anyway. "I'm not idolizing you, you doofus."

Oh. Well, that was... good. Except not.

"But you said --"

"I was praising God for what *He's* done in you, David," she said. "Just like you said back in your sermon at that conference. It's not you. It's Him and what He's done. And if it sounded, to your egotistical ears, like I was singing *your* praises, then maybe you need a reality check. I would say you're a good guy, David, but there are *no* good guys. Scripture even says that. We're all just a bunch of train wrecks."

Ouch. And true. He could hear Paul Connor all over that theology.

Cammie had been listening in church all those years, obviously. And now, she was taking a sledgehammer to his pride. Which, you know, was probably more warranted than the wonderful things she'd said about him earlier.

"Oh," he managed.

"You're going to hear me say a lot to those students over the next few years," she continued on. "And you'll do well to remember that when I speak well of anyone, you especially, I'm really speaking to the goodness of God in putting any goodness in any of us. So don't worry about being on a pedestal. You weren't ever on one. Even *before* I knew the whole business about your voyeurism."

"Wow, voyeurism is a really harsh word," he muttered. "But point taken."

They watched one another for a long moment.

And for just a second, he saw shame in her eyes.

His breath caught. He was the one who should have been ashamed. Treating her like he had back then, spying on her... yet, here she was all these years later, looking just a little insecure, looking more than just a little hurt, looking like he had failed her somehow.

This wasn't what he'd intended.

"I'm so sorry, Camille," he said softly. "For back then. For assuming now that --"

"You know what, David?," she sighed. "Just don't. Just... please."

What a jerk. What an egotistical jerk he'd been, on top of being a rotten, hormonal, little boy. What a great way to start this new season of ministry, outing himself like this, for who he really was, and alienating her through no fault of her own.

"Camille," he said weakly. "I was wrong. Then and now. Please forgive me."

"You know," she said, letting out a deep breath and still not meeting his eyes, "that was a long time ago. And I'm blowing everything out of proportion anyway, probably."

He wanted to tell her that she wasn't. That she had a right to be irritated with him, not just for then but for now and how prideful he had become after just one affirming comment from her.

But before he could say any of it, she gave him a weak smile, clearly trying to cover up the hurt he'd caused. "So, are we finally ready to head out to Swakopmund?"

Cammie

The drive was quiet.

David Connor. Just another jerk.

The truth? Well, she probably *had* been putting him on a pedestal. It wasn't hard to do, given what his job was here, given how well he'd done it, given how much she admired his heart, and given how attractive she was finding him.

That was mortifying, honestly. The way she felt was mortifying, because he was like her little brother. And just as she was telling herself to get over it, that he wasn't really her brother and all... well, then, he'd come out and very nearly acknowledged that she had a crush on him, that she was checking him out, and that she thought he was amazing.

And then? He told her that he was a pervert.

Even as they drove across the country, she recalled any number of nights when the peeping situation could have happened, pulling her jacket tighter around her and glancing over to him as he drove silently.

Good on Paul Connor for coming down hard on him for that. And good on David for having learned his lesson. And good on her for vowing to hold it against him for a good, long while. That would certainly take care of any crush she was feeling for him. As if! His attractiveness had plummeted with the vision of his geeky self standing on his bookshelf checking her out.

Except not. Because even as she shot him glares, she had to admit that he was still... well, really cute.

Seriously, Cammie? Good grief...

And he was remorseful. She could see that, too. Convicted and regretful. Very, very sorry.

No one was inherently good on their own, but David Connor had plenty of good in him, all thanks to Jesus, all given because of grace.

She was being too tough on him.

"I'm sorry again," he said softly as she continued watching him.

"You know, David," she said, "you were just a dumb kid."

"I was," he said.

She looked out the window, thinking about how she'd been plenty dumb herself back then. Hanging out with Charity and Hope, dismissing David and his geeky friends as being practically non-existent, ignoring them most of the time they all were in the same area, much less the same house. She remembered laughing as Charity and Hope had talked about David as though he was still an annoying kindergartener, even when he'd been nearly a teenager.

Annoying kindergartener nothing. He'd clearly been more grown up than she'd figured. She'd underestimated him, that was for sure.

She glanced over at him again, still frowning as she did so.

"I'll make it up to you," he said, glancing at her hopefully.

"You don't need to," she said, reasoning that it was dumb to hold onto a grudge, especially one stemming from something that had happened so long ago. And especially since David was so obviously a changed man. "It's okay, David."

"I just said I'd make it up to you," he said. "And you told me no."
A long pause. "Don't you even want to know what I was
planning?"

At this, at the eagerness in his voice, she had to fight back a smile.
"Well, is it something good?"

"Oh, yeah," he said. "It will have you completely forgiving me and
thanking God that He ordained for you to come here and join the
work going on."

"Yeah, about that," she said, looking over at him, "I talked to
those girls. Katrina, Laina, and Elizabeth."

"Good girls," he said, releasing a breath, clearly relived that she
was moving on with him. "Very faithful in all that they're doing
with the church out in Swakop." He smiled. "Though they do
tend to roll their eyes just a little when we go back to sports and
roughhousing and --"

"I can imagine," Camille noted. "But they did tell me about all the
ways your ministry here has changed their lives. This is real,
meaningful work. I can't wait to jump right in."

She watched as he smiled at this. "Sooner than later," he said.
"School starts next week. They'll be coming back to town in a few
days."

"They mentioned that," she said.

"The hostels will be full again, and Swakopmund will change
completely. From a fairly empty tourist town to a teenage
wonderland of sorts. Students just waiting to hear the Gospel and
carry it back home with them on school breaks."

"And you get to be a part of it all," she said. "Excuse me, *we* get
to be a part of it all."

"That's exactly right," he said.

"I want to see where it all takes place," she said. "Can you take me by and show me where you have church, where you do your group meetings, where you throw your parties?"

"Well, there goes the surprise," he said, sighing dramatically. "That's how I was going to make it up to you."

"That works," she said, smiling at him at last.

"But before that," he said, "I'll take you for your first helping of fish and chips, right on the beach."

And this? Sounded even better.

"Awesome," she said, settling into her seat and anticipating her first glance of the ocean.

David

They'd arrived at the coast just half an hour before sunset.

David had rushed through buying the best fish and chips in town, chatting with Camille as they'd walked into the shop together, then hurried back out again to his truck. He sped the entire way back down to the beach, stopping just in time to jump out, lead her over to the seawall, and point to the horizon as she sat down.

The sun was just beginning to slip down into the water.

"Amazing," she had said, her eyes bright as she watched it. "You get to see this every day, huh?"

He did. And he'd not once stopped and thought it "amazing" as she'd said, given how many other "amazing" things he saw here.

After they'd eaten, he took her from one amazing location to the next, telling her stories about how his ministry here had started, where it was going, and what his days looked like. In her eyes, he saw it all anew as she took in what he was saying, as she looked around at the places where God had done the work, and as she sighed contentedly.

"Amazing," she had said again.

And it was. It really was. He was more excited for this new school term now, given who would be here to see it all alongside him, given how well she'd already connected to the girls in Tsumeb.

They had talked all the way to the Botha house, where Kait lived with Piet's mother, Ana Marie.

"Will I meet her tonight, then?," Camille asked.

"No, actually," he shook his head. "She's in the States visiting her brother for the next few months. Then, she'll be going on to Asia to visit her other son."

"Wow," Camille murmured. "World traveler."

"And you would know," he pointed out, smiling as he pulled into Ana Marie's driveway. "Anyway, it was a surprise to us that you're... well, you're a woman, obviously. Which I know, obviously."

Obviously. David kicked himself a little for sounding like a dunce.

Camille only looked at him, no offense or chiding in her eyes.

"Anyway," he said, "your living arrangements had to be changed in light of that. Kait suggested that you stay here, if that sounds okay."

"Oh," Camille said, looking to the house. "Well, that should be fine, I guess. It's been a while since I've had a roommate... but it'll probably be nice to have Kait around to help me adjust, huh?"

"Probably," David said. "We do a lot of work from here anyway, so it should be convenient."

"Great," she said. "Then, I'll go ahead and get my bags --"

"Oh, no, let me get it all for you," he said, already getting out and going to the back to get everything for her, leading her up the walkway as she protested and offered to help him.

"Camille, it's fine," he said, his hand already in the air, ready to knock on the door --

When it flew open on its own.

"There you guys are!," Kait practically yelled at him. Her eyes fell on Camille. "Well, welcome home, Camille. Come on in."

David watched as Camille moved into the house, taking stock of everything around her. "Oh, this is beautiful. David was telling me that this is Piet's mother's house?"

"Ja," Piet said, coming out from the kitchen, smiling. "The house I grew up in. David, let me take those bags for you. Kait said you wanted to go over plans for the party. We've already got everything set up in the kitchen ready to go."

"When's the party?," Camille asked, smiling, even as Piet left the room with her bags.

"David told you all about them, huh?," Kait asked.

"He did, and the teenagers did as well," she said.

"Teenagers?," Kait asked. "Did you get to meet some of them in Tsumeb?"

"Yeah," David said, smiling. "She's already BFFs with all the girls."

Camille smiled at him appreciatively. He loved that look on her face.

120

"I'm so excited to meet even more of them," she said.

"Well, the party is set for tomorrow night. Right, David?," Kait asked.

"That's the plan," he said. "If we can get everything sorted out and ready."

"Already done," Piet said, coming back in. "Kait and I came back from Tsumeb early and spent most of the afternoon working on it all."

"Then, what's left to do?," David asked. "Let's go ahead and finish it up so we're ready."

They all made their way into the kitchen, where bags and boxes of all kinds of supplies were laid out. School supplies, personal items, snacks, and Bibles on every surface in the Botha kitchen. Kait showed them all what had been done, David made some recommendations, and in no time at all, all four of them were gathered around grouping things together, separating everything, and getting it lined up and ready for the party. Halfway through their work, Kait slipped her phone into the radio and started a playlist.

It began with a song about Texas.

David looked up to find Camille smiling at him.

"I come all this way, only to hear about home," she said.

"I hate this song," Piet noted.

"But it's about home," David said. "And you don't hate it. I taught you to dance to this one, Piet."

Camille raised her eyebrows at this.

"He did," Piet acknowledged.

"Yeah, and he taught Ana Marie as well," Kait said, grinning. "She was so besotted with the way he danced that she told him she'd marry him. Told him he could be Piet's new papa and all."

"Who's your daddy, Piet?," David grinned over at him.

"Ja, well," Piet grumbled, "that's enough of that."

"What dance did David teach her?," Camille asked.

"We'll show you," David said, reaching out for Piet. "Come on, dance with me. Camille's watching, too, so make it good."

"I do not want to be the woman again," Piet said, frowning, coming closer to him. "You must let me lead, David."

"I would," David said, "but you're pitiful."

"I'm a great dancer," Piet swore, taking David's hands anyway, allowing himself to be led.

"Not with this," David said.

"Camille, do you know how to do the funny dance he always does?," Piet asked her, grinning, even as David began dancing him around the room with a smile on his face. "Because Kait had never even heard of it."

"Well, it depends on what you're doing," Camille asked, smiling as well, watching them. "But, yes, I think I know that one."

"Yeah," David said, letting go of Piet, hoping for a better partner as he glanced over at her. "She taught me this one herself, so there's no need to demonstrate any more of it for her."

And as she acknowledged this with a nod, his mind went back to that lazy Saturday afternoon when Cammie knocked on his bedroom door.

He was lying in bed, a game controller in his hand, creating the perfect NBA team using their roster of real live players... plus a player of his own creation. He deleted Trent Patterson right off of his team and put that new player, a rookie named David Connor, in his place.

The David Connor on the screen was a big dude. Huge muscles. Over seven feet tall. Handsome, if he did say so himself. And way better than any other player out there or any other player that had ever lived, quite honestly.

David Connor, NBA star.

The pounding on his door began only a few minutes into the championship game with David Connor already putting points up onto the board. He ignored the knocking for a long while, pretending not to hear it, until it was clear that the person on the other side wouldn't take a hint and go away.

"What?," he said, a groan in his voice even as he made his way to the door, thinking it was Charity, with bossy instructions from his mother, forever relishing the opportunity to pick at him.

He flung open the door, ready to really tell her off.

But his voice caught when he saw her, Cammie Evans, standing there instead.

He was twelve. And she was over at the house all the time, just like she'd always been.

But it was different now. It had been different for a while. Because Cammie was different.

Taller. Prettier. Looking very, very grown up.

David? Well, not so much. Everything David Connor the fake NBA player was the real David Connor was not. Short, too skinny, and kind of weird looking.

He was kind of like a hideous elf, standing next to a supermodel princess, here with beautiful Cammie Evans. He was sure she noticed the incongruity between the two of them.

It only made it seem more strange and disconcerting, the way that his heart raced whenever he saw her, even if he did well to never let her see how she affected him.

"David," she said with some urgency, reaching right through the doorway and pulling him out of his room. "I need you."

Oh, glory. She needed him. And she was touching him!

He didn't even ask any questions as she dragged him down to Hope's room. Anything Cammie needed him to do, he would do. Anywhere she wanted him to go, he would go. Just as long as she didn't take her blessed hand off his suddenly favored arm.

His attention was only momentarily torn from her beautiful face when he got to Hope's room and saw his sisters holding one another in an embrace.

He frowned at this and opened his mouth to question what was going on, when Charity said to Cammie, "Okay, show us."

And Cammie took David's hand in hers and put his other hand on her waist.

He very visibly swallowed... and started sweating. This was a dream. Surely this was a dream, and he was going to wake up any minute now --

"David," Cammie said, authority in her voice. "I'm going to lead this time. But you figure it out so that you can lead next time."

"What?," he asked, certain that if this *was* a dream he wouldn't be sweating nearly this much. "What are we doing?"

124

"Dancing, David," Hope muttered. "Charity and Cammie have dates for the Homecoming dance. And Charity doesn't know how to dance. We're trying to teach her some basics, at least."

But David had been caught up on something else. "Dates? You have dates?"

"With seniors!," Charity squealed.

Cammie smiled a little at this as well.

"Older boys?," David asked, still holding onto Cammie, hating the idea of anyone else standing this close to her, holding her like this. Especially not taller, older, manlier guys who didn't resemble elves. "Is that a good idea?"

"Probably not," Hope said dismissively. "Well, go on, Cammie. Teach us. Use David. Show us what to do."

David didn't much like the idea of being used.

But if Cammie Evans was going to be the one using him --

"Got it," she said. "Okay, David. Stand up straight."

He did... and it put him at eye level with her chest. He tried in vain to find anywhere else to look.

"The rhythm is one, two, one," she said as he continued to stare.

"One, two, one," he said, finally closing his eyes so he could concentrate for a moment.

One of the twins flipped on the music as he continued chanting the rhythm to himself, his eyes closed, even as Cammie began to move and he began to move with her.

And as she moved rather gracefully beneath his hands and he attempted to focus, he found that for all that he couldn't do as a dweeby, awkward, little guy... well, he could do this. Elves could dance, apparently. He moved closer to her, continuing on in the rhythm she'd started for them, keeping pace right alongside her, and opening his eyes at last, smiling to see how she beamed at him.

"Do you see how easy it is? Even David's a natural," Cammie said to his sisters, even as she reached out and messed up his hair, letting him go for a moment, much to his disappointment.

"She keeps stepping on my feet," Hope groaned. "Charity, you're like a graceless cow."

"Hope!," Charity gasped. "Did you really just call me a cow?!"

"Well, if the hooves fit," Hope said. "Seriously, all over my feet. You're going to look like a fool at that dance."

Charity, panicked at the thought, began whining to Cammie. "I need to see it again!"

Cammie nodded, then looked to David. "Okay, you lead now. Now that you've figured it out. Think you can do that?"

"I can do anything for you, Cammie," he said, so ready to be her dancing elf.

"Okay, then," Cammie said, missing the look in his eyes. Thankfully. "Here we go."

And he danced and danced, twirling Cammie Evans around and around, praying that God wouldn't let that song end and that Charity would never figure it out so that he could spend the rest of the night just like this...

"I remember teaching you," Camille said, all these years later, all grown up, smiling at him now in Swakopmund. "Tried to help your sister."

He nodded. "You did, but she was hopeless."

126

"She didn't even end up using those skills anyway," Camille shrugged. "She spent the whole dance in a dark corner of the gym, kissing the creep of a guy who took her."

Kait raised her eyebrows at this. "Wild preacher's daughter."

"Yeah," Camille and David said together... then smiled.

"But you danced that night, right?," David asked, wondering who her date had been back then, hoping he had treated her better than Charity's date had treated her.

"I did," she said. "But just one dance. I went with a guy from the church. He was too nervous to even hold my hand. Or call me again after that one date."

David was glad for this. And as the music continued on at the Botha house, he grinned, going for levity, even as his heart pounded.

"Well, we need to show Piet how it's really done. Because he makes a miserable woman."

"Thank you for that," Piet muttered, even as David held out his hand for Camille.

And she took it.

"You lead this time, huh?," she asked, glancing up at him.

"I'd love to," he answered, draping his arm over her shoulders, just as she drew closer to him.

"Well, you're taller than you were last time," she noted, a gleam in her eyes as she smiled.

"Yeah, I'm staring at your forehead now, instead of..." And he stopped the thought, but not before Camille could raise her eyebrows at this. "Never mind."

As the music continued on, sounding so much like home with this woman who had been so much a part of who he'd always been, David found himself pulling her closer, his lips just a breath from her cheek. Cammie Evans...

"I think you've been practicing," she chided softly, squeezing his hand.

"Better than I was at twelve, huh?," he asked.

"I think so," she breathed, just as the song ended.

Camille backed away, still smiling at him.

"Well, that song was a lot shorter than I would have liked," David said, very simply, his eyes still on her.

"Too long still, though," Kait said in her no nonsense voice, as Camille's eyes regrettably drifted from his. "Let's get the rest of this work done so we can all go to bed at a normal time, huh?"

And David went to it, still remembering the feel of Camille Evans in his arms.

Cammie

She'd stayed up too late the night before.

Once David and Piet left, she'd had time to talk to Kait, one on one.

And now that she knew Kait had been very deeply involved in the board and its matters, Camille had a whole lot she wanted to talk about with her.

The same was true going the other direction as well.

"I was by myself in Brazil, for the most part," Camille said, answering Kait's question, as they talked about where she'd been, what all she'd done. "But there were ten of us in Russia."

Kait nodded, grinning over the Dr. Pepper she held in her hand. "I read that in the list of jobs you'd held. And all ten of you were women. Crazy."

"Not so much," Camille shrugged. "You know the numbers. How it goes."

She'd always go back to this, no matter where she was. It was almost as if she was holding up her willingness to go, her willingness to put herself far away from home and a normal life, as a credit to her spirituality. When she'd go back to the US on furlough and meet men in ministry, it was always a thorn of sorts to her, the way they'd acknowledge what she did with nods and affirm that they were glad they weren't called to that.

She knew it was wrong, but she was proud of it. Proud that she was one of the few who went.

And at the same time, she was resentful. Because it cost so much.

She'd felt the truth of that as she'd seen Piet kiss Kait goodbye earlier.

This was what it cost. Regular relationships.

"It is a bit skewed," Kait acknowledged. "Which is what's so unusual about being here. There's David, of course. A man who could have any ministry job he wanted back in the US, with his father being who he is."

Camille caught this mention, just as she had the earlier mention, up in Tsumeb, of Paul Connor.

"You know about David's dad?," she asked.

Kait looked at her for a long moment. "Everyone in the convention knows about Paul Connor. Or they will, at least."

Somewhere in the back of her mind, Camille registered something odd about this comment. Sure, Paul Connor was a big deal back home, but he certainly didn't garner the interest in Kait's eyes as she had mentioned him.

Before she could question it, Kait was already back to the subject that Camille could (and did) talk into the ground.

Men. And how they left the work of foreign missions to women.

"So, there's David here," Kait said. "Unusual. A single man in a career position. And before him, years ago? The pioneer missionary from the board was a man. Single, too. Served for ten years here, all by himself, never even leaving Africa when he was on furlough."

"Good for him," Camille murmured. "That's commitment."

"Commitment or stubbornness," Kait shrugged. "But he was the only one in *all* the board's personnel, way back then. The only single man serving in a career capacity. The rest were short term or married."

"Or women," Camille said. "How many single women were serving in career roles at the same time?"

"Seventy-eight," Kait grinned. "But maybe that was a direct result of the way the board advertises itself. We name our foundations and our organizations for single women missionaries in our history who paved the way... not men."

"Single women," Camille said, thinking of the very ones she'd seen quoted, from centuries past, who were the very faces of overseas ministry for their convention. "And even those ladies pointed out that it was a shame that the men wouldn't stand up and do more."

"That they did," Kait nodded. "And that's what the board promotes. A bunch of spinster ladies living for Christ overseas and browbeating and shaming the men into being men."

Camille bristled just a little at this description. Spinster. Browbeating. Shaming.

"Doesn't mean the men aren't culpable for ignoring the call overseas," Kait said.

"They are culpable," Camille noted.

"But you've got to wonder what came first. The chicken or the egg? Us teaching little boys that our missionary heroes are women, or the lack of men willing to go with that stereotype hanging over their heads?"

No easy answers, obviously.

"Well, here in Namibia. Single men. That's the history," Camille murmured.

"Yeah," Kait smiled at her. "Of course, that one single guy before David didn't stay single. He was here for ten years by himself. Then, the board sent a woman in a temporary position to do something that wasn't part of any of his strategies at all. Irritated him plenty, probably, but didn't stop him from marrying her and spending thirty years with her here."

"Wow," Camille breathed. "Does that happen often?"

"No," Kait said. "Personnel who've been single that long or even just as long as you, working on the field... they stay single." She shrugged. "Which is good. Makes it easier to serve Christ if you're sold out and content with never marrying. Husbands, kids -- they tend to compete for your loyalty."

"Mmmhmm," Camille murmured, feeling, at the same time, inexplicably sad about being lumped into the category of forever single missionaries and proud that she was able to serve Christ without distractions. "Well, good for the board. Here in Namibia. Having David, one of the very few single men out there, working here so faithfully."

Kait had grinned at this. "Oh, yeah. And you know how they like to brag about the men. More so than the women."

Oh, yeah, Camille knew about this, too. Politics, perceptions. The board made itself look more favorable, thought it made Christ's commands to go to all the nations more palatable if they could hold up men who had other options yet still embraced it as their calling.

This was irritating as well.

Because in a career where she'd given everything to be faithful, she was still heralded less than a man would be in the same situation. Because men were still heralded in a way that women weren't.

There was some chauvinism there, definitely. And if she wasn't more convicted about the fact that she felt the need to be heralded at all for serving Jesus, of all things, she would have been more righteously indignant about it all.

Of course, she was already righteously indignant enough about it.

"Well, good for them," she muttered to Kait.

She'd remembered it all again the next day when they'd arrived for the party.

There were students everywhere. Word of mouth had done its work amongst the regular teens, and the news about this party had spread to what certainly felt like every student in town, all of them having just arrived from the north like a swarm.

Camille spent the time moving from one task to another, getting things ready until Kait finally waved her away.

"Go meet them," she said, her hands full of the packages she and Piet were busy getting out to the students. "David's got a whole crowd over by the seawall. Go over and meet them."

Camille did this gladly, having hoped for the opportunity all afternoon and having been disappointed when the tasks kept her from it. She made her way to David's side where he began introducing her around.

She'd parted ways from him thirty minutes later, so into conversations with a huge group of girls, all of them firing one question after another at her about life in Texas, giving her suggestions of places to see in Namibia, and already forming relationships that she was certain would define her life here in this new place.

She was so into all that they were discussing that it took a long moment before she realized that someone was singing and playing a guitar.

It took her a few more moments after that to connect that voice to David Connor.

His speaking voice had matured, so it just made sense that his singing voice would have as well. And while she'd only known him to be able to play a few chords (and that was bad enough), he'd obviously figured out how to do a little more.

He was actually quite good.

As he sang familiar songs -- familiar to Camille, familiar to the students there -- he found her eyes in the crowd and gestured her up with a nod of his head.

"Maybe Camille will sing harmony for us," he said, even as he continued playing, smiling over at her.

She could do this easily enough, and so she picked up the song with him, seamlessly joining in what he was doing.

As the song continued into another and Camille began to worship from her heart, she thanked God that He'd sent her here, to a place where she seemed to fit right in.

David

Well, everything about that had been thrilling.

The party had gone off well, like it always did. But it seemed like there were even more students this time. David had reconnected with every last one of his students from the last term and had met at least one hundred others, invited them all to the next event, and had already started the task of trying to memorize names, which of the three schools they attended, and how he could get in touch with them.

And then, there was Camille.

She probably didn't remember the days he'd played in the youth praise band back in high school, always pushed back into a corner because he was just learning and just getting good, but he'd been only a few feet away from her every week when they'd open up for the Sunday school hour. He'd always watched her, listening to how she sang so perfectly on pitch, and being so thankful that he knew her and knew how her words were authentic.

Cammie didn't just sing about God. She knew Him. He knew it from the life she lived beside his sisters, from the way she served Christ, and from the joy in her life.

All these years later, he still knew it, as she joined him, as she finally saw him as they worshipped alongside all of those students.

What a thrill.

Just as the crowds were beginning to disperse, he turned to tell her just a fraction of this, but his attention was re-directed to the elderly man who approached them.

"Brother David," he said loudly in a thick accent, reaching out his hand for David's hand.

"Brother Tobias," David grinned. "How are you, friend?"

"Doing well," he said. "These students! Where have they all come from?"

"Your neck of the woods," David grinned. "That's where."

Tobias looked over at Camille and raised his eyebrows. "And who is this?"

"This," David said, grinning, "is Camille Evans. A new missionary from the States."

Tobias regarded Camille with a raised eyebrow. "Sho," he breathed. "A woman?"

David could see a flash of irritation on Camille's face about this. How many times had she already heard it from everyone?

Probably too many times.

"Yeah," he laughed. "And we sure did need her out here. Camille, this is Pastor Tobias Nujoma. He comes down from Oshakati and his church there a few times a year to do some work in the refugee camp just north of town."

"Oh," Camille smiled. "I've heard a few things about it. David drove me by earlier."

"Which he should not be doing," Tobias said. "Not safe there for a woman." He shook his head at David. "Would have been much better if they had sent a man, Brother David."

"I don't know about that," David said, glancing over at Camille, worried about the look on her face.

"Women are better suited for other things," Tobias said with some authority. "Church work is men's work."

"The work of Christ is all of our work, though, isn't it?," David asked. "And that's church work at its very essence, friend. Jesus Himself had women disciples."

"But the twelve were men," Tobias noted. "As was fitting. And the epistles say plenty about women and their place."

And before David could continue on with this conversation, knowing that there were no easy answers in two different cultures on a subject that David's own culture was grappling to understand itself, Camille spoke up.

"I have more experience than David does," she said, in a voice that was surprisingly sour, given how sweet the words were that she'd offered to Christ only moments earlier in song.

"Do you?," Tobias asked, surprised by this outburst.

"Yes, and perhaps David would have gotten another male worker in here if men weren't, on the whole, abysmal failures at answering the call of Christ."

Oh, wow. That was harsh.

Tobias apparently thought so as well as he narrowed his eyes at her, then glanced over at David.

"Well," he said.

David could see Camille opening her mouth again. And while praying for forgiveness for this, even as he did it, he interrupted her. "Hey, Camille, can you check and make sure that Kait doesn't need any help?," he asked.

She cut her eyes at him, sensing that he was brushing her off.

But she did as he asked, turning on her heel and leaving them both behind.

Camille

That man. That man had *not* been right to say what he did.

She'd heard more of the same before. Church work was hard work for a woman, to be expected to fade to the background, to follow a man...

"What was that?," David asked, reaching out and grabbing her arm not even a minute later.

"That?," she asked, gesturing to the awful man who was now joking around with the teenagers. "That was the same old song and story I've heard my whole career."

"Probably," David said, looking annoyed with her.

Annoyed. With *her.* And not that loudmouthed, awful man!

"But what you said," David continued. "What was that?"

She resisted the urge to roll her eyes at him. "That was me. Standing up for myself. Standing up for every woman who's ever had to listen to that."

"By pitching a fit?," he asked.

And at this? She did roll her eyes.

"Was I just supposed to stand there and listen to that?," she asked.

"You were supposed to be Christlike and kind, even in the face of that, Camille," he said. "Did it do anything to further your witness to the grace of Christ or to correct his assumptions about women and their place in Christ's work when you bit off his head like that?"

"I hardly think I bit off his head," she huffed, feeling just a tiny bit of remorse for having -- yes -- bitten off the man's head.

Because it didn't help anything, honestly. It felt great, but it didn't do anyone any good. Only made the man's point for him, likely.

David sighed. "I'm not saying he was entirely right, but --"

"Well, good," she said. "I'm glad I'm working with someone who thinks I'm worth something. Even if he can't stop talking about how I was supposed to be a man."

"Camille," David said softly. "I told you that it was a *good* thing that God sent you."

"I know," she said, still thinking of the words she'd heard, in so many places, about how disappointed people seemed sometimes to hear that their missionary was a woman, to hear that the missionary speaker back home in the churches was a woman.

Guess she can speak at a women's banquet. That's what they'd say, with such disappointment in their voices. Camille always wanted to shout, "You can have a man speak anywhere if any of you men will actually get up and go do the work!"

She could get so angry about it all.

"Then what was that?," David asked again, looking quite shocked by all that had happened.

"This is hard work," she said to him. "Always expecting to fade into the background and follow someone else --"

"That's the work of ministry," he said. "We're all called to fade into the background and follow Christ."

True enough. But wow, she didn't want to hear it because it convicted her, very nearly began to correct the wrong ways she was thinking about her work.

So, she tried another approach.

"You can't tell me that you're not here because you're a man. That they didn't work hard to get you here because you're a man. And Paul Connor's son at that."

That caught his attention.

"That has nothing to do with why I'm here," he said. "And I get that you're irritated with the gender dynamics that go on. I'm sure you've had plenty of time to stew over it all. I remember you mentioning it back at the conference."

She had mentioned it. And she had years of time to stew over all of it before then, of course.

"But you're not going to let your irritation over things that you can't change right now ruin what you're here to do," he said. "I'm not going to let you sabotage what Christ wants to do through you."

"You're not going to *let* me," she said, hearing the snide side of her voice.

"I'm not the enemy," he said. "And I don't know what's going on in your head and how you've been hurt, or what expectations you already have that you're projecting onto me, but it's clear that you unintentionally despise men who are trying to do the good work of the Gospel out here. And what you said likely hurt the relationship I've built with that pastor. We're all on the same team, and you just did your best to work against it."

And this? Hurt. Because it was true. There was pride on her part, most definitely, for doing the job that most men wouldn't. So much so that she'd failed to see that it wasn't a gender issue at all, that David was here, doing exactly what she was doing, with the added responsibility of being in charge of it all, with all the demands and stresses that involved.

She was one of those stresses, doing what she'd just done.

"I'm not the enemy, Camille," he said softly. "And I'm certainly not some goofy kid you knew years ago who can't get it right. As I'm sure you were ready to tell Tobias. Drag down the men around you so that you look better."

"That wasn't my intention," she said, just as softly.

"I don't know what your intention was," he said. "But can we agree to something?"

"Yes," she offered, already beginning to wish that she'd never said anything at all.

"You," he said, bending down to look her in the eye, "are just as valuable to the purposes of God here as I am. Maybe more. Because you're right. You're bringing more experience to the table."

That's not what she'd meant. She hadn't meant to insult him. She'd only meant to prove herself.

To someone who didn't really matter anyway...

"David, I --"

"But," he said, cutting her off, "that doesn't mean that I don't have an appointed role here."

"Board-appointed?," she asked, thinking of how they would classify this relationship. Camille could just imagine. David in charge, the big man leading the clueless little woman, because men were always in charge, even if they were in short supply all over the world, and --

"No, God-appointed," he said. "Tobias said a lot of things that weren't entirely right, but he hit some of them head-on. Like how it isn't safe for you to do the same things I do here sometimes. How there are some definite Scriptural guidelines for church leadership. How men actually aren't worthless."

"I didn't say that," she gasped.

"Can you trust me?," he asked. "Can you see past the geeky little kid from New Life-Dallas and trust that I'm following Christ, that I'm taking my cues from the Lord, and that I want to lead this team here? I swear, Camille, I'm not going to discount your opinions and your wisdom along the way, but I have a responsibility to you. And it's not just board-given. But I'm responsible for you because Scripture calls me to lead in what's going on here and to do my job as a man of God and shepherd of the church He's established here, actually caring for those under my watch. Which includes you."

She said nothing for a long moment, thinking of the responsibility he already had, already felt called to here, was already fulfilling.

She thought about how there was some freedom and goodness in that, in being someone under his watch care.

She'd never, in all of her years, thought about it like that.

"David, I --"

"Just pray about it," he said. "Not the enemy, Camille. I'm so not your enemy here."

And he left her alone to think about it.

David

Two hours later, he was finally back at his cottage, done with the whole event.

But his mind hadn't been on the success of it all.

His mind had been on Camille, on the way she'd felt slighted by Tobias's words and likely years of the same unfair assessments by the board and the church at large... and the way she'd bitten back.

Unfair, yes. Not that she'd been right to say what she had, but she'd had a point. David had watched in high school as boys much less capable than her had been asked to lead the group and how Cammie had sat by and had probably nursed some bitterness in her heart because of this.

To think that she felt this way about him, though, that she thought him less capable... well, it hurt. He was her friends' goofy kid brother, yes, but he felt called here, called to this ministry, called to lead this team, and called, since he'd seen her in Tsumeb and welcomed her, to look out for her, protect her, and care for her as much as she would allow him.

Stupid David.

She didn't need that or want that, likely. But it didn't change who God had called him to be here.

Just as he was wondering how they would carry on with this between them, this irritation, this inequality of sorts, he got a text on his phone.

His first text from Camille, who had only just gotten her new Namibian phone that morning.

I'm sorry.

Before he could even text her back, she responded again.

I want to follow you as you follow Christ.

And David breathed a sigh of relief, all while feeling even more responsibility, hearing that such a capable, competent woman, ordained by Christ for the very same tasks that he was called to, was going to be looking to him as a leader.

He texted her back, praying even as he let his fingers move over the screen.

We'll follow Him together, Camille.

SWAKOPMUND

Cammie

Winter turned to spring, and spring turned to summer.

And there was sand everywhere.

Camille still wasn't accustomed to the grainy sand that followed her wherever she went. She'd adjusted to seaside life fairly easily, but she was still surprised to find that no matter how careful she was, how tedious she was in cleaning her space in the house she still shared with Kait, how meticulous she was in keeping the sand from her hair and her body... well, it was still always there. In crevices and folds in her purses and clothes, in between her toes, always under her fingernails, and in every step she took.

It was particularly noticeable after a weekend of camping in the dry bed of the Swakop river. She and David had taken seventy-four teenagers down there, where they spent hours singing praise songs, studying Scripture, and just hanging out, continuing on in the relationships that had been forged since David had arrived in Namibia and in the months that Camille had been by his side, ministering with him.

She had sand in her hair and the smell of smoke from the braai the night before still in her nose as she continued hugging students farewell back in Swakop, unloading David's truck.

But she didn't care about the sand. She only cared about the conversation, so familiar now after all these months, that David was having with a student who had just joined their group for the first time that weekend.

She listened inconspicuously as she continued to work.

"It's a hard thing to get," David was saying. "How God is judgement and grace, all at the same time."

"Brother David," the young man responded, breathless as he'd been towards the end of the time they'd all spent together, as he'd begun to ask questions, as it was evident that God was doing something in his heart, "I've done many wrong things in my life."

"We all have," David said. "But God is merciful, ready to forgive."

"Not the God I know," he said. "It is all judgement and Hell. That is all I've ever known of church, of the Bible."

"God is entirely just," David said. "And He does judge. And He does send people to Hell. We're all earning ourselves Hell, every day of our lives, living in sin."

Tough words. True words.

"Even if I do good, though," the student said. "Even if I do more good than anyone around me, I still earn Hell?"

"You sure do," David said. "So do I. My good's not good enough for God. All the good in the world's not good enough for God. He's holy. Perfect. There's no measuring up to His standard."

Even tougher words. Still just as true.

"But you said that God forgives!," their young friend gasped.

"He does," David smiled. "That's the mystery, isn't it? That He judges, and that He's right to do so. But He's merciful. Grace without reason, without our earning it, all for His glory."

The student watched him for a long moment. "I don't understand how He can be both."

"Think about it like this," David said, and Camille smiled from where she worked, knowing exactly what he was going to say, having heard him say these words so many times already to so many students as he led them right into hope. "You committed a crime. A bad crime. Think of it in your mind."

The student thought for a moment. "Okay."

"And you're before a judge. He has to punish you. You broke the law. He'd be a horrible judge if He didn't sentence you to a punishment that fit your crime. So, He does. BAM. Verdict delivered. Then, He comes down from the bench. Comes to where you stand in your handcuffs. And He takes them off of you. And He puts them on Himself. And He says to you, *I will take your punishment for you*. He pays for your crime. You did nothing to deserve that. You deserve the punishment. You deserve to pay for the crime. But He took it for you. He delivered the punishment, and He Himself took it. That, my friend," David said, leaning down and looking in the student's eyes with a smile, "is what God has done for you."

The student simply nodded, obviously overcome by this explanation. "I will think on this, Brother David."

"Good man," David said softly. "And I will pray for you as you think on it."

Camille turned away once again as David said goodbyes, leaving the two of them alone in his driveway as she continued unloading all the supplies they'd taken with them.

She felt his familiar arm drape over her shoulders and felt her heart kick up a beat and her smile deepen as his familiar drawl very nearly spoke right into her ear.

"I think he gets it," David sighed.

Camille looked up at him, squinting in what was left of the sunlight, just as the sun was settling down on the ocean. "I think you're right," she said, her arm around his waist for just a moment, squeezing in agreement. "But," and at this she dropped her arm back down and picked up the ice chest she'd just unloaded, "it might take him a while to figure it out."

"Camille," he chided, taking the ice chest from her, "let me get that."

"I've already unloaded almost everything," she said. "Lifted much heavier things than that."

"You should have waited on me," he said. "Waited for me to be done talking, so I could have helped you. But --"

"I didn't," she said, looking over all she'd done. "I never do."

"So determined to be a team player," he murmured, grinning at her.

"I'm a great team player," she affirmed.

"You're half the team all by yourself," he agreed. "I'll start dragging all this stuff in if you'll get the house opened up."

"And start cooking dinner?," she asked. "There was some leftover beef from the braai in that ice chest. And I just might have stocked your pantry before we left with some very special items from my last care package."

"Care package," he scoffed. "What did your church send this time? Gold and diamonds?"

Her church was always sending her care packages. David had never even gotten one from New Life-Dallas. He wasn't bitter... just very curious about all the packages she got, claiming that he loved living vicariously through a real missionary.

The thought made her smile even as she looked at him.

"Better," she said. "Tortillas and salsa."

His mouth dropped open. "Get out."

"Well, if you don't want me to share --"

"I didn't say that!," he protested, a slow grin building on his face.

She loved that smile. She loved that face. There wasn't much that she didn't love about David Connor, honestly, all these months later.

Love... really?

So strange, feeling this way, battling with this, wondering what she was even thinking when she looked at him and felt herself falling, more and more, every day.

It had been a slow thing, building with time. But it had been easy. So, so easy.

Those first few weeks of working alongside him, her attention had been entirely devoted to the teenagers she'd gotten to know, and in the times she would prepare for events and to organize things with David, her focus had been on the work entirely.

Except, of course, for those moments when they'd talk about home, about growing up together, about the same vision they shared for the work here.

He'd been a friend. A really good friend. Camille had assumed that they'd spend most of their time as a foursome -- Kait, Piet, David, and Camille. But Kait and Piet had their work all over the country, and as their responsibilities increased, the time they all spent together had lessened, leaving Camille with only David.

It made her wonder how lonely his work must have been before she came along. And it made her lean on him more and more as they saw lives changed, as they lived life together, and as she found herself dreaming of the life she might have with him.

Crazy. All of it. But the feelings were there. On her part, at least.

Who knew what David Connor was even thinking half of the time...

"What are you thinking, David?," she asked even then, as he had closed his eyes, right there in his driveway, smiling.

He was weird like that sometimes. She could see in his grownup face, darkened with three days worth of beard, ash from the fire, and, yes, sand, the same kid he'd been.

"I'm thinking about fajitas," he said, laughing out loud.

"Where are your keys?," she said, laughing with him. "I'll go in and get it started."

"In my pocket," he said, still holding onto the ice chest.

She looked down at his pocket briefly, wondering at the wisdom of just reaching out and fumbling around in there.

"My bad," he mumbled, obviously considering the same thing as he put the ice chest down and fished them out of his pocket for her. "Here you go. Fajitas straight ahead."

After turning and unlocking the door, she made her way into his cottage with him following her close behind.

This place was like home with all the time she spent here, honestly.

She knew where everything was. She knew just where to put his keys so he'd find them, right next to where he kept his phone charger, right beside where he'd plug in his laptop. She knew just where he kept the cookware she'd need to fix dinner for him, right under the cabinets that held the truly hideous dishes he'd bought at the Namibian equivalent of the dollar store his first week here. She knew how many steps (fifteen) he'd have to take to go and throw his bag of sand-filled, soot-covered clothes into the laundry hamper in the bathroom. She knew just how he'd look as he did so, glancing at his face in the mirror, predicting the words he'd say just as he shouted them to her --

"I've got a beard! I've turned into Paul Connor!"

She'd heard this before. These weekend camping trips were a regular thing.

"Mercy," she heard him mutter.

And she smiled as she could see him in her head, gaping at just how much he did look like his father as he stared at himself.

"Shave, then! Right now!," she called to him. "The world can only handle one Paul Connor!"

"No need to yell at me," he murmured, just over her shoulder.

And there he was, fifteen steps later, smiling at her in the kitchen.

Even looking just like Paul Connor, his smile was all David. The sight of it connected a thousand memories together in her mind, each of them sweet and perfect, all of them centered around him and how much he meant to her now...

"Seriously, David," she said, forcing her gaze from his, looking into the ice chest, and pulling out the meat. "It'll take me a while. You can get cleaned up while I cook."

"I'll get the rest of the stuff in," he said. "You can start washing your clothes here, if you want."

"That'll make for a late night," she called after him. "I'll be here for hours finishing it up."

"I don't care," he said, already outside grabbing more things. "I like having you here."

And she liked hearing that.

Even as she heard the shower start a few minutes later, she smiled and went to work.

David

He started the shower and pulled his shirt off over his head.

Then, he stuck his head back out the bathroom door and checked, just to make sure.

There she was. Camille Evans, standing in his kitchen, pinning her hair up as she peered into his fridge, humming a little tune under her breath... and smiling.

That never got old. That smile. No matter how many times he checked to make sure she was real -- that she was Cammie Evans, here with him -- it was still a thrill.

He shut the door, grinning like a stupid fool, thinking about the past few months and how many times he'd had to double check, just like that, hardly believing that life had turned out like this.

He stepped out of the rest of his clothes, still smiling even though his bathroom was now covered in sand, and stepped into the shower, thinking on the last few months.

There was the work. Camille knew it in part, but she didn't know the whole of it, even though he'd attempted to explain to her how much things had expanded this term. Three years worth of work, with the added bonus of a helper made to fit here so perfectly, had been the conduit of so many blessings. The group had doubled in size from the last school term. He'd picked up another three classes at the high school, with Camille coming along to teach beside him. They were running two discipleship groups, each with forty teens, and two more Bible study groups for the junior high students. The camping trips were more frequent, as were the trips to the beach, the meet-ups around town, and the evenings spent visiting the hostels.

And the church. Oh, the church. David had baptized thirty students in one term. They were already reevaluating the space they had as every week, more students poured into the building, as they ran out of seats more often than not, as God changed so many hearts.

Camille was there, right with him, through it all. She was so good at what she did, just like he'd suspected she would be all those years ago when she'd first mentioned missions to him.

Thinking about her, like he was prone to do all the time these days, made him rush through his shower. He could still hear her in the kitchen, even as he shut off the water, wrapped a towel around his waist, and caught the stupid look on his face as he looked in the mirror.

He was in love with her. Anyone could see that in the moon-eyed, dopey look on his face.

Except for Cammie, of course. Praise God she couldn't see it because she'd be icked out and weirded out, likely. And would get on the first plane out of here.

David Connor. Charity and Hope's weird little brother. She'd made that pretty clear back in Tsumeb when he'd so idiotically insinuated that she was idolizing him.

Seriously, David?

At this, he frowned, even as he began shaving off the beard.

It was all for the best, probably. Her not knowing anything about how he felt because it's not like it would change anything.

And she was too good of a teammate to risk changing anything anyway. She was half the team, as he had said. Because she was. It hadn't even been a team until she came, and now, he felt like he could conquer the world with her by his side.

She'd always been a good teammate like that.

His mind drifted back to a Wednesday night back in Texas, right after their youth Bible study. Jay had gotten all of the students to pair up by drawing names out of a hat -- high school boys and high school girls, so that the girls wouldn't break off into their cliques and so they would keep the guys from getting bored and losing interest.

David had been ecstatic that he was a freshman now and that it put him with the older kids, which meant that he would get to bypass the stupid game of charades that the junior high students always had to play.

Instead, he would be playing... charades.

There was a collective groan as Jay made the announcement.

"You are the loudest bunch of kids," he said, waving away their irritation. "Each boy come up and grab a name to see who your partner will be. We're going to do this on a point system. The two teams with the most points at the end of the half hour will war it out for a really great prize. So, keep your fingers crossed that your partner is a winner."

David got in line behind all the really tall dudes in the youth group... which included just about everyone except for him. The girls watched them from the couches, already taking up their spots, laughing to one another, likely over who would get stuck with the three freshman boys.

The other two freshman boys were a better option than David himself was. He knew this from the comments he heard. But he ignored it because he was actually good at charades.

He'd show them all that weird little David Connor was actually a real catch.

"Charity Connor," Brian Willis, a senior who was on his school's track team, wrestling team, football team, basketball team, etc, etc, said as he held up the scrap of paper with David's sister's name on it.

Charity practically cheered in response as Brian exchanged a coy grin with her, and she moved over to make room for him.

More girls. Freshmen, sophomore, junior, senior girls, all paired up.

"Hope Connor," Jeff Morris, a junior who was in his school's marching band, his school's choir, his school's orchestra, his school's musical theater team, etc, etc, said as he held up the scrap of paper with David's other sister's name on it.

Hope studied him critically for a moment as he did likewise. And she didn't move over to make room for him, leaving him to sit on the floor.

By the time David finally got up to the hat, most of the teams were already together and already talking through strategies.

He reached in, said a little prayer, and lifted up his scrap of paper. *Cammie Evans.* Glory.

He refrained from saying that part out loud, thankfully. "Cammie Evans," he squeaked, grinning, even as several other girls laughed at this, including Charity.

Poor Cammie. He could see the disappointment. But still, she moved over and patted the seat next to her.

David took it with a smile, looking up at her as he settled in. Wow, she was so pretty...

Despite the distraction, once the game started, he and Cammie managed to get every single one in record time. No matter who was the one giving the clues and who was guessing, they moved quickly, never missing a beat.

"You're good at this," she said to him, grinning. "We just might get whatever lame prize Jay has, huh?"

"I hope so," David said, thinking that he'd already gotten the prize when he'd drawn her name.

They came up on the final card. They watched Hope and Jeff totally miss the word on their card -- patience. Which David would have figured, since Hope had none of that, as evidenced by the glare she gave her partner when he just couldn't get it.

"Okay, easy win for David and Cammie," Jay said, as he handed David the final card. "If they can just get this one before time runs out."

David looked at the card. *Love.*

As he bit his lip, thinking on how to best show this, given all the different kinds of love that are out there, he watched Cammie as she sat forward and studied him.

He could pretend to rock a baby. There was love there, between a parent and a child. He could grab up Charity, who was making eyes at Brian and vice versa, and stand with his arm around her. There was love there, between a brother and a sister. He could point to Jay and to his wife, Christy, who sat beside him. There was love there, between a husband and his wife.

But when he thought of love... he thought of how he felt looking at Cammie Evans, even as one side of her mouth quirked up in an inquisitive grin, no doubt as she wondered what was going through his mind.

"Okay, I'm ready," he said to Jay, handing the card back.

"And your time starts.... now!," Jay exclaimed.

And despite the laughter he knew it would create, the talking people would do about silly David Connor and how weird he was, he went right ahead and did what he knew she would understand.

David Connor fell to one knee before Cammie Evans, reached out for her left hand, and pretended to slide a ring onto her finger.

He could see the different words rushing through her mind, even as the group giggled around them. *Wedding, proposal, husband...*

"Love," she said softly, grinning at him. "That's what you meant, wasn't it, David? Love."

Love. What a crazy thing to be thinking now, all these years later, as he finally finished shaving.

He gave himself a good, hard look in the mirror, still hearing Cammie's voice singing quietly in his kitchen, before he turned around, got dressed, and went out to meet her.

Cammie

"So, Paul Connor is gone, thankfully."

Camille heard his voice and turned around to get a good look at him.

His hair was still a little wet, evidence that he'd hurried out here to her. He'd thrown on a T shirt and some jeans, giving definition to all the parts of him that were so different than the weird little guy she'd grown up alongside. He smelled so good. She barely refrained from closing her eyes, leaning up against him and taking in a long, slow whiff.

And his face? Clean-shaven and handsome enough to send her pulse racing.

So weird. So, so weird, feeling like this.

He smiled at her, as if he could hear all that she would never say. That just made her heart beat faster.

"I always liked Paul Connor," she said, taking a breath with the joke.

"Well, glory be, Cammie Evans," David drawled, imitating his father perfectly. Wow, Camille could remember Paul Connor saying that to her when he'd ask her something about the sermon over lunch at the pastor's house, when she'd answer correctly, and when he'd gesture to her as if to say *someone got it.*

She had. She always had.

"Glory be," Camille said right back to David.

"You liked him," he noted. "He was likeable some of the time, at least."

"But as far as Connor men went," she said, "I always liked you best."

157

"Bull," David said after a long moment.

"Okay, maybe not," she laughed. "Not back then, at least. But I do now. And I'm glad to see that face instead of Paul Connor's."

He had no idea just how glad she was to see him, every day of her life here.

"Well, I'm honored," he said with an exaggerated bow.

"And you smell better than you ever did back when you were twelve," she smiled, looking back down at the meal she'd been making.

"Though I didn't thirty minutes ago," he said. "You never know how dirty you get out there until you come back to modern plumbing."

"Hmm," she murmured, watching him from the corner of her eye, like she did so often these days.

"You can shower here if you'd like," he said. "If you'll excuse all the sand I left all over the place back there."

"I'll be content to just get my laundry done," she said. "After we eat."

"Fajitas," he said, grinning, leaning over her shoulder to watch what she did.

Him, this close... thrilling. She closed her eyes and shook her head just a little at the surprise of this, a smile still playing on her lips. The temptation to just lean up, brush her lips across his cheek --

"What can I do to help?," he asked, completely without a clue.

"Um... help me carry it all to the table, huh?," she said softly, forcing her mind back to where it needed to be.

And he took care of it all for her, somehow managing to pull out her chair at the table for her, even with his arms full. As soon as they were seated, he reached out for her hand and prayed over the meal, just like he'd done all the other times before.

He mentioned the student he'd been talking with earlier, praying for him to think on these things, asking God to move in his heart even more, and saying, above all, that he would trust the work to the Lord. Like always.

"Amen," Camille said, even as David gestured for her to fix her plate first. "Eager to see how it all unfolds with him."

David grinned. "Yeah, and with all the girls you were always in such deep conversation with this weekend. I'd come by to see what was going on, and they'd all stop talking as soon as they saw me. David Connor, conversation killer."

"Just Elizabeth and Esther, being girls," Camille said, thinking of the two girls and the drama going on with them.

"What was up?," he asked, reaching over to begin his plate as well. "I mean, if it's not so serious that you've been sworn to silence."

"You know how girls work," Camille chided.

"Two sisters," he said. "I'm practically a girl myself."

Not quite, Camille thought, watching him serve himself a huge helping of everything she'd set aside for this meal.

"Well, I can share with you as long as I can stay vague," she said. "Boy problems."

"Boys are generally a problem," David nodded at this, falsified wisdom in his voice.

Camille thought of the problem, that the boys these girls were around weren't saved, weren't born again, weren't living for the Lord. How they knew it was a problem, dreaming about a future with a godly man when godly men seemed to be in such short supply. Even with the group that David was leading, the church that they were seeing grow, the boys were less serious about the faith than the girls were.

It was just that way sometimes.

Boy, did Camille ever know that.

Well... she had. But ever since that first night at that party, David confronting her with his guitar on his back, real sincerity in his eyes even as he'd said difficult things, she'd seen differently.

Godly men weren't in such short supply after all. Not here, at least. Not when it came to David and who he was, who she'd seen him be all these months. In every encounter, every relationship, every word of Scripture shared here in his ministry and in his life, she'd seen the godliness in him.

When she wasn't trying to prove a point about women on the mission field or her own capabilities, she was content to work alongside him. He valued her opinion, looked to her as an equal, and didn't ever talk down to her. The natural and shocking outcome to that had been that she'd followed him gladly when he'd taken up leadership, when decisions had to be made, when everyone was looking for someone to give direction, someone to speak truth from Scripture.

She looked to David, too. And she was so surprised to find that there was tenderness in the way he led, in the way he ministered even to her here, and how he had somehow become her pastor over the last few months.

She hadn't said one word since that first night about men and women, about their roles in ministry, or tried to reason away Scripture about it all.

She'd simply done the work of the ministry that she'd been called to do, comforted to find that it was under David's watch as well, and that he looked out for her in ways she hadn't known she wanted someone to.

He was, very frankly, changing all of her opinions. And her world, if she was honest about it all. It was no wonder that she had feelings for him now that exceeded anything she would have thought possible.

"What did you tell them?," he asked, his mouth full. And she found herself smiling, thinking about him talking with his mouth full so many times when she'd gone over to the Connor house for dinner, and he'd spent the whole meal trying to keep her attention.

Hey, Cammie, so are you going to the movies with the youth group next weekend? Me, too! Maybe we can sit next to each other on the van ride over there, huh?

That boy... grown up into the godliest man she'd ever known.

How strange. And wonderful, of course.

David reached for a napkin, remembering his manners, even as he swallowed and wiped his mouth. "My bad," he murmured. "But it's fajitas. I can't help myself."

"You're fine," she said.

"So, the girls," he prompted. "What did you tell them about problematic boys?"

"I told them," she said, "that this is not the time in life to be concerned about boys. That they have a whole long list of other things that should be taking priority. School, serving Christ, becoming the best women they can be for His purposes."

"Sounds like good advice," David nodded.

She took a breath at this. "I could hear my parents even as I was saying it, though, you know," she said softly.

At this, he looked up at her. "Did they say that?"

"Oh, yeah," she answered around the bite she'd taken. "Go to college. Get a degree. Get a job. Take care of yourself. Then, Cammie, then look around and see who's walking the walk right alongside you."

David watched her for a long moment. "Well, that's great advice."

"Must have been," she sighed, "because I took it to heart. And I did everything they said to do."

She thought about how she had. About how she'd done everything right and how it hadn't changed what she wanted. She thought of Chelsea, about how critical her parents had been of her young marriage, the choices she'd made because of Kyle, and how every negative word had made an impact. Not on Chelsea, who was happy, but on Camille, who heard their words, who began to see things like marriage and having a family as secondary, as not as spiritual, as something she shouldn't want if God alone was enough.

She still wasn't sure how to sort it all out. Especially now, so far from home, still single... sitting across from David, who had her feeling things she wasn't sure she'd ever felt.

"You did everything they said?," he asked, taking another bite.

"Yeah," she nodded. "College, then right onto the mission field. From one assignment to the next to, and I quote, feel out the possibilities. Meanwhile, my sister rushed right into marriage at eighteen, dropped out of college, started having babies too early… she did everything wrong. And she's blissfully happy. And I'm here half a world away, wondering what in the world I'm doing with my life."

He grinned. "You're doing great things with your life," he affirmed. "Changing the world for Christ. I see it every day. See what He's doing through you."

And this felt so inexplicably good, hearing this affirmation.

"I hope so," she said softly.

"But," he said, "there's something else."

"Something else?," she asked.

"Something else that you want, obviously."

And there was. And she wanted it when she looked at him, more than she wanted it when it was still some unnamed, unknown part of her future.

David Connor. A future with him in it.

How crazy was that?

"What did you want?," he asked.

She took a breath, ready to be honest. In part, at least.

"Marriage, family… things that seemed foolish when compared to what I could do for God," she said. "Which is dumb, isn't it? As if anything I could do is something He needed from me. Or that He couldn't have worked through me if I had still gotten everything I wanted."

David nodded at this, silent for a long moment. "Could have been," he said softly. "You'd have been happy, I'm guessing."

"Maybe," she said. "Or not. Because even as I was doing what I should have done by everyone else's standards, I looked around. I was always available. Chelsea just lucked out and found her happily ever after earlier on. Me? I never did meet anyone. Might have just gone for it if I did, and I'd be no different than her." She thought of her sister and the home she'd made. "Happy, that is."

"You're not happy?," David asked.

"Happy enough," she said. "Happier here than I've been anywhere else, that's for sure."

And it was true. And she felt the truth of it even more as David smiled at her.

"Not that I'm unhappy at all," she said, trying to explain, "but we all probably have something that could make us happier, don't we?"

He nodded at this.

"Besides," she said. "I wouldn't be here if something else had worked out."

"And that," he said, smiling, "has made me happy. You being here."

She appreciated this, even as she looked back down at her plate. "Because you got fajitas tonight."

"There is that," he conceded.

And she laughed along with him.

"So, no one, huh?," he asked, taking a breath.

"What?," she asked around another bite.

"You never met anyone," he clarified.

"Dated around a little," she shrugged, thinking about the few boys in high school, a few more in college. A few dates with some, several with others, and no real relationship, no lasting and meaningful relationship to speak of at all. "Nothing serious, though. Ever."

"What about that kid from youth camp?," he asked, looking over at her curiously.

Kid from youth camp. She was drawing a blank, unable to recall much about him, apart from that last night when he'd made her cry by kissing some other girl, how David had been the one to cheer her up.

"Jeremy something," he said.

"Was that his name?," she asked. "He cheated on me. Last day of youth camp. You were there. You remember his name. That's better than me, so surely you remembered that little unfortunate detail as well."

"I did," he said. "But, you know, maybe you worked it out."

"It wasn't that serious," she said.

"Oh?," he asked, a sparkle in his eye. "Because you told me back then that you were going to go onto the mission field. That he was, too, and that it just might be God's doing that He had called you both at the same time. God's very will that you and this boy had gotten together for His glory among the nations."

She rolled her eyes. "Oh, that sounds like me, David. Very fatalistic about the will of God."

"You were," he said, still smiling.

"But that was long before I started delivering fiery edicts about inequality between the sexes in church polity," she said. "Not too long, though, because I think his moral failure played a big part in my view of men called to ministry."

"Way to go, Jeremy," he said. "Messing things up for the rest of us."

"Not you," she said, smiling over at him. "You were never lumped in with him."

He grinned. "So, where did he end up? God's will for you? Your happily ever after and all?"

"Haven't seen him since youth camp," she said. "As it turns out, those sweet words and kisses weren't as serious as I thought they were at the time."

"You kissed him?," David asked, obviously surprised by this. "I mean, it's not my business... but you kissed him?"

"Yeah," she said, watching him curiously.

And for a brief moment, David looked like he had back at that youth camp, aghast by her romantic choices, how she was supposedly meant to marry him instead.

Wow, she hadn't thought of that conversation in years. But it came back to her as he watched her, that wounded expression on his face, and she could remember very nearly every word David had said that night.

It struck her as odd, how she couldn't remember much of anything about Jeremy, but she could remember David so well. Sweaty, squeaky-voiced David, following her around youth camp...

"Well," he said softly. "Didn't realize things got that exciting at youth camp."

"Well, I probably shouldn't have been acting like that," Camille said, suddenly embarrassed by how easily she'd given her kisses away to a boy she hardly knew. At youth camp, of all places. "It probably would have helped me focus more on what I should have been focusing on if I'd set some better boundaries for myself."

"You were plenty focused anyway," David said, shrugging.

"Maybe. And it wasn't all that exciting," she said. "Teenage boys. And older boys." She sighed, thinking of how little she felt for all of the men she'd dated, all the men she'd kissed.

There weren't many. There hadn't been many. But David watched her with such sadness even as she said this.

It made her rethink every last one.

"Glad and sad, all at the same time to hear that," he said.

"To hear what?," she asked.

"To hear that there was never anyone who left you feeling something exciting," he said. "You deserved exciting. Still do." At this, he smiled at her again. "I hope you know that now, grown up Cammie."

She looked over at him, her heart warmed by his smile and by the sentiment. "I'll bet you're exciting," she said softly.

He raised his eyebrows at this, and she heard, belatedly, how he could have taken what she'd said. What she meant, honestly, but...

"Well, I mean," she said, stumbling over her words, "I'm sure you've made many girls happy over the years. You grew up just as soon as I left town, so... years and years of you with girls, and..."

She stopped short, not really liking where she was going with this. David and other girls. Other women. David with anyone but... well, but her...

Not right, somehow. And disturbing, in and of itself, that she was thinking this.

"Yeah," he said, not even noticing her discomfort. "There were girls. Not too many in high school. Late bloomer and all. And I wasn't sneaking around youth camp, kissing like everyone else apparently, because I was spending all of my time those last two years teaching the junior high group."

"Your time was better spent then," Camille murmured quietly, imagining the David she'd missed out on, learning youth ministry as he did it, while everyone else his age went on with insignificant things.

"But I dated around in college," he said. "Seems I wanted the same things you did. Marriage, family. Things that were good. And *not*," he said, looking to her to emphasize his point, "things that were unspiritual to hope for."

She was more inclined to believe him, each and every day, the longer she stayed single, honestly.

"Was there anyone special?," she asked. "Back in college?"

"No," he said, shaking his head. "And I was serious about Christ and knew that a godly marriage was worth pursuing. So, I did. Took out lots of girls, kept looking for the right one. Never got serious with any of them. Never even kissed any of them."

Her eyes widened at this. "Are you serious?"

"Dead serious," he said.

"You've never kissed anyone? You're twenty-five, and you've never kissed anyone?"

"Remember that purity study?," he said, smiling. "That my dad forced me into after..."

"Yes," she said, blushing again. "My pink underwear sealed your celibacy. Wow."

"Not your underwear, per se," he laughed. "But... in a way. Kinda. Thank you, Camille."

"Well."

"I got it," he shrugged. "Talking through purity with Jay. I got it. I understood I was saving everything for the glory of God. Covenanted to do just that, even before girls got all that interesting to me, honestly. And it made a difference. And if I wasn't serious about a girl, wasn't planning on forever with her, I wasn't going to make any physical overtures towards her. So, I never did. And would you believe," he said, smiling, "that it makes a difference in what I'm doing here? To be able to speak purity from experience to all of these students who face some really hard issues because of immorality?"

She could see a difference. Had already seen it many times. He lived what he believed, and it inspired others.

"So, I'm not very exciting," he said. "I think that was the word you used."

"You," she said, thinking of David committing himself like this, treating the girls he'd known with such respect, honoring God. "This... propensity to be such a gentleman, to be so godly..." She shook her head at the enormity of it.

"What?," he asked. "What are you thinking?"

And she thought of how everything David said lately left her feeling more than she had counted on when she'd joined him here unknowingly.

"It just makes you sound more exciting," she breathed, even as he smiled softly at her.

David

He'd walked her back to the Botha house much later that evening.

Much, much later, after more meaningful words, sincere looks, and joyful laughter between them, as David reminded his heart, again and again, that this was Cammie Evans.

Camille Evans.

And he was David Connor. The geeky younger brother of her best friends.

Yeah. Perspective.

He'd walked her the mile there, her clean laundry in a bag he wore over his shoulder, and she'd turned from him at the door... and couldn't get in.

"Locked," she murmured. "Kait turns in so early." She looked over at him and bit her lip. "And she's a light sleeper. I'm totally going to wake her up just as soon as I unlock the door and walk in. Even though she sleeps way down the hall."

"How's it been going, having a roommate?," he asked.

"It's like having a roommate," she said, smiling softly. "Haven't had one since college. Eons ago, you know."

He hadn't thought of how this might be a change for her, how it might be anything less than ideal.

"Kait keeps strange hours," she continued, searching through her pockets for her key. "And she's really loud when she's at home. I like going over to your house. It's nice and quiet with you."

She'd had more than a few opportunities to do that. They'd practice the songs they were going to do for the worship sets there in his living room. They'd go over the lessons they were going to be teaching sitting there on his back porch. They'd spend hours talking in his kitchen over the meals she'd made for him.

And there had been more than a few evenings like the one they'd just spent, where she'd do her laundry at his house instead of the laundromat, sitting with him for hours, them keeping one another company.

He could remember every detail from the evening they'd just spent together after they'd eaten, when she'd pulled out a deck of cards and thoroughly whipped his butt at every game he could name, laughing behind her hands at him when he'd tell her he wanted yet another rematch.

She'd granted it to him every time, and he'd been so thankful, not for another chance to be beaten by her but because it meant she stayed with him a little longer.

He loved having Cammie at home with him. He hadn't realized just how lonely he was until she came along.

"You were going to be my roommate, you know," he said, thinking on how wonderful this would have been.

She narrowed her eyes just slightly at this. "What?"

Realizing how she had taken what he'd said, he laughed. "Well, when we thought you were a guy. Which you're not. Obviously."

Obviously, David. Keep right on helping yourself out by thinking about how Camille Evans is so clearly NOT a guy.

"Oh," she said, sighing. "That explains why you all had to change up plans when I came here. You were expecting me to live at the cottage with you."

The very thought. Cammie there in the mornings, in the afternoons, at night...

"Well, that would have been fun," she said. "We could have had a pajama party every night, just like in the old days."

This wasn't helping him, imagining this. Cammie, smiling at him from behind a hand of cards, wearing something very cute and tiny, throwing down the cards, crawling over to him, and --

"Although that would have been weird for two guys," she said thoughtfully.

And now, he was having trouble thinking clearly at all. That's how messed up he was around Cammie Evans.

"Oh, well," she said, oblivious to all that was running around his mind. "Still thankful for a place to stay. Even if it's with Kait and not you."

"Hey," he said, trying to distance himself from all the thoughts running through his mind. "There's another mission house, you know. Here in Swakop."

"Really?," she asked.

"Yeah," he nodded. "Piet owns them all, technically. But he still calls them mission houses, still has them set aside for ministry. I didn't take it when I moved here because it's so big. But it belonged to the missionaries who were here before me. A real home. I mean, it needs a woman's touch. Totally undecorated now and left really bare, but..."

She watched him with great interest, tears pooling in her eyes.

"Camille," he said, "are you okay?"

"I could decorate it," she said. "I could make it into a real home again."

"Would you like to do that?," he asked.

"More than you can possibly imagine," she smiled. "Yes. This place, it's..." She looked over to the beach, biting her lip.

"It's what?," he asked.

"I mean, I know there's not a career position for me to even work myself into," she said. "Just the temporary one. But this feels like it could be long-term. Like I could finally go long-term. Those students, what's going on here, the possibilities --"

"Incredible," they said together.

"Yeah," she said.

And he thought it as well, how incredible the work was, how incredible it would be if she would covenant herself to it for the long-term.

Incredible.

"And I've felt like... like a guest, staying here," she said. "Like I can't make a home on my own. And I know it's just in my head, the need to do that --"

"I get it," he said. "It's something we should've thought about."

"No, David," she said softly. "You've been so good to me. Everything has been perfect."

He was thankful to hear this, so glad to know that she was happy here. And that he could make her happier by giving her a place to call her own.

"I'm glad, Cammie."

"So, yes," she sighed, smiling at this. "Yes, I would love to set up a home here."

"Then we'll make it happen," he said, resolving then that he would take care of it as soon as possible.

Cammie

He did make it happen, less than a week later.

"Got the keys from Piet," he told her the night that they were doing their last Bible study of the school term.

"The keys?," she asked, her attention pulled in several different directions with all they were doing to close out things with the students. Then, with realization, "Oh, David, the keys to the house?"

"Yes," he said, smiling. "I can take you by tonight and let you see it all."

"We won't have time," she said, wishing that they did. "We'll be up here so late, saying goodbye to everyone. Merry Christmas. All of that."

They would be. Every evening led to another couple of hours spent chatting with the youth, leading into early mornings where Camille and David were both worn out, able just to make it over to the Botha house, where he'd drop her off for the night and make plans for the next day and whatever they had on the calendar.

"Maybe we will," he said. "And if not, there's tomorrow. Either way, we'll get you moved in before Christmas."

Oh, the very thought. Having a home of her own to celebrate Christmas in.

"Is Kait going to be offended?," she asked, thinking of the last week in particular, when Kait and Piet had been around Swakopmund more. As the holidays neared all over the nation, their travels were dwindling down to a slower pace until the new year. She and David had spent more than a few evenings with the two of them, hearing about the plans they had to travel out to South Africa and meet up with Piet's mother, who was coming in for a surprise visit, along with Piet's uncle and aunt.

"Kait was there when Piet gave me the key," David said. "She wasn't at all offended. It would take a lot to bother her, you know. She seemed glad to hear that you're thinking about the long term, that you want a place of your own here."

And she did. And the long term was on her mind all night long, of course. Even as she chatted with the students who filled the building later that evening, even as she and David led them in several worship songs, and even as David opened up Scripture to the book of Acts, his message about being sent with the Gospel clear and precise.

Camille loved the passage, about being witnesses to the goodness of Christ, in all the places He was calling His disciples. It didn't end there, though. Not with the disciples two thousand years ago, not with the teenagers there in Namibia. Christ had gone a step beyond calling. He had equipped them, going so far as to dwell in them, to be their helper, and to live in them so that His truth would be proclaimed. He would do the work of changing lives, and the world would change forever.

David said it perfectly.

Camille had loved sitting under his teaching those last few months, as he'd led newcomers through the book of John and as

175

he'd walked the students who'd been with him for years through the book of Romans. She'd felt herself reminded of truths she'd known from childhood, encouraged by the truth of them here, and challenged in fresh ways by the way David exposited them. How could the same passages, some of which she'd had memorized for years, still impact her in new, relevant ways?

She wasn't sure. But she craved these times spent in Scripture, with David Connor sitting on the edge of the stage in the building where they lived and breathed God's Word, hearing what he had to say.

"So, as you're going in the next few weeks," David said, "back to those places where you've come from, back to where God has raised you up, back to what you knew before you knew Christ like you know Him now... well, know that He goes with you. That He's called you towards home for a very distinct purpose, and that He knows exactly where you're going so that you'll share His truth with others and lead them into salvation as well."

The students watched him, some of them nodding and even more of them looking quite terrified.

"Brother David," a young man named Shati said uncertainly. "My parents will think I've joined a cult."

There was a little bit of nervous laughter from some other students, along with worried glances over at David.

But David relieved them all when he himself laughed. "I would imagine so," he said. "It's a difficult thing for someone else to understand, how God has been speaking to your heart, you know?"

"It's impossible," Hatutale, another one of the boys, shared. "My family will not understand it."

"May I tell you something?," David asked.

And the students nodded, as did Camille, as they all leaned forward in their seats, eager to hear one of Brother David's stories.

"I told my father, back when I was seventeen, that I was going to live in Africa one day and share stories about Jesus with teenagers." At this he grinned as the students around him smiled back. He was doing it, obviously. Just like he said he would at seventeen.

"And you have, Brother David," Esther said.

"Knew I would," he answered. "But my father wasn't so sure. I told him what God wanted me to do, and he told me that it was a waste. That my life would be a waste."

Camille suppressed a surprised gasp at this. Of all the sermons she'd heard in her life from Paul Connor, she'd never heard anything but praise for the mission field, admiration for those who went, and urgency for more to go.

But perhaps it was different when the one being called was your own. Still, though...Paul Connor, saying that his son's life would be a waste?

It was hard to grasp.

"Is your father unredeemed?," Shati asked.

It wasn't as hard for these students. They had no idea who Paul Connor was like Camille did. They only heard that he was a father and likely compared him to their own fathers, many of whom were unredeemed, living without Christ even now.

"Oh, no, Dad's born again," David said. "But he has his own ideas about the way God should work. And his son, in Africa? Not the way he thought it should be. So, in the same way your parents might not understand what God is doing in your life... well, my father didn't understand what God was doing in my life."

Elizabeth raised her hand. "Brother David, what does he think now?"

David smiled sadly. "Does it matter what he thinks now?"

"He's your father," Shati said softly.

"He is," David nodded. "Just like your fathers are your fathers. And you will want to share with them, because you love them, because Christ tells you to. But, friends, you will be obedient to Christ, despite what your fathers think. You must answer to the Lord before anyone else on the earth."

Good words. Such good words.

Such hard words, Camille knew, after a lifetime of pleasing her parents, pleasing her teachers, pleasing the board.

David had learned it early, apparently, this way to be free from needing to please his father, who could never be pleased as long as David did what Christ had called him to do.

"You need to honor your parents," David said. "But when their expectations lead you from Christ, you need to follow Jesus first. You can still love your parents even as you do that. And you should love them for the glory of God. But He is first. Always. And you must remember that in all of your relationships. Friendships, marriages --"

And at this, there were giggles from the girls.

Camille gave him a smile even as she shook her head. He rolled his eyes at this and smiled at her.

"Yes, even that," he said. "Even the people you love most dearly in this world can never take the place of Jesus. I hope if we've learned anything this term, we've learned that. And if you love Him, you can certainly live for Him, even if you're not here."

"We can share His truth, even when we're all alone," Elizabeth murmured softly.

"We can. We can do all things through Christ, for His glory. Why is that, Camille?," David asked, finding her eyes, nodding encouragement at her, at the answer he knew she would give.

"It's because we don't do the work," she said softly, thinking of all that they'd seen happen, even in this short while. How much David must have seen as well, before she even got here.

"And how is that?," David asked.

"God does it through us," she answered. "It's all Him. Not us."

"Exactly," he murmured. "And that's our prayer for you. For all of you. That as you go home, He'll do the work of changing hearts as you follow Him and love Him."

And with that, he began to pray over the students, for what they would face as they went home as new people, made new in Christ, transformed for His purpose, on mission for His glory.

Camille felt so much, loving these students, even now, even as she reached over and put her hands on their hands, their shoulders, squeezing, knowing them so well, already missing them, desperately hoping for the best for them.

It was another two hours before she was alone with David, waving to the last student, even as he shut down the building.

"I didn't know that about your dad," she said, bringing them back to the words he'd spoken about Paul Connor and the waste he thought his son's life was.

"Not a story he likely shares from the pulpit," David nodded, locking the door and turning to her.

"I'm sorry that he did that," she said. "But I'm glad you did what you did, David."

And at this? He smiled. A genuine smile. "Some of us didn't do what our parents wanted us to do, did we?"

She had. But she was challenged even now to begin to think about life and pleasing God, doing things the way He would have her do them, and being open to the blessings He had for her.

"You still did something good, David," she said very sincerely, thinking of all the students already preparing to go back onto their mission field. "Something very, very good."

David

He insisted on taking her by the house, just for a look.

It was past midnight, but he didn't care.

Neither did she, as the door opened and she took it all in.

"Oh," she sighed, her face glowing in the dim light. There were some light bulbs he'd have to change out. The furniture needed to be uncovered. Some windows needed to be opened so the place could air out.

But Camille was obviously seeing none of this. Only the potential, the promising reflection of it in her eyes as she turned to him.

"Already," she said softly. "Three steps into this house, and I can tell that it's perfect."

"It can be home," he said, nodding, looking it over as well, just a little regretful that he hadn't decided to live here himself three years ago. Seeing it through Camille's eyes made it seem warmer, more welcoming... home.

She turned from him with a grin and took off into the house. "Look at the kitchen!," she said, making her way in, flipping lights on. "Open plan, just like this. I can cook and look out over the living room. When you come over for dinner, you can actually lay out on the couch and talk with me while I get everything ready."

"Already an invite to come over for dinner," he said. "I accept."

"And the pantry!," she shouted, hardly listening to him. "Look how many shelves are in here! And they left some food..." She glanced back over at him. "We'll probably need to clean that out, huh?"

"First thing we'll do when we move you in," he said.

"Already an offer to move me in," she said. "I accept."

Before he could comment on this, she was moving down the hallway.

"The master bedroom is huge!," she called out to him even as he followed her down the hallway, peeking in rooms as he went.

"Four other bedrooms as well," he said, opening doors so she could look at it all. "Big house."

"How many children did the last missionaries have?," she said, breathless as she came up next to him.

"Just one," he said. "It looks like that was her room. This one looks to be an office, and those two..."

"A guest room," Camille said, wandering into it. "Maybe another one, too?"

"Yep," he affirmed. "And another bathroom. Three in all."

"Unbelievable," she murmured. "It feels like half the town could live here. Even the hallways are big."

And at this, she twirled around in a circle, right down the hallway.

Beautiful. So beautiful. He smiled as he watched her.

"David," she said, touching his arm, still looking around, her eyes not meeting his. "This was a real home. With a family. I mean, I can picture it. All the love and happiness here. And I can make it a home again."

He watched her as she spoke about family, as she talked about what she could make of this place...

And his heart began to imagine her here, with a family of her own, ministering just like she was now, except with children. Her own children. Enough children for every room in the house, all of their tiny shoes and backpacks and little socks and school uniforms and books and toys and everything they'd ever need or want strewn all over the hallway. Doors slammed as little voices called out to one another, maturing and aging over the years, looking for Mom, looking for Dad.

Camille, in the kitchen, in this hallway, in these rooms, getting everyone sorted out, reading books, playing on the carpet, bringing in laundry, cooking meals, helping little ones to get dressed, talking about important things the older they got, studying Scripture with them, teaching them about Jesus with each and every word.

Camille all over this house, a family of her own, making her life here.

And where would he be?

Right there with her. Her family... his family.

As he watched her, he wanted it more than he'd ever wanted anything.

She didn't know any of it, though, as she threw her arms around his neck, hugged him, and said, "David, it's perfect. Thank you."

Camille

It was perfect.

She thought it again as she and David set about airing out the house, cleaning in all of the neglected corners, and making plans.

They'd found a lot in the attic, so many things stored away when the last missionaries left, saved for whatever was going to come next, long before Camille even knew where Namibia was or that it was even a place.

She'd found the dishes in a big box in a far corner of the attic, and David had helped her carry them down to the kitchen, along with all that she'd need to cook any number of meals for an entire room full of people.

Or just David. There were plenty of meals, just the two of them, and Camille could picture so many more even as they began washing each plate, every skillet, the pans, the bowls, all of the silverware, and the glasses that were all in perfect condition.

"A window above the sink," she murmured as she washed and he dried, pointing out to the street, the view beyond of the ocean. "Just how I would have built this house if I had built it myself."

He looked out and smiled as well. "Next dish?," he asked, holding his hand out for it, ready to rinse and dry, always trying to stay two steps ahead of her.

They'd been here before. Not here as in this house, but here as in doing this, just like this, so many years ago.

It was the summer of her senior year, and the Connors were going down to the beach for a little break. It would be a whole week away from Dallas and the church for the majority of the family but only a couple of days for Paul Connor, who would show up later, after several important meetings, mid-week services, and obligations.

Cammie had been invited along, and the three girls had spent whole days lying on the beach, talking about how awesome college was going to be and how they couldn't wait for those days to begin.

The two Connor girls, with Phoebe's fair skin, had gotten bad enough sunburns after just two days that they were soon housebound and slathered in aloe vera, cursing the beach from where they laid in their beds, dramatically requesting that the rest of the group bring them food and drinks so that they wouldn't have to move more than absolutely necessary.

Cammie was a little sick of them after just a little while of that, quite honestly. So she volunteered to help David do the dishes one night while Phoebe took care of the twins.

"They're such drama queens," he said to her as soon as she'd handed him a dish towel and submerged her hands in the soapy water. "Oh, my skin is pink! I'm dying, I'm dying!"

She'd hidden a smile at this, recalling the twins saying this exact thing to one another as they'd taken turns showering earlier that day. "A little more than pink," she murmured. "Charity is actually red."

"You didn't burn at all," he said. "You tanned."

And she looked down at her arms, noting how dark they'd gotten, glancing up at his face for a moment. His skin had darkened as well.

"You, too," she said.

"Some of us are made for more tropical climates," he noted.

"Probably," Cammie said. "And I'm glad for it. I love the beach."

"Me, too," he said. "I'm totally going to live by the ocean one of these days."

"Galveston," she said, handing him a fork she'd just cleaned. "Or Corpus Christi maybe. South Padre Island."

"There are beaches beyond Texas," he said. "A whole world full of beaches."

Cammie doubted she'd ever see them. "This one is nice enough, though," she said.

"It is," he grinned. "The company makes it even better."

"What are you talking about, you little weirdo?," she asked. "You didn't even bring a friend with you on this trip."

"I did bring a friend," he said. "You're my friend, Cammie."

"Ha, ha," she said, handing him a dish to dry. "Of course, I am." Except not really. Not in any real sense.

Sure, she hung out with him when she hung out with his sisters. And they talked more than she talked to most boys.

But still. Friends?

"Yeah," he said, drying off the plate and grinning. "Charity and Hope brought a friend the last time we went to the beach."

"Yeah, I know," Cammie answered. "They brought me."

"That's right," David said. "So, this time? It was my turn to bring a friend. Mom asked me who I wanted to come with us. I told her I wanted you to come."

She watched him for a second. "Nu-uh."

"Yuh-huh," he shot back, holding out his hand for another plate. "You're way better than anyone else I could've picked."

He was for real. The little turkey had actually been the reason why she'd been asked to go on this trip.

She wasn't the guest of Hope and Charity... she was David's guest.

Weird.

"What did Charity and Hope say when you asked to bring me?," she muttered, bothered by this for some reason.

"They thanked me," he said. "Thought I did it for them."

"Well, how nice of you," Cammie said, casting him a glance, waiting to hear that he was joking.

"Yeah, they thought I did it because they think I don't have any friends. But I do," he kept on.

She handed him another plate, thinking of his entourage of odd friends. Now that he was in high school, he seemed to have found a clique. A nerdy clique but a clique nonetheless. "You've got plenty of friends. And you're all a bunch of dorkasauruses."

He laughed out loud at this, and she couldn't help but smile. "Dorkasauruses. Sounds cool."

"Totally uncool," she said. "But there are plenty of you. Should've brought one of them when your mom said you could bring someone."

"Why would I do that?," he asked. "Bring someone from my group of dorkasauruses, or bring *you...*"

And the way he said *you* had her looking at him with something close to alarm.

Surely he wasn't...

No.

"It was an obvious choice," he said, taking the next plate from her hands. "You're the best friend I've ever had."

She would think about that conversation as the summer progressed and David spent more time around her, annoying her, making her wonder at what he was thinking.

Youth camp had been the pinnacle of that.

You're the best friend I've ever had.

Camille thought about his words, even as she handed him another dish in Namibia, watching him as he grinned.

"What?," he asked. "You kind of left me there for a second."

"Just... spacing out, I guess," she said, pulling the drain stopper out of the sink. "That was the last dish, David. Thank you."

"No problem," he said, leaning up to put the final glass into the cabinet, right where she'd directed him earlier on. "You're all set."

"Except I don't have any food yet," she said, glancing away, trying not to notice how great he looked, even dressed down like he was, putting the hand towel back on the counter and grinning over at her.

"Hey, come on," he said, grabbing her hand and pulling her across the room. "I gotta show you something you didn't know."

"Oh," she murmured, surprised by his hand in hers. "Sure."

"It's about the pantry," he said, grinning.

"Oh, well," she said, very nearly shaking her head against all the crazy things she'd been thinking. "Expired food. I know all about the pantry."

"Doubtful," he said, stepping into the small space and pulling her in with him. "You know about that door, but did you know that there's a second door?"

"Really?," she asked, the door behind her shutting on its own, throwing them into darkness.

"Why did you shut the door?," he asked softly... and glory, he was just inches from her face as he said it.

David Connor...

"I didn't," she stammered. "It shut behind me. Let's open it and get some light in here, at least, so I can see the other door --"

And the doorknob was stuck. Or locked.

"Well, I can't open it now," she muttered, rattling the knob beneath her fingers. "Seriously. It's not moving."

And she could feel him reach around her, his arms very nearly embracing her, as he tried it as well.

"I probably need to fix that," he noted.

"Is there a light in here?," she asked, thinking that it would be easier to breathe if she could see him standing this close to her, instead of just feeling him... or maybe not. Maybe that would make it harder --

Click. Click. Click, click, click.

"Burned out," he said, so close to her that she could feel his warm breath against her cheek. "Or broken. I probably need to fix that, too."

She thought for a fleeting moment how easy it would be to turn and kiss him even as he was contemplating what all he needed to do for her. There was plenty he could do for her, all right, starting with putting his arms right back around her, and --

"There's a second door," she said, irrationally panicked by what she might find herself doing in this dark pantry with her old friends' kid brother and all. "You said there's a second door. So, we're not trapped."

And she swore for just a second that she could feel his lips near her cheek even as she kept blinking, praying for sight so that she could see if David Connor was actually this close to kissing her, and --

"Oh, yeah," he mumbled, and she could feel him move just a little. "The second door. Yeah, it leads straight out into the garage, which is kind of a weird feature. But nice, especially if you're unloading a lot of groceries, and --"

And at this, he opened the door, flooding the pantry with light, then shut it again, sending it back into darkness.

"Why did you just do that?," she asked, a nervous edge to her voice.

He let out a long breath. She could feel his chest moving against her arm. This pantry was tiny, too tiny, and --

"I asked Piet to come out and fix the garage door. Rig up an opener for you so you could drive in without getting out to lift the door," he said.

"Well, that was sweet, but what does that have to do with anything?"

"He's out there right now. In the garage," he said.

She didn't get it.

"So?"

"Kait's out there with him," David sighed.

Camille could guess what that meant. As infrequently as Kait was at the Botha house these days, given all the trips she made around the country to do medical clinics, she was still there some of the time, as was Piet.

And they were, quite frankly, all over one another most of the time. It was no wonder Kait had wanted a roommate with Piet's mother overseas, and it made perfect sense why they always found a third party to go up north with them.

Models of moral purity. Going to ridiculous lengths to maintain some accountability. Setting and respecting physical boundaries for themselves.

Except, of course, when they were unexpectedly left alone in a room together or in a random, empty garage.

Oh, well. Camille had embarrassed them before and wasn't embarrassed to do it again. So, she reached over, accidentally grabbing David's hip in the process (talk about embarrassing) and opened the door to let them know they had an audience...

And shut the door again without saying anything.

"Well, that's a little more involved than what I was expecting," she said simply.

"True that," David added. "She looks like she's attacking him."

"He seemed to be okay with it," she murmured.

"Yeah, Camille. Welcome to my life for the past three years."

"Great," she swore under her breath. "How long are we going to be stuck in here, pretending like this isn't happening?"

He peeked out again. "Uh… a while," he whispered with a grin. "Wow… get you some, Piet."

"David!" She reached out and closed the door again.

"What?," he laughed. "He re-roofed an entire house for her a few months ago. Excuse me, we both did. I think he's due a few kisses as a resounding thank you. No one's doing the same for me, so good on Piet for getting --"

"Good grief, David," she said. "Are you still twelve?"

"No," he managed around a giggle that just reinforced her assertion that, yes, he was still twelve. Then in a lower voice, "All grown up now, Camille."

Well, she knew this. Knew it better than she had pressed up against him in this tiny space, even as he made a move to open the door again.

She hit him on the arm. "Stop watching them!"

"I hope to accidentally startle them," he said. "Besides no matter what it looks like from here, I'm sure it's all very chaste and that she'll tell him in another couple of minutes, surely, that they need a time out. As far as moral purity in tempting situations goes, those two could write a book. Really admire that about them, but honestly? They just need to get married. And then get a room."

"It's so dark in here, though," she murmured.

And like that? There was light. From David's cell phone, which he held out towards a shelf.

191

"Better?," he asked softly, even as she watched him looking over all of the shelves, admiring the way he looked in such soft light, so close like this, so near to her that she could grab him and do to him what Kait was doing to Piet out in the --

"What?," he asked. "What's that look for?"

She couldn't tell him the truth, obviously. So, she picked a point over his shoulder and gasped, making it up. "David! There are Twinkies in here!"

"Where?," he asked, brandishing his cell phone in his other hand now, moving gingerly, yet still almost knocking her into a shelf. "There's not enough room in here for me to turn around —"

"I know," she huffed. "Your armpit is in my face, David."

"Maybe your face is in my armpit —"

"Here," she whispered irritably, putting her arms around him, her head against his chest. Ooohhh. That was nice. "Can you move now?"

She could feel his heart pick up its pace. Before she could wonder at that, she heard him laugh. "Oh, yeah… hey, Twinkies!"

"That's what I said!"

"Well, they're supposed to have a shelf life of, you know, forever," he noted.

"Makes you wonder what they put in them, doesn't it?," she asked.

"Yeah, but that's good news for you," he said. "Something you don't have to throw out. Must have been a treat the Boyds picked up on furlough…" He moved his cell phone again to get a better look. "And they're expired."

"I thought they didn't go bad?"

"Apparently they do."

"What a waste."

"Hey," he said, putting his arms across her shoulders. "There are other things, though. Canned goods. They don't go bad. Enchilada sauce. Salsa."

"I miss real Mexican food," she groaned quietly.

"I seem to remember that you were a big fan," he said. "Breakfast tacos especially."

She grinned up at him, saw him smile at her in the little light they were getting. "Yeah, the kind with the –"

"Papas rancheras," he noted.

"How do you remember that?," she whispered, still smiling at this.

"That vacation down to the beach," he said. "I'd go with Mom to pick up breakfast for all you girls. And I always made sure to get your favorite."

"Did you?," she asked, surprised by this, amazed that he'd brought up that same vacation she'd thought of earlier that very same day.

He'd been thinking about it, too.

"You were my guest, remember?," he grinned.

Oh, he remembered. Oh...

"The best friend you ever had, I think," she said.

"Yeah," he said, surprise in his eyes that she remembered it as well.

And what was there to say to that? Except the truth. *David Paul Connor, I think I'm in love with you. Which is weird and all, because --*

"I'd do anything for a breakfast taco right now," she said, saying anything -- blasted anything -- except what she was really thinking.

"I can get you a Twinkie right now," he said. "Would that be equally thrilling?"

"An expired Twinkie," she noted.

"Hey, you take what you can get. And better desserts than what they try to pass off as desserts around here. It's like they don't even use sugar in their pastries."

"That's true."

"It is."

"But still, an expired Twinkie might make me sick," she said, biting her lip, considering it.

"Still worth it, though, right?"

Oh, yeah. "Fine."

"Let me grab one," he said, turning her around and reaching out for the box. "Can you get your hands up to hold it while you eat –"

She tried, inadvertently whacking him right in the face and sending his cell phone flying.

"Oh, David, I'm sorry," she murmured into the darkness.

"Yeah, put your hands back," he said, unwrapping the snack cake. "There's just not enough room without me getting the fury of your fists. And I can't even get on the floor to crawl around and find my phone now."

"I didn't mean to hit you," she said.

"I know that. Here," he said, holding the Twinkie up next to her lips. "Trust me."

And so she did, taking a bite… and groaning. "That's incredible."

"Is it?"

"Mmmhmm. Real sugar, David!"

"Well, I've gotta try it now, too," he said. "Mind if I take a bite?"

"Free world," she said. "My germs, your germs, no biggie."

He took a bite… and groaned with her. "Praise God…"

"Tell me about it," she said. "Give me another bite."

"Here," he said, then gasping. "Well, I didn't tell you to eat the whole thing, Camille! You almost got my fingers."

"Mmmnnuuuhhh," she mumbled, her mouth full.

"Okay, then," he said, fumbling around in the dark for the box. "Since you ate most of that one, I get a second, right?"

"I get a bite of that one, at least," she murmured around the bite, all out grinning as she felt him laugh beneath her hands.

And just like she had so many times when they were younger, Camille reached up, without thinking, feeling her way up to his face, putting her hand in his hair, meaning to mess it up like she had.

Silly David Connor. Just like the younger brother she'd never had.

Yeah, right.

She knew he was nothing of the sort, not by a long shot, not for a long while now, even as he stilled and, though she wouldn't have thought it possible, moved closer to her, her hand still in his hair.

"Hey, Cammie," he said, his voice low and deep, as her heart raced.

"Yeah?," she breathed, waiting for words that would indicate what he was feeling, if it was what she was feeling, if it was even okay that she was feeling anything at all --

And suddenly, the pantry was flooded with light. She'd barely registered the open door, Kait on the other side brandishing a shovel, running towards the door, and Piet poised to run *away* from the door he held gingerly in his hand, when David's arms pulled her close protectively, his hands covering her head, even as he yelled, "Whoa! Whoa! Kait!"

"Oh, wow," Kait sighed heavily as she stopped mid-stride, dropping the shovel loudly. "Oh, wow, wow, wow." She put her hands to her knees and let out a deep breath.

"Shame, man," Piet echoed, finally relaxing and looking like he wasn't about to run away screaming.

They all stared at one another for a long moment.

"Do you mind telling me what you were going to do with that shovel?," David finally exclaimed, his arms still around Camille. Not that she was distancing herself from him, of course. In fact, she moved even closer even as he continued staring at their two friends.

"I heard something! Piet and I both heard something!," she said. "I thought a snake had made a home in there. I was going to take care of it while Piet --"

"Was here for backup," he said, standing taller.

"Yeah," Kait said, rolling her eyes. "Good thing he fixed the garage door so it'd go up. Otherwise, he would have run straight through it. Left Camille a giant Piet-shaped hole in her garage door."

"Scared us to death," David murmured... still holding Camille in his arms where she could hear his heart racing just beneath her ear.

Wonderful. She wasn't complaining. She would never complain about this. Ever.

"What were you two doing in the pantry?," Kait asked, watching them suspiciously.

"What were you two doing in the garage?," David asked, turning her question back on her.

Again, they all stared at one another.

"Fixing the door," Piet finally offered, glancing over at Kait. "What was that noise?"

"David dropped his phone," Camille said, looking up at him, wondering at the look in his eyes...

"Yeah," he said, slowly letting her go, hesitation in his face as he did so.

Hesitation because he wanted to still hold her? Or hesitation because he realized what it looked like, how close he'd been to her?

"We were cleaning out the pantry," he murmured. "And the door locked behind us. And we weren't going to come out here because --"

"No way," Kait breathed. "Are those Twinkies?!"

And the opportunity to say or do much else was cut short as Piet and Kait crowded around them and forced them apart.

David

Christmas Eve. The interdenominational service for the entire town.

David hadn't gotten an invite to be a part of the celebration his first year in Swakopmund. He'd gone, though, as an observer, understanding only snippets of the festivities, as Piet, Ana Marie, and Kait took turns translating for him, sitting in the big middle of the crowd, then holding candles, singing Silent Night in Afrikaans.

It had been his first Christmas away from home. The students were gone to all corners of the nation by that time, with school over, and he'd parted ways with the Botha clan, them never guessing that he was going to go back to an empty cottage all by himself, where he would celebrate Christmas with Jesus and no one else.

The two years in between had been different.

He'd been established enough to be included in the services. So, Christmas Eve was work, just like it had been for his father back in the US, of course. He'd rejoiced at the opportunity to celebrate, to worship, to share from Scripture, and to be who God had called him to be.

But still. At the end of it all, he went home. Alone.

Merry Christmas.

This year was looking to be different already.

It was summer in Swakopmund, and Camille had dressed accordingly in a long sundress, a denim jacket thrown over it, and flip flops.

"Christmas on the beach," she had grinned when they met up. "How cool is this?"

"Totally cool," he'd affirmed as they made their way out of the parking lot and into the outdoor amphitheater, talking through the passage he would be sharing and the songs they'd be singing together as they led worship, even as she grinned up at him, telling him how excited she was for this Christmas.

Totally cool. He thought it again as he watched her talking with Tobias, the pastor from the north that she hadn't spoken so well of just a few months ago.

She'd obviously made things right with him, in the interim, in those few times he'd come to see David and his work in Swakopmund during the school term. She had changed things so that she could be more effective here, and he felt such appreciation for her as he finally caught her eye and she smiled over at him again.

He felt it even more and more, as she led worship alongside him later, as they sang the Afrikaans songs together, the tunes familiar, the words so new. He'd spent more than a few evenings teaching them to her, all out lying on her couch and laughing at her as she'd mangled the language so spectacularly. After she'd demanded that he get back up and stop laughing, telling him that she'd tell everyone that he wet the bed until he was a second grader (she *knew* that?!) if he didn't stop, he'd sat up and tried again.

He'd finally had to reach out, hold her face in his hand and show her how to move her mouth to make the sounds.

The Afrikaans was sounding so much better only moments later, but David could hardly hear it over the pounding of his heart as he watched Camille's lips form the words again and again.

She'd looked over at him at one point during the worship set, and he knew she was thinking the same thing he was thinking. His hand on her face, him watching her lips, her watching his...

It was the best Christmas he'd ever had.

As they were closing up for the night, several of the pastors in town came by to chat with him, even as Camille was talking with the teachers from one of the schools. One by one, the teachers left, leaving Cammie to watch him... then, wave goodbye to him as the pastors continued gabbing on and on.

He made a move to leave them, but she'd waved him on, understanding in her smile.

He felt the disappointment, watching her leave, knowing that she was doing it because she thought he had plans.

This happened every year, after all, with everyone around him just assuming what wasn't true. That he had plans. That he had someone who wanted to be with him.

But this year? He *did* have plans.

His plan had been to spend Christmas with her.

"Brother David?"

And his attention turned back to the group of pastors, as his heart followed her.

Cammie

She went back home afterwards. Back to the house she'd made her home.

She had done Christmas by herself before, obviously. There had been several Christmases, in fact, spent overseas on her own, celebrating in her own way, with care packages arriving long after the season, quiet holidays spent reading, thinking about what she was missing back home.

There had been a quiet comfort in it, though, in knowing the sufficiency of Christ, even alone like that, and she had weathered it well.

But here in Namibia, what was the point of staying by herself and celebrating by herself when David was here, too?

He'd made no mention of what was ahead for him that evening after the service, and as she'd watched him get caught up in conversations with the other pastors, she realized that perhaps he already had plans. He probably spent Christmas like this every year, and she had assumed too much to think that he'd be on his own, all too eager to have her join him.

He'd been here three years, after all. Three Christmases. Three services just like that. He had plans, of course. So obviously. And he hadn't intentionally left her out.

She left before he could include her.

Maybe she left too early, huh?

She bit her lip even as she turned the Christmas tree lights on and made her way to the master bedroom, opening a chest of drawers and thinking about how she could change into her pajamas, camp out on the couch, and spend this holiday listening to music, thinking about the States, trying not to think about David, trying not to wonder if that had been disappointment on his face as she'd turned away...

Surely not.

Camille rolled her eyes. Stupid. This was stupid. Why was she wondering anything when she could just go back to where she'd left him, make an excuse for why she'd had to run home, and go with him, wherever he went?

It didn't make her look desperate, did it? Too eager to be with him?

Who cared? She wanted to spend Christmas with him. Not just anyone. *Him.*

Even as she left her bedroom and grabbed her keys off the counter in the kitchen, she thought of Christmas Eve at New Life-Dallas, where she'd conclude the candlelight service every year by hugging Charity and Hope, talking over what they hoped to find under the Christmas tree, always turning to find David, smiling at her and saying very simply...

Merry Christmas, Cammie.

She went to the front door, intending to walk the short distance to the amphitheater where David would surely still be waiting...

... only to run right into him.

"Hey," he laughed, just as her face hit his chest and his hands moved up to catch her arms.

"Oh, hey, David," she breathed, feeling foolish even as she got her balance back. "Wasn't expecting you."

He let go of her arms, and she felt the loss. How stupid was that?

"Probably not," he said, stuffing his hands into his pockets. "I'm sure you have somewhere to go tonight."

And there it was. That strange something in his eyes that she'd seen more and more often lately. Expectation. Hope. Maybe more...

"I don't," she said. "I was coming to find you. I don't have anyone to spend Christmas with, David."

He seemed surprised by this. Surprised and... pleased maybe.

"Me, neither," he exhaled. "I've spent the last three Christmases by myself."

So had she. More than that.

And they understood one another better than they had, better than most people would understand either of them. Christmas alone.

Not anymore.

"Spend this one with me, then," she said.

And he smiled. He smiled.

She very nearly burst into tears at this, at the enormity of the feelings that rushed over her as he smiled.

"Sounds great," he said.

So he followed her back into the house, neither of them saying much of anything, until she stopped him at the kitchen.

"I made you a gift," she said, thinking about the time she'd taken this afternoon away from him, decorating her house, thinking about him, hoping that he'd be here...

... just like this.

"You *made* something?," he asked. "I'm honored."

She waved away the praise, reaching out for the box she'd put aside earlier, here on her counter. "Well, it's not much, but I thought you might appreciate it."

She held the box out to him, nervous about what he'd think, what he'd say. He took it with a smile and a peek inside, a bigger smile breaking out on his face, just as he laughed out loud.

"Christmas cookies! Made with sugar!" He lowered his voice and put a hand to his mouth. "Did I say that out loud? Because sugar just --"

"Doesn't taste right here," she said. She grinned at him. "Thought it was just me, but the sweets here --"

"Aren't sweet enough," he finished for her. "I mentioned it in the pantry the other day, with the Twinkies and all." And at this, he stuck one of the cookies into his mouth. Didn't even take a bite -- just stuck the whole thing in his mouth.

She could so clearly see twelve year old David Connor in the move, remembering times when he had done this very same thing.

"Oh glory," he mumbled, his mouth full. "Is that cream cheese icing?!"

She smiled, almost hearing the boy he'd been in the words. "Yes."

"Well, happy birthday, Jesus," he murmured, sticking a second one in his mouth. "And thank you, Camille." He reached out and hugged her, holding her close for a few moments, then backing up and smiling down at her. "I'll try not to eat them all tonight." And with this, he popped a third one in his mouth. "But I'm making no promises."

"Your cookies, your business," she said. "Want something to drink with it?"

"Sure," he murmured, even as she turned to start making something for them both.

"Hot chocolate okay?"

"The more sugar the better," he said. "Love how you're all settled in here. Love that it means I'm getting fed on a regular basis."

She smiled at him over her shoulder as she set the water to boil. "Happy to do it," she said softly.

He had no idea just how happy.

"I have a gift for you, too," he said, reaching in his back pocket for a small wrapped package. "I was going to wait until tomorrow, but... well, here it is."

"Can't wait for Christmas morning, huh?," she asked.

"Never could," he said, grinning. "And Charity and Hope ruined Santa for me, so there was no need for patience."

"Oh," she sighed sadly. "They told you Santa wasn't real? That's so mean."

"Santa's not *real*?!," he gasped.

She narrowed her eyes at him. "David..."

"Just kidding. And I was in the seventh grade when my dear sisters let me in on the big secret," he said. "I think they thought I would never figure it out." He handed her the gift. "Go ahead."

Camille smiled as she began to tear the paper away. And she lifted the lid of the box, feeling her heart race just a bit at the bracelet winking up at her.

"Oh, David," she murmured, pulling it out and studying it, "it's beautiful."

"Called your name," he said, smiling. "Knew you needed it to mark your first Christmas here."

"Sure did," she answered, slipping it on, fastening the clasp, and peering at it more closely, her breath catching at what she saw.

"David... are those diamonds?" She looked up at him with surprise.

"Very tiny Namibian diamonds, yes," he said. "You needed a piece of Namibia. And these beat just random rocks, I thought."

She was speechless for a moment by the generosity and thoughtfulness in this. "And I just made you cookies," she said.

"That was worth more than diamonds," he said, eating another one. "Trust me."

"Thank you," she said softly. "Thank you for this... for everything."

They watched one another for a long moment. A comfortable moment that felt like home. Not unlike this place, which Cammie had tried her best to make into a home.

David broke her gaze to look around, just as the water began to boil on the stove. She went to get their drinks ready, even as he stepped into the living room where the tree she'd dragged from the attic was decorated with lights she'd found and generic ornaments she'd bought at the grocery store until she could make some of her own for the long-term.

"This looks amazing," he said. "You've done a great job in making this place nice again. And the Christmas tree..."

"Thanks," she murmured, bringing their drinks to the coffee table. "Found a whole bunch of handmade ornaments with the name Marie on them. Figured they were special to the last family, so I boxed them up, called the board for a forwarding address, and shipped them out."

"They should get them in three months then," David nodded. "They'll be glad to have them, though."

"Actually, they've already gotten them," she said. "I sent them with DHL. Had them insured and got a confirmation number so I'd know that the package got there."

David looked back at her. "Wasn't that expensive?"

She smiled. "Yeah, but worth it. Must have been something they thought they had to sacrifice and leave behind. I mean, there were little reindeer ornaments made out of plasters of tiny hands. Her little name scrawled on the back in marker. Special things, you know. They likely had to sacrifice so much to be here for so many years, and it just seemed a shame that they'd had to sacrifice anything going the other direction, you know?"

He stayed silent, staring at her.

"What?," she asked, wondering if she'd overstepped some invisible bounds, finding out this much information on the past missionaries, sending them the ornaments without asking anyone.

"Thank you for doing that," David said softly. "That was really thoughtful. I would have never thought to do that."

"You're too busy being thoughtful when it comes to things like buying diamonds," she said, holding up her wrist. "Happy birthday, Jesus, right?"

"Happy birthday, Jesus," he affirmed. "And thanks again, Cammie."

She smiled at the name. "Hey, your sugared drink to wash down your sugared dessert is going to get cold."

"Can't have that," he said with another smile, and she followed him, joining him as he made his way over to the couch. She'd only left the Christmas tree lights on, keeping the rest of the lights off in the living room, and the effect was festive, something that felt like home.

Not unlike David himself, whose smile reminded her of so many Christmases past, all spent at New Life-Dallas and their candlelight services.

"Great service tonight," she murmured as they sat down on the couch together, and he picked up his mug. "Reminded me of some other Christmas Eves."

"Christmas Eve candlelight service," he said. "Every year of our lives, huh? Not unlike tonight."

"Yes," she said, "but it's summer."

"Which is not all that different from Christmas in Texas," he noted.

"But still. And the service was all in Afrikaans. Call me sentimental, but I'd love to hear it in English."

"English," David said thoughtfully. "The same English Jesus Himself spoke."

She grinned at this. "And He spoke English with a Texas drawl. At least in my mind, after hearing Paul Connor sermons my whole life."

"What you need to do," David drawled, "is open up your Buy-bulls to the first chapter of the book of Ez-uh-ruh..."

"Buy-bulls," Cammie smiled, thinking of this. "You sound like him. All grown up like you are."

David glanced down at this, a pleased smile on his face. Not for the comparison to Paul Connor, obviously, but for the acknowledgment that he was all grown up.

"Well, he was something," David said. "Still is. Still will be."

"The same yesterday, today, and forever," Cammie sighed. "Like Jesus."

David laughed out loud at this. She joined him in his laughter, blushing as he watched her appreciatively.

"Well, not quite," he said.

"Not quite," she said, thinking of all those years at New Life-Dallas.

Big thoughts, deep thoughts... complicated, now that she knew the man who had been born out of it all. She could think of Paul Connor and how he sounded one way on the platform but was someone else in his home all those times she visited.

David was the same in both places. Before a group of teenagers, right here with her...

"And how," she said, wondering at how constant and consistent David was now in her life, "did your dad manage to sound like that from the pulpit and sound entirely different in personal conversations? He wasn't even from Texas originally."

David smiled at this. "All put-on, for the most part. But would you believe that the put-on accent he did for the Big D crowds actually *is* my legitimate accent?"

She could believe it. David sounded the same, just with a deeper voice now, but she'd noticed his accent even more here. Slower than Kait's clipped English, more drawn out than Piet's proper accent...

David sounded like home.

What an odd thought.

And what a comforting one as he smiled at her here in this home she'd made for herself that was becoming as familiar to her as the one she'd left, all because he'd gone out of his way to reach out to her.

"Yes," she said simply, thinking on this. "I want to hear it."

"My accent?," he asked. "Does it even sound like an accent since you sound the exact same way, you hillbilly?"

"I do *not* sound like a hillbilly," she laughed.

"You sound like me," he said. "Freaks Piet out probably."

"Yes, well," she murmured. "Sounds like home. And I want to hear it. I want to hear you read it."

"Read what?," he asked, his smile certainly indicating that he had a guess.

"Read the Christmas story for me, David," she said. "Right from your Buy-bull and all. It's a tradition, you know. Our New Life tradition."

He nodded, pulling out his phone and pulling up the Bible. "Maybe it'll become our new Namibia tradition, huh?"

And she smiled at this, earnestly praying in her heart that it would become just that.

"I'd love that, David."

David

He showed up again on Christmas morning.

They'd said goodbye only a few hours ago, sitting together on the porch, listening to the church bells all over Swakopmund chiming the arrival of Christmas.

It could be a lonely time. Cammie was obviously feeling it a little, as she wanted him around more and more lately.

Why else would she want him around? Not that he minded. No matter why she wanted him around, he'd be there.

But he'd wondered if there was something more going on. Probably just a figment of his very active imagination and all of his pathetic boyhood hopes. Because when she smiled at him, he very nearly reverted to his twelve year old self, sweating and having trouble breathing, very nearly giggling, *well, glory be, Cammie Evans.*

Smooth. So smooth. Even if she caught him smiling at her all moon-eyed, at least he'd been careful to not say anything and embarrass himself.

Unless, of course, she was feeling something, too.

Maybe...

She'd told him as he'd reluctantly left the night before that he was, of course, completely welcome and very much expected to come back the next morning.

He was glad for the invitation. And Cammie herself seemed to be as glad about his acceptance as she opened the door and grinned at him.

"I made you a huge breakfast," she said by way of greeting.

Cammie Evans and food. A whole day ahead of them with just this.

He'd never had a better Christmas.

"Merry Christmas to you, too," he said, hugging her, knowing that he was using the holiday as an excuse to touch her. And she was okay with it, apparently, as she held him close a moment later, seemingly unwilling to let him go.

Homesick, probably. Nothing more than loneliness. Maybe.

"Well, come in," she said softly, backing up just enough to look him in the eyes, her arms still around him.

Seriously. Maybe. There had been that afternoon in the pantry. Then the night before. And every moment in between, with this look on her face...

He'd seen that look before.

He was going to be late to his first high school class. World history. It was first period, and it was somewhere -- yes, somewhere -- in this ginormous building that was bigger than his junior high and elementary school combined.

There were three stories at this high school, and the building had to be three miles long. (Maybe more!) He'd been astounded to discover that his freshman class had 1,438 students, but that was nothing compared to the shock of arriving on campus and discovering that the sophomore, junior, and senior classes were just as big.

He was glad to be in high school, finally, of course, but... wow, he was so lost. Where in the world was his first class?!

He'd hoped that Charity and Hope would help him out a little, but beyond the ride they'd been forced to give him in the little SUV they shared, they'd pretended like they didn't know him, purposeful, important seniors that they were, disappearing into the crowds as soon as they left him at the door.

He looked back down at the computer printout with his schedule, wondering which direction he should even go as floods of students passed by him on every side.

"David Connor!"

He heard her voice before he saw her, and relief washed over him as soon as his eyes met hers.

Cammie Evans. Grinning at him, even as she reached out and messed up his hair... then pulled back her hand with a grimace.

"How much gel did you use this morning, David?," she asked, studying his hair with curiosity.

"Too much probably," he said. "Wow, am I glad to see you, Cammie!"

"Oh, yeah?," she asked, already distracted, as people passed them both, calling out greetings to her.

He took the opportunity to look her over. He saw her every week, of course, almost every day during the summers, but this would be different, going to the same school she went to. He'd scowled at the prospect of wearing a uniform (what public school did that anyway?), but looking over Cammie's fitted shirt, her little skirt...

Uniforms were good.

"You're glad to see me," Cammie said, waving back to a group of girls then looking at him. "Why is that?"

Because I'm in love with you, obviously. And you're wearing a really short skirt.

He refrained from saying this.

"Because I'm lost," he said instead. "I don't know where my first class is."

She smiled at him. "Happens to the best of us," she said. "Happened to me my first day here, too. Where are you heading?"

And she looked at his schedule and began walking him that way, explaining how the building was laid out, checking over his other classes, telling him that he'd lucked out with his Spanish teacher but that his biology teacher was really hard and --

"Hey, Cammie."

He was a big dude who came out of nowhere and slung his arm over Cammie's shoulders, very nearly knocking David over in the process.

"Hey, Owen," she said, smiling up at him.

Oh, him. A guy from church. Another senior. Pretty popular, too. Charity said it was because he was "haaaawwwwhhhhttt," but David didn't see what that mattered since the guy had the intelligence of a gorilla. (And he was very nearly as hairy as one, too.)

"You make that uniform look good," Owen said, giving Cammie a slow smile.

And David wanted to kick himself for not having been the one to say this to her. Especially when he saw how it made her beam, just a little.

That look in her eyes. She didn't *like* this monkey, did she?

Owen finally saw David scowling up at him. "Hey, little man," he said. "Didn't see you down there."

"I'm helping David find his world history class," Cammie said, still giving Owen that look.

That look. David couldn't help but stare at her a little, seeing the way she looked, how much more beautiful it made her, how he --

"Is it just me, or do the freshman get smaller and smaller every year?," Owen asked, no longer even looking at David.

"Maybe," Cammie giggled.

Ugh. Go away, monkey man. Go away, go away, go away...

"I'll catch you at lunch," Owen finally said, ducking away with a smile, heading the opposite direction for his own class.

And Cammie watched him leave, that same look on her face.

"Uh... Cammie?"

She looked down at him finally. "Oh, sorry, David. I didn't realize you were still here with me."

Half a lifetime later, he found himself seeing the same look on her face as she looked up at him and said, "David, are you still here with me?"

That look on her face, as she was looking at him...

"I hate gorillas," he said softly... wanting to kick himself a second later for his idiocy.

She watched him for a long moment. "Okay," she said, laughing just a little.

"I'm just saying," he shrugged, letting her lead him into her house finally. "Gorillas. And really hairy guys. They're gross, right?"

She made a face at this for a second, as he pulled her chair out for her then sat down in the chair next to her. "I guess," she said.

"Exactly," he nodded, thankful that somewhere along the way stupid, ugly, gorilla Owen had messed up somehow and hadn't ended up with Cammie forever because she was right here, right now --

Reaching out and touching his face with a grin.

Whoa.

Maybe, huh? Because there was that look.

"I kind of like my guys clean shaven and all," she said, clear nervousness in her voice, even as she rubbed her thumb lightly over his cheek. "Not hairy and... well, gorilla-like."

And David forgot all about the food on the table. He was going to say something. Finally. He was going to --

The doorbell rang.

Of course.

"Are you expecting someone?," he asked, making a move to answer the door for her.

"No," she said, standing with him. "It was just going to be us."

Before he could say anything about how that was great with him, she walked past him and opened the door.

"Geseende Kersfees!"

Kait and Piet. David thought about slamming the door back in their faces, not wanting to share a minute of this holiday with them, wanting Cammie all to himself, especially now that she said she didn't like gorilla men either.

But before he could pretend like they'd never even been there, Cammie came up behind him, laughing. "Hey, welcome back!"

"Thanks," Kait breathed, grinning as she stepped in and put down her ever-present messenger bag.

"I didn't realize you were coming back so early," Cammie said. "You said after Christmas."

"Cut the trip a bit short," Piet answered, shaking David's hand as he came in, too, with a curious glance towards him... almost apologetic as he did so.

Well, good. He should be apologetic. Should be sorry for walking in right when David was ready to tell Cammie everything.

David took a breath, willing them to go away again, even as he said, "Well, merry Christmas, y'all."

And Kait turned to him, something strange in her eyes. "Merry Christmas, David." She glanced over at Piet with some concern, reaching up to put a strand of her hair behind her ear nervously.

Well, that was weird. Before he could wonder why she was watching him like that, why Piet was watching him like that, too, Cammie gasped.

"You're wearing a ring!," she said, grabbing Kait's hand.

"Oh, that," Kait said dismissively, looking down at it herself. "Yeah. A Christmas gift from Piet."

"You're getting married?," David asked Piet, who had gone from looking apologetic to looking downright euphoric.

"Nee, man, we are already married," he said.

Cammie looked between the two of them, her mouth rounded in shock. "What?"

"Well, he asked," Kait sighed, as if this was taking too much effort to explain it all when she had something else on her mind clearly, even as she glanced back at David. "And rather than planning some elaborate wedding that will ensure that my dear, psychotic mother will come here and taint the entire African continent with her presence --"

"Nee, man," Piet laughed.

"-- well, we just went ahead and made it legal in South Africa. Which I'm told makes it legal here. And if we can get the good parson David here to have us say some vows and sign a paper for us, it'll be legal in the great state of Texas... and the rest of the States by default, I guess." She shrugged. "So, yeah. Married."

They all watched her for a long moment.

"What?," she asked.

"After three years of putting him off," David said, "you just randomly married him the same day he proposed?"

"Fine by me," Piet said.

"And I haven't been putting him off," Kait argued. She looked over at her... husband. Wow. That was weird. "And after three years... well, I was sure. Finally. So, there you go."

"Congratulations," Cammie said, grinning over at David.

And he could understand it at least in part. With Cammie looking at him like that, he could understand eloping, running away with someone --

"You're just in time to have breakfast with us," she said, looking over at the table.

"Oh, no, we don't want to crash your party," Kait said.

Good. Then, go away, David almost said.

"I made plenty," Cammie assured them. "David and I don't mind."

Well, actually, he did mind. But he and Cammie would have other moments by themselves.

He opened his mouth to assure them that it was okay (even if it wasn't), but Kait interrupted him.

"No, really," she said. "We just wanted to come by and..." She looked over at Piet.

What was up with these two?

"David, we've been in touch with the board," Piet said softly.

The board.

He thought this odd but not worth all the looks. "Oh? Is everything okay?"

"Everything's great," Kait said. "Just perfect, actually. They want you to go back stateside on New Year's to give some speeches. You know, while all of the students are back up north and you're not as busy."

He didn't want to leave here now, obviously, not with Cammie here. But a short trip to make some speeches and shake some hands wasn't any big deal.

"And they want Camille to go with you," Piet added.

Even better.

Cammie grinned over at him. "Free vacation to the US?," she laughed.

"We can do that," he said, grinning back at her.

"There's more to it," Kait added, picking up her messenger bag, looking away from David with guilt in her eyes. "Have you talked to your parents recently?"

He hadn't. He'd intended to call them that very night, to wish them a merry Christmas, but it hadn't been a priority. He'd left home three years ago and had distanced himself from the drama of the church, the convention...

The convention.

"What kind of meeting will I be going to, Kait?," he asked, getting an uneasy feeling about it all.

"A convention meeting," she said. "To present your father to trustees and leaders. And to secure their votes for his presidency."

He wanted no part of that. He didn't want any part of promoting his father and his business, because it had nothing to do with life here, and --

"It's also an opportunity for you to tell them about Namibia," Kait continued on calmly. "This is our chance to get more funding for our work here. Even more workers. They'll have to listen to us now because Paul Connor's son is on our team."

And suddenly, it all became clear to David.

He could remember how they'd pursued him. Kait and Piet both, with phone calls and emails, even though he was just an average youth minister, with no real, paid experience or education towards this kind of work. He could remember how they'd been vague about what had gone on in Namibia, about what their long-term goals were --

"You," he said. "You lied to me."

"What?," Kait asked. "I never lied to you."

"You said you just stopped working for the board. Retirement for the last missionaries. You aren't part of the board anymore. Then, why are they contacting you?"

She glanced back at Piet.

"Kait, what's going on here?," David asked again, fearful of the response.

"Well, first of all," she said, "I never lied to you. I did work for the board like I told you. And then, I stepped down. And now... well, now they've asked me to do some work here, in getting you ready for the next thing."

"The next thing?," he asked. "And what do you mean, 'they'll have to listen to us now'? What happened here? What happened to the last missionaries?"

Could it be that his father had known something back at that steak dinner?

"They forced the others into retirement three years ago, David," Piet said quietly. "Tried to close out all operations indefinitely here. But there was work left to do. And then, Mark told Kait that Paul Connor's son had put in application with the board, and --"

"You knew who my father was," David said quietly as Piet tried to avoid his eyes. He turned to Kait. "And the only reason you wanted me here was because of him. You saw his name. Not mine. His. So you went for it. Not for the work. But because of what the exposure would do. Because of what would happen when he became president of the convention."

Kait was unapologetic. "I did," she said. "I worked there for years, and when I came here and saw what was inevitably going to happen, I knew it would only be short-term, the loss of all workers. I knew I could eventually figure out a way to get workers back in. Would have taken years, probably, but I could have done it. Starting with just one fulltime worker. The right one. And if we could make him successful, we could force the board's hand. They need workers here, they need the visibility, and the whole infrastructure needs the funding. And then we heard about you. We went after you. We wanted you on the field. They wanted you on the field. And so they gave us funding for one missionary, and we made sure you wanted Namibia."

David swallowed, thinking on what she'd said before she'd spoken about what anyone wanted. "*If* you could make him succeed. You think I couldn't do it on my own."

"No, David," Piet said. "You did. We knew you could. But Kait's right. We were all in on making you a success. Not for you but for the future of ministry here. And for the lives that were changed. The board was watching. We had one chance. And you did it. And now, you're going to tell them, with your father giving approval, the whole convention turned towards Namibia, and.."

But his words faded away, as David considered something more horrible than the news that he was who he was because Paul Connor was over it all.

Cammie. Had she been in on it, too? Had she been pretending, just like Kait and Piet had?

Was she pretending even now, reaching out, touching his face, saying so many wonderful things to him?

"Did you know?," David asked her, hurt in the words.

"I had no idea," she said. "I didn't even know you were here. Or the situation."

"We brought Camille in without knowing that there was a connection at all," Kait said. "We couldn't even find New Life-Dallas anywhere on her information."

"My parents moved when I went to college," she said softly. "Chelsea was with Kyle at their church, so none of us were still there." She looked to David. "That's why I didn't see you for so many years. I had no reason to come back to Dallas, with my parents gone."

He nodded at this, doubt in his eyes.

"I swear to you, David," she said softly. "I didn't know anything about this."

And he believed her. His eyes darted back over to Kait's. "Why Camille, then? If you didn't know anything about her connection to New Life-Dallas? Why did you pick her?"

"She knows enough people at the board because she's been moved around so often. That's why we wanted her. Of course, at the time, we didn't know she was a woman, that she knew you, any of it. We just knew where she'd been, what she'd done. She was just a list of former jobs, without a name. She was almost as good as you. You were our connection to Paul Connor, and she was our model missionary."

David looked over at her, thinking about how the board had reduced her to just her work. How she'd stood on her own in that, how her value had been in what she'd done.

Not who she was. Because she wasn't Paul Connor's kid.

That's what he'd been reduced to. Simply part of Paul Connor.

Kait sighed, the stress evident on her face. "And then, she showed up. I picked her up at the airport, saw that she was young, pretty, well spoken. I knew the two of you would look good together for the rest of the convention to see. It was almost better that she was a woman." Kait shrugged. "But it was just a lucky coincidence that she knew you beforehand. We didn't know anything about that. But now, having her present with you will connect the rest of the dots. The board will listen. The trustees will listen. People will want to see personnel sent here. Money sent here. Paul Connor's son is leading our team. Everyone can get behind that."

"But I'm nothing like him," David said. "And I don't want to be."

"Doesn't matter," Kait said. "They'll be looking for reasons to have anyone connected to him up on the platform. They've already made arrangements for John to speak about his church, about what he and Charity are seeing happen. Knew they'd look good up on the platform with your nephew, with her expecting again, giving proof to the fact that the convention's not dying. It's being built by young people, young families —"

She knew everything. Kait knew everything about his life back in the States. And his nephew, his niece...

"No way," David gasped. "The baby... did Charity know? Did they know that this was going to happen, that dad was coming up for the presidency? That they would be promoting him, too? Is that why they got pregnant again —"

"I'm sure they wanted their children, David," Kait said calmly. "The convention couldn't force them to have children, obviously. But there may have been a suggestion, about how it would help your father's election process, how it would look... encouragement to go ahead..."

"Oh, my goodness," Cammie breathed out.

"What have they done to Hope?," David asked, his voice cracking.

"They haven't done anything to anyone," Piet said. "And Hope already made your father look good. Living at home, serving at New Life —"

"They encouraged her to stay, didn't they?," David cut in. "To stay close, since I was going overseas. That way, he had one child in pastoral ministry, one overseas, another at home being the dutiful single daughter. That's it, right?"

Kait frowned. "They didn't make decisions for any of you. But, yes, they might have suggested it to her. Given her reason to consider changing her plans. But that's life. And to believe otherwise, to believe that we make decisions unaffected by those around us, is just naïve. Would you be here if things were different? I don't know. It doesn't even seem like a question worth asking at this point because you're here."

And he was who he was. Would he be the same had he not been born into the Connor family? Most assuredly not.

Who would he even be? Who was he now, if David Paul Connor, missionary to Africa, had suddenly been reduced to David Paul Connor, son of the man behind it all?

What was the point of even asking?

"So, the question isn't how you got here but what you're going to do now," Kait said calmly. "Not for the convention. Not for your father. But for Namibia. For Christ and His purposes here."

David watched her silently.

"This is the beginning of something good," she said. "You'll see it eventually, David. How you've done more for Namibia than you can imagine." She handed Cammie a magazine. "And I've done most of the hard work for you already. You just get to go in and celebrate it."

"Oh, my," Cammie murmured, holding the magazine up to David.

The Legacy of Paul Connor. A picture of both Connor men, smiling under the headline. It was a recent picture, taken on the trip when he'd unexpectedly met up with Cammie again.

Kait had her people working on it even then.

"You're his son, of course," she said trying to reason with him, "and you and Camille both grew up under his pastorate. And everything here has been a success. The board wants you to present for them, be their star. They wouldn't send anyone else. I suspected it was going to happen like this. I knew three years ago that your father was in line for this. And then? Your name showed up for appointment, David. When we needed exposure, for the convention to hear what was happening here, Paul Connor's only son shows up looking for a place. It was like God gave you to us at just the right time."

"Why didn't you just tell me?," he asked. "In all that time you were telling me about the needs here, practically begging me to come... why didn't you tell me the real reason? It wouldn't have changed the real needs here."

"Would you have come to Namibia?," Piet said. "If you'd known why we pursued you, why the board allowed you to come in a career capacity, even with your qualifications as they were —"

"Which they weren't, huh?," he asked. "I got this job because of my dad, didn't I?"

"It doesn't mean you weren't the right man," Piet said. "Or that you haven't been better than we could have ever hoped for. Or that we weren't friends, David —"

"Or that God hasn't done a lot through you," Kait added. "Which is what it comes down to, right? Even you can agree to that, right, David? That the gospel came first. And that God was going to work through you. And He has. But originally, yeah. You were picked because of your father. And you're here now because of him."

He'd done it. Paul Connor had followed him to Africa.

How? How had he done it? How could David ever stand on his own?

"Cammie?," he asked weakly.

"I'm with you, David," she responded.

And without an explanation, he left the house, with Camille following him.

Cammie

She didn't have to ask him if she could go along. He didn't even look back as he opened the door to the truck and helped her up, then went around to the driver's side, starting it up and leading them away from her house, where Kait and Piet would likely eat the breakfast she'd made for David and continue on with plans to reduce him to nothing more than his last name.

Oh, David...

"He was right," David said softly as he drove. "My father. He was right when he said that something was off with everything here. I mean, he said it the last time I saw him. Said there was something not quite right with it. With the board's involvement, with personnel, with what was left behind here in Namibia. How can he be such a jerk and still have such clear discernment, half a world away?"

Camille thought back to David's sermon at the youth event, back when she'd wondered over how he could be who he was now. "David, you never named the country where you served. Back in the US. You left that out." She looked at him. "Was it because of your dad? The convention?"

"It was stupid," David said, shaking his head, not meeting her eyes. "But I figured the more generic I could keep it, the less it would change my life here. It was enough to know that Paul Connor's son was on the field. If I went around talking about the specific place... they'd know about it. Everyone would. Not just the board. Everyone. And people can't stay away when they hear about Paul Connor. I just wanted my own place, you know?" He looked up at her. "I know it's selfish. Especially with all that Kait

227

said could happen here if the rest of the world just knew what God had been doing. But I just..."

"Just didn't want to be in the spotlight," Cammie said.

"Well, I was," he said. "Back there at that meeting, where we saw each other. So, what was it all worth anyway?"

"You weren't, though," she said. "You kept this quiet. No one would have known. Until now, of course. But I understand, David. I really do."

"And they only asked me to that thing because of him," David added, shaking his head. "I thought it was because of what I'd done. But none of it has been because of that. It's all been because of him."

Cammie thought about it all, about how it was true likely, even as David pulled off the road, put the truck in park, and hit the palm of his hand against the steering wheel. Hard.

She jumped a little.

"I'm sorry," he mumbled. "I just... I just can't get away from him!"

"I'm sorry, David," she said, reaching over to take his hand. "I'm so sorry."

"I was so excited when I came here. So excited that I was doing this on my own," he said. "That I was finally in a place where I was who I needed to be, who I could never seem to be in his shadow. And now? Now, he's suddenly the reason behind everything I do."

"He's not the reason," she said. "Jesus alone has been the reason. And, David, who's to even say that as we go and share what's going on here that it has to be about your dad at all?"

"It's all for him," David said, insistent.

"That's their plan," she answered, "but God can still work through that, can still show the convention what's going on here, can open the way for so much more to be done. It wasn't right what they did... but God can still use it. For your good, for the work here... for His glory. And I think He will."

He watched her sadly. "Do you even want to go back to the States now? Now that you know you'll just be a part of it all, too? Being puppets for Paul Connor and for the board both?"

"I'll do whatever you want me to do, David," she said sincerely, meaning it with everything in her.

"Why?," he said. "Why would you follow me? Why would you trust my judgment? I'm not qualified. You heard them say it. I've just been everyone's puppet. Kait and Piet's puppet. The election committee for my father. My father himself. Why would you do anything I think you should?"

"Because I trust you," she said simply. "And because you're leading this team."

He looked away again. "I'm sorry that you've been dragged into it all, too."

Dragged into what? This mess? Sure, that was bad. But dragged into being beside him as he went through this, as he fought his way out of all the feelings, and as he tried to be who Christ called him to be, despite all of this?

There had been no dragging. She'd walked into it willingly.

And she'd stay in it willingly, if it meant staying by David.

He took a deep breath. "When did she say we're doing this?"

"New Year's."

He laughed humorlessly. "Didn't give us any time to think it over, did she?"

"A few days," Cammie murmured.

"And that," he said, pointing to the magazine in her lap. "How long has everyone else known about that and not told me?"

"It's a January release," she said, looking at the date. "No one's gotten it yet."

"Except my dad," David noted. "He probably knows all about this."

Probably. Cammie thought about it, about the rest of the Connor family getting news about David coming home for a visit, probably even now.

Oh, David... Cammie thought it even as she looked at the magazine.

Kait had done her homework.

She had somehow gotten her hands on the glossy spread in the convention magazine early as well, likely because half of the pictures looked to be ones that she had taken. *The Legacy of Paul Connor* was emblazoned at the top, with a picture of David and his father at New Life-Dallas, taken sometime fairly recently. Scattered throughout the article were pictures of David growing up, pictures of him at the church, and a picture of him in Namibia, with a group of teenagers.

Cammie put her hand on that last one, overcome once again by all that she felt for him, after all this time. Before she could say anything, David sighed. "Pretty sure she had me airbrushed in that one."

She looked closer. "No, David," she said softly. "That's how you look."

"Well, she totally airbrushed that one," he said, pointing to one of them both, seaside, David with his guitar, grinning, and Cammie squinting into the sun.

"Not enough," she groaned. "Look at me. Why did Kait let them put that in there?"

"Looks good," he murmured. "Especially next to that one."

Cammie studied the picture for a long moment, trying to place it. She was sitting on the steps in the sanctuary at New Life-Dallas, barely sixteen, wearing shorts and a T-shirt, her hair in a ponytail, and a brightly colored name tag on a lanyard around her neck. Cammie. And over her shoulder was David, dressed in basketball shorts and a ratty old shirt, with his own name tag wrapped around his head.

"VBS," she exhaled finally. "We were all scheduled to work with the kindergarten class. Me, you, Charity, and Hope."

"And Charity," he said, "came down with mono."

"The kissing disease," Cammie whispered, just like she had back then, smiling up at David, giggling even as she did so.

"Good grief, Cammie," he said sarcastically. "Are you still twelve?"

"Some days," she murmured, still grinning.

He rolled his eyes. "Yeah, and then Hope came down with the kissing disease, too. Leave it to her to get mono from her twin sister. It was the longest summer of my life with the two of them so sick."

Cammie laughed out loud at this. "And they left us to handle the class by ourselves. It's like they knew those five year olds were all living terrors!"

"They were particularly rotten," David affirmed. "Evil from birth, like my dad would've said. And he was right."

"You were so good with them, though," she said. "So sweet and gentle with them, even at your age. And you'd sit there during the Bible story and look ten times more interested than they did when I'd teach them about Jesus."

She remembered the way he had looked there at New Life-Dallas, three five year olds in his lap as he listened to the story, as he clapped and sang along to wee sing songs, and as he ran around the gym with them all chasing him, trying to teach them the rules of dodgeball.

Such good memories. Such incredible, life-defining moments, spent at that church.

"I have so many good memories there," she said softly.

He exhaled. "The Legacy of Paul Connor," he murmured.

And she swallowed the words she hadn't been brave enough to say, even as David started the truck back up again.

And all of my best memories have you in them, David.

THE CONVENTION

David

He was on his way to do Paul Connor's bidding.

Again. Just like he had his whole life.

They'd gone back to Cammie's house later that Christmas and had jumped right into the plans Kait had made. They needed some horrific missionary costumes, traditional Namibian clothes, being made for them at her request, because the board loved seeing their missionaries look like missionaries.

Whatever that meant.

Kait had also had their flight details, their schedule of events, their accommodations, and all of their transportation arranged. She'd even gone and gotten Camille a bottle of the magic happy pills she needed for anxiety on the flight.

Those magic happy pills had knocked Cammie out in Walvis Bay. David had very nearly had to carry her onto the plane in Cape Town, where she'd snuggled up against him and slept for the first half of the long journey.

Things weren't all bad, honestly, he thought, as he looked down at her.

Not that things had progressed there. Not that he'd had a chance. He'd been so preoccupied with all that had been upended about his life, his purpose, and his work that figuring out things with Cammie had taken a backseat.

She'd been courteous to Kait and Piet while David had been curt. She'd listened to him complain about them, about his father, and about the whole mess, never quick to give a solution, always eager to hear him.

"We can't hate them forever," she had said.

And what she had really meant was, *You can't hate them forever, David.* Because she hadn't hated them for it. She'd seen their reasons, knew that they wanted to see Christ glorified in Namibia, and understood it.

But Cammie didn't know about Paul Connor, about how none of his plans had anything to do with Namibia, about how he would just as soon pull their only missionary out from under them if he could so that he'd stay on top at New Life-Dallas.

Well, not their only missionary. Because David wasn't alone out there anymore.

He smiled at this, even as his mind raced with all that waited for him in the States, as they made their one stop on the flight between continents.

The change in noise volume on the plane, as people moved around and stretched, broke Cammie out of her haze.

"Where are we?," she asked, glancing up at him and moving closer, her head on his chest.

He wasn't alone. Praise God, he wasn't alone.

"We're halfway there," he said softly. "In Senegal. They're refueling the plane."

She groaned, and he smiled, tentatively reaching out to smooth down her hair.

"I thought maybe we were there already," she sighed. "I still have so far to go."

"I know," he murmured.

"I'm a nervous flyer," she told him again. "You should've gotten me drunk, David."

"Mmmm," he sighed. "I did get you some water so you could take your magic happy pills. Remember that? Back in Walvis Bay?"

"I do," she said, reaching her hand up to his face, outlining his lips with her finger, making his heart pound as she did so. "I'm probably doing this because I'm still drugged."

"Regrettably, yes," he said, smiling underneath her fingers, wishing for all the world that she was really doing this on her own. Then, holding her hand still, he kissed each finger softly.

"Did you take my pills, too?," she moaned softly, and his heart clenched at the sound.

"No, Cammie, this is all me," he sighed, still beaming at her, putting her hand to his cheek.

"Cammie," she said. "I like that you still think of me like that. Even if you were a little pervert who saw me in my underwear." A pause. "And even if you're still imagining me dancing around in your head. Shame on you..."

"I'm a guy," he said. "I try to fight it, but you know."

"Just as long as I'm by myself up there," she sighed.

"Only you," he whispered. "There's never been anyone but you."

"Wow," she groaned again. "I really wish I could remember this conversation. So great."

"Maybe we'll have it again," he said.

"Maybe," she sighed, laying her head on his shoulder. "Remind me, David. Remind me."

"If you remind me to remind you," he said, lacing their fingers together. "Deal?"

"Then, it's not going to happen," she murmured. "I won't remember to do that."

"I know," he said, kissing her on the forehead, glad for this, glad that he could feel the freedom to say these things now, if not ever again.

"Why wouldn't you want me to remember?"

He watched her for a second, almost wistfully. "Because I don't picture you dancing, up in my head, you know. And I didn't back then. Not too often, at least."

"Hmm," she said, confusion on her face. "What do you picture? And why does that have anything to do with me remembering?"

"I picture you with the high school girls," he said. "Sharing with them, giving them everything you have, teaching them to love Christ like you love Him, like you did when you were in high school. I remember that, watching you in youth that last summer, when I finally got to join the group. You were so serious about following Him, and when you talked about Him, I could hear your heart so clearly. You had the most beautiful heart. You still do."

She said nothing for a long moment. So long that David said, "You're out again, aren't you?"

"No," she said. "That's the most wonderful thing anyone's ever said to me. Why wouldn't you want me to remember that?"

He thought about all he was facing, all that he'd been facing for so long in this. He thought about how helpful she was in the work, how helpful she was proving to be even now.

How much he needed her to face everything going on back home.

"Because I need you," he said softly. "And I can't be scaring you off by telling you that I'm really, really into you."

"Maybe I'm into you, too," she said.

He'd thought a few times that maybe, just maybe, she felt something more. But he was David Connor... and she was Cammie Evans.

He was just a man whose only significance was in who his father was.

"And maybe it's just the magic happy pills talking," he said, swallowing.

"David," she said, her eyes closed, "maybe you need to just take a chance. Tell me how you really feel when I'm not on my magic happy pills. Because maybe the Cammie on the magic happy pills feels just like the one without them. It's entirely possible."

"Is it?," he asked, daring to believe her.

"Maybe the Cammie off the magic happy pills wants to make out with you," she said, grinning, her eyes still closed.

"Well, that Cammie sounds very exciting," he said, grinning as well.

"Exciting," she murmured, pulling him closer. "She would definitely be that to you."

"Oh, yeah," he laughed softly.

"David?"

"Hmm?"

"Maybe," she said, so softly that he had to move closer to hear her, "the Cammie off the magic happy pills... maybe she loves you, huh?"

Maybe. Maybe just a fraction of how much he loved her.

When he looked down at her, thinking of all the things he'd say and do if he was someone she'd only known in this context, as two people living their lives for Christ half a world away, instead of the boy who was even now doing the bidding of the past...

... well, he saw that she was fast asleep. Her head on his shoulder, her hand on his chest, and her mouth turned up towards his.

He smiled, pulling her closer, kissing her forehead, and falling asleep right beside her.

Cammie

She woke up with her face in his shirt.

Her lips were lingering over his heartbeat, slow and strong, reassuring and right. She smoothed her hands out on his chest and glanced up at him, trying to discern just how asleep he still was.

His eyes were closed, with his eyelashes just barely touching his cheeks. His mouth was just slightly open, his perfect lips just inches from her forehead. She debated moving her hand from his chest so as to touch those lips again... but even she couldn't deny her poor hand the pleasure of resting where it was.

She remembered everything they'd said to one another. She remembered David, kissing every one of her fingers, telling her he needed her, expressing how he felt about her beyond the work. She let out a small sigh at the magnitude of all she was feeling in thinking through it all, and David moved in response. With his eyes still closed, with him still asleep, with his arms still around her, he pulled her closer, and put his nose to her hair, breathing her in.

Mmm... yes, yes, yes.

What was good for the gander was surely good for the goose, so around the pounding of her heart, she closed her eyes and breathed him in as well, stretching up to his neck, taking in all of him.

She had no idea how men, stuck on an airplane for this long, were supposed to smell... but heaven help her, she concluded that the world would be a glorious place if they all smelled like David Connor.

"Cammie?"

Her lips were on his neck. And it was long past the point of blaming her lack of inhibitions on her drug use. (Though it had worked as a great excuse earlier when she'd been coherent enough to store in her heart every word he had said. All those lovely, wonderful, amazing words...)

Her mind raced for a moment, grasping for an excuse. There were none. So, she simply smiled and said, "Good morning. Or afternoon. Or whatever. I have no idea where or when we are."

"Somewhere, sometime," he murmured, watching her face for a long moment, wonder in his eyes.

They simply stared at each other.

"Are you --," he asked, just as she asked, "Are we --"

Silence again.

"Go ahead," he prompted.

"Oh," she said, swallowing. "I was just going to ask..." Her mind was drawing a complete blank, especially as David tilted his head to one side and watched her for a long moment.

"Going to ask what, Cammie?," he asked softly.

Cammie. She loved that name. She loved hearing him say that name.

"Uh, yeah," she mumbled. "Are we anywhere close?"

He nodded, looking at his watch. "About three hours out probably," he said.

And he continued watching her, curiosity in his eyes. She would've loved to ask him what he was thinking...

"What?," he asked again, his voice barely a whisper.

Pull it together, Camille. He has enough to think about without you acting on all of these feelings that...

"I was just wondering," she said, "what the plan is once we get there."

He took a quick breath. "They'll have someone pick us up and take us straight to the convention center. Have to wear our fancy, Kait-approved clothes," and at this, he grimaced, "then on to makeup and hair and all of that."

"Fancy," she smiled.

"And they'll have us say a few things before the dinner meeting. Just the Texas convention leaders at that one. We'll do the presentation we put together."

"And then?," she asked.

"The big time," he said softly. "I'll be up there preaching for the general assembly. And my family, I'm quite sure."

"And me," she said. "I'll be sitting on the front row, cheering you on."

"I'll just watch you, then," he smiled. "Pretend we're back in Namibia and that this is no different than what I'm really called to do."

"Your biggest fan, right here," she said, blushing only after she'd said it, surprised to hear herself offer so much.

David said nothing for a long moment. "I have a movie on my laptop," he murmured, pulling it out from the seat in front of him. "Wanna watch with me? It'll make the time go by more quickly."

Well. That was that.

She nodded, a little deflated by all that he hadn't affirmed, all that he hadn't confessed, all that he'd left unsaid...

... but not unexpressed, she marveled, as he murmured "come here," pulled her back into his arms, and kissed her softly on the forehead, even as she took the earbud he offered her and slipped her arms around his waist.

David

Best. Trip. Ever.

He was certain that he would never go anywhere ever again without Camille Evans.

All that he'd doubted before about what she could possibly feel seemed to vanish moment by moment as they crossed the globe, as she pulled herself closer to him, as she reached for his hand, and as she looked up at him with wonder.

She'd been looking at him like that for a long while, but he'd never let himself think it could mean anything. Not really.

Not until that flight, of course. And all that she'd said and clearly meant, as evidenced by the way she'd sat with him and held him close, as if she had no intention of ever going anywhere without him ever again.

Bolstered by her proximity and all the clear signals she'd been giving on the long flight, he finally went with it and took the lead.

Pulling her under his arm through passport control, whispering down into her ear when he needed to ask her which bag was hers at the luggage carousel, holding her hand as they waited for the convention people out by the curb, and touching her bare shoulder just a little longer than necessary as she'd scooted next to him on the crowded seat in the van.

She'd responded to every move he made with encouraging eyes, full of hope and affection, as she looked up at him.

Seriously. Best. Trip. Ever.

They'd regretfully been forced to part ways once they got to the huge convention center. She'd looked back and given him a sad wave as a woman took her off for hair and makeup and to change, as a man did the same for him. He'd spent every minute of that time rushing himself and rushing those around him, until they led him to a makeshift green room set up right behind the ballroom where the Texas convention would be eating in another thirty minutes.

Every minute without her was a strange new kind of torture now that he knew she felt something, too. He paced and kept looking towards the door, which mercifully and finally opened.

And there she was. In a Herero dress. Complete with the giant hat and everything.

"I look ridiculous," she said very simply, a murderous glare in her eyes that was likely meant especially for Kait.

"You look beautiful," he said diplomatically, having learned more than a few things living with nothing but sisters.

That, and he really meant it. Even in the outrageous getup, she was beautiful.

She frowned at this. "She let you wear something normal," she groaned.

"Well, it's a linen tunic," he said, looking down at the bold prints. "Not really even Namibian, I don't think. But it matches your dress, which is *totally* Namibian. For the past two hundred years. And for only a small subset of the population."

"Our students don't dress like this," she said, a little whine in her voice. "I've got a corset on under this. Victorian era, David. Why do the Herero women put up with this?"

He was trying to keep from imagining this when she pointed at his pants.

"Cargo pants," she said. "And flip flops. Why, Kait, why?"

"I know," he said. "I look good. Except I don't get a fancy hat like you."

"I don't think white girls are supposed to wear these," she said, looking at her hair critically in the mirror set up for them. "I mean, I don't have enough hair to support this. My neck is hurting already. Is there some way to adjust this so I don't fall over halfway through the presentation?"

"Here," he offered, stepping up behind her, "let me help."

"Because you know so much about women's hair," she muttered.

"Two sisters," he reminded her. "I actually know what a bobby pin is."

"Good," she said, "then just take them out altogether. I'll leave the hat behind. I'm sorry, Kait, but I can't do it."

He smiled at this, removing it carefully, then gently loosening more and more of her hair as he took out one pin after another.

Lock after lock tumbled down, one curl after another, David's fingers pulling them loose with tenderness and careful attention, even as he thought of every youth trip they'd ever taken, where he would lean forward to the seat where she was sitting with his sisters, where she'd turn to face him, where her hair would brush against his hand. He thought of every camping trip in Namibia, where he'd put the truck into four wheel drive, lean his arm over the seat and look backwards, his hand always brushing against her hair from where she sat, hiding her eyes so that she wouldn't have to witness them backing off into a giant hole or something equally catastrophic.

So many amazing memories. All in this woman, right here. All with them together.

"Hey," she said, bringing his attention back to her eyes even as he worked on smoothing out her hair and she looked at the two of them in the mirror. "David?"

"Yeah?," he asked softly, just as he finished pulling down the last curl.

"I think Kait was right," she breathed. "About the outfits, at least. Look at us. We look good together."

And he stopped what he was doing and watched their reflection. With complete confidence, finally, he slipped his arms around her, leaning his chin on her shoulder, just as she pulled his arms around her, leaning her head against his.

And there was wonderful freedom in this, in finally just letting it happen. She relaxed in his arms, and he pulled her closer.

"This okay?," he murmured.

"Yeah," she breathed. "I remember what you said on the plane, David."

He watched her cautiously, thinking of all that he'd said, feeling like he could be more to her than who he was. "I meant it."

She sighed, glancing up at him nervously, even as she pulled his arms tighter around her. "I don't normally let myself get involved with anyone," she said.

"Never the right guy," he murmured.

"No. Never," she said softly. "And if I let myself... if we... well, this will be serious, David."

"It already is, Cammie," he whispered, continuing to hold her.

Cammie

She let herself enjoy him.

Being held, being touched, being close like this, to David who she'd known all of her life, who she was only just now discovering, as he kissed her cheek, brushed his face against hers softly, even as she closed her eyes and let herself memorize every detail.

And while there was something deep and intimate about holding one another, there was something very pure and rare in it, in knowing that they knew the best part of one another, a oneness in Christ, in mission, in feeling this way.

What a gift, on top of so many others.

So, with her heart pounding, she let him turn her around and felt her heart rejoice as he finally leaned in and kissed her. Nothing about it, about putting her hands slowly into his hair, opening her mouth beneath his, and allowing him to pull her closer, felt unnatural, unusual, strange. Everything about sharing this moment with him felt right, good, inevitable. And as he smiled and murmured "Cammie" in between kisses, she had a brief flash of who he'd been all those years ago, when she never would have imagined that she'd be in love with him now.

David Connor. So right. Right now. Forever.

She would have stayed there the rest of the night, honestly, being held, expecting nothing more, reveling in just this, agreeing silently with him, through lips and hands, mouths and fingertips, that they were more than they'd been.

And his smile. She could feel him smiling. She'd been too overcome at first to do much but breathe, just breathe, but only a few kisses in, his smiles were so insistent and familiar that she found herself smiling under his lips as well, murmuring, "David Paul Connor..."

"David Paul Connor! Yeah! You! With the goofy headset! We're looking for David Paul Connor!"

They broke away fractionally at the sound of the loud voices wafting in their way from just outside the green room.

"Charity," she whispered to him, still smiling at the twinkle in his eyes as he stared back at her.

And then, another voice piped up.

"Seriously, no one here has any idea what's going on. This is a logistical nightmare. Way to look professional, Texas."

"And Hope," David whispered back, putting his hand to her face, sighing, looking at her with unabashed adoration.

He leaned in and kissed her one last time, even as his sisters' voices carried on, just as loud as they had been in Cammie's memories.

Without needing to explain it or make apologies, she and David let go of one another at the same time and turned to face the door, just as it sprung open to the Connor family.

Cammie recognized each twin instantly.

"David!," Charity shrieked, running towards him, which was quite the feat, given how advanced her pregnancy obviously was. The curvy, mature shape she'd carried so well in high school had naturally, beautifully changed to this – motherhood. Happy, healthy motherhood, where every curve and dip had a purpose as evidenced by the way she carried herself now and the little boy her sister carried for her.

Hope looked very nearly the way she had ten years earlier. Entirely different from her twin, slim and fit, with David's height and her mother's smile, even as she hugged her nephew while she smiled over at Charity, who was laughing in their brother's arms.

She was followed by her mother, Phoebe, a woman who had always seemed regal and well refined to Cammie... and now seemed older, tired. Her eyes didn't even drift Cammie's way as she looked at her son, sighing and pulling a tissue out of her purse.

And then, there was Paul Connor.

He saw Cammie instantly... and smiled.

"Cammie Evans," he said. "Glory be."

And before he could elaborate on what exactly he meant by this, Charity and Hope both turned to her and gasped.

"Cammie!," Charity exclaimed, moving to her now. "We heard! Well, we saw... the magazine. The article about you. My word! Of all the people in the world --"

"You and David, in the same place," Hope said, crossing the distance between them, hugging her old friend. "You look great, by the way."

"But that dress is doing nothing for you," Charity piped up, coming over to embrace her as well, a wink in her eye.

The past. Forgiven and forgotten. Or close to it.

"It is a rather unfortunate choice," Phoebe murmured. "But you look lovely, Cammie. A little flushed maybe, but --"

"All for show," Cammie managed, her cheeks blushed even more, as she went to patting Charity on the back. "The dress. The makeup. They did it to David, too."

"And he has lipstick on his face," Phoebe muttered, finally pulling out that tissue, licking it, and attempting to wipe David's mouth for him.

"Mom, please," he blushed, embracing her to avoid the tissue.

"They put makeup on your father for the convention presentations, too," she said, rubbing his back. "But he draws the line at lipstick. You should tell them that you do, too."

"Most definitely," Charity said. "And it's a bad color on you anyway. Looks like they put the same color on Cammie. Glory! Who have they got doing makeup around here?!"

Cammie blushed and looked from one Connor woman to the next, wondering if they were seeing the covert glances David was sending her way as he attempted to wipe her lipstick from his lips.

But they were oblivious. Thankfully.

Paul Connor? Wasn't, given the way he kept grinning... and raised his eyebrows at his son with an affirming head nod and a glance back over at Cammie.

Discerning. So discerning. And unnerving.

"Well," she managed, hearing the shrill edge to her voice, not for what she felt for David but for it all coming out right here and right now before the meeting even really got started, "I'll leave you all to catch up before we've got to leave for the dinner."

David opened his mouth to protest, actually stepping closer to her, but Charity spoke before he could.

"Mercy, no, Cammie," she said. "You're with the family tonight. Giving your presentation alongside David. Then joining us at our table. Just another Connor."

At this, Hope laughed loudly. Inappropriately, actually, given that no one else knew why she was laughing.

"Goodness, Hope," Phoebe murmured. "What?"

"Just remembering that time Cammie went on vacation with us. That big lodge thing. You know, with the water park inside?"

Cammie remembered it. They'd spend all day in the pool and half the night. She'd leave the room she was sharing with the twins, already dressed in her swimsuit, and head down to breakfast. It never failed -- David was always there, every morning, where they'd sit together and eat themselves full then head to the pool. They were the only ones there for at least an hour before the rest of the resort showed up, and they'd take turns doing flips off the diving board and racing one another back and forth up and through all the stairs.

She'd acted *his* age on those mornings, suddenly maturing and ignoring him as soon as his sisters arrived.

But it had been fun. She'd remembered that.

"I remember that," Charity grinned. "And Cammie's wristband. They didn't even ask. Thought the three of us were sisters. Cammie Connor. You were one of us for a week."

"In spirit and in name," Hope affirmed, grinning even brighter. "Cammie Connor."

"Cammie Connor," Phoebe smiled softly, remembering.

"Cammie Connor," Paul laughed, looking over at his son.

But David was watching her, not even aware of the appraising scrutiny of his father. "Cammie Connor," he breathed.

"That's me," Cammie managed. "Well... it was me. For a week."

"And it will be again," Hope said.

"Pardon?," Cammie asked, her pulse racing as she was certain that everyone was staring now and could tell what she was thinking. Being in David's arms, running her hands up his chest, telling him, very sincerely, as he smiled down at her, "I take you, David Paul Connor..."

250

"Tonight," Charity said. "Come and have dinner with us. One of the Connor family."

She took a breath, glancing over at David, releasing it when he nodded.

"We need to be heading that way," Phoebe said, already turning and heading out, putting her arm through Paul's as he led them away with Hope and Charity following him.

And David reached out and squeezed her hand in his for just a brief moment as they followed as well.

David

The presentation went well.

David could imagine poor Piet holding his bleeding ears half a world away as Camille used her very poor Afrikaans to make the jokes they'd planned out.

"Buy a donkey, David, for that great introduction," she'd said as he told the big room full of Texans just exactly how Cammie had found her way to Namibia, after zigzagging her way through continents.

"What kind of donkey should I buy?," he asked. "They have a wide range of them in Namibia."

"Ha, ha, ha," she'd deadpanned, then laughed, her real laugh. "No, you see, that's Afrikaans. Baie dankie. It means thank you. Ladies and gentlemen, David here is fluent after three years, after building a youth ministry from the ground up, and after being the board's representative to Namibia."

"And it won't end there," he said. "They've got us on a plane going back tomorrow, right?"

"Before we can even get adjusted to the time difference," she said, grinning.

They'd gone on to be serious, to take turns telling stories about their students, about the church they'd established, and about what the future looked like in Namibia.

David had been glad to see the interest there, letting his eyes roam right past his family's table, trying to focus on what he was here to do. *Share about Namibia. You're more than Paul Connor's son. God has led you to this place right now to bring Him glory.*

He knew that. He knew it fundamentally because he knew that about God. He knew it even though things were difficult right now because Cammie had prayed it over him, even as she'd helped pin the microphone on him.

She was so cute, grinning and entertaining the audience, charming them even as she gave them a true picture of what life was like on the mission field. As David watched the crowd, he thought about how right Kait had been. The Texas delegation was eating this up -- the attractive, young couple talking about Africa.

They concluded their presentation just as Paul Connor stood to say a few words himself.

Of course.

This was why they were here. Show the happy people, the very important happy people, how wonderful Paul Connor is, how he's got the whole world in his hands practically, and how he can lead the convention.

"Well, glory, y'all," Paul said, taking the handheld microphone at the front of the room while looking over at his son. "I feel like we've all just taken ourselves a little trip to Africa, don't you?"

His words were followed by applause, a few amens, and many appreciative looks and smiles. David smiled back, having played this game his whole life, standing next to the man in charge, knowing how to look good in front of an audience.

So did his sisters, he noted, as he looked out to see them doing the very same thing at the family table.

Growing up had not spared them from this.

They would be doing this for the rest of their lives. Or the rest of Paul's life. But even then, there would likely be libraries dedicated in his name, seminary buildings to hang his portrait, and New Life-Dallas to include him in their list of saints of the faith.

Even death would not be able to keep a hold on Paul Connor and his legacy.

Paul seemed to know it, even as he beamed at the audience, watching them hang on every word he uttered.

"David here," he said, with his hand on his son's shoulder, "is my only son. If you didn't know that."

Miraculously enough, there were a few gathered who didn't know it, as evidenced by the gasps and murmurs that followed.

"And I tell you," he said, great severity on his face, "that it is a sacrifice of the highest order, that God has ever called his mama and me to make, to relinquish him over to the Lord, for His purposes overseas."

Oh, glory. Paul Connor was making David's call to the mission field his own personal cross to bear. Or his sacrifice to the Lord. Take your pick.

David barely refrained from saying, "Wow, Dad," right out loud.

"But we do it," Paul said adamantly, continuing to take it just as far as he could, "as unto the Lord. And He's glorified through it. And I believe that He has even bigger things for my son. As he's been faithful in these things, God's just gonna lead him on to bigger things."

David knew just exactly what his father was thinking, easily guessing what "bigger things" Paul had in mind.

"And this sweet gal here," Paul said, looking over at Cammie.

David could only imagine how the term "gal" had Cammie cringing even as she did a great job of keeping a smile plastered on her face.

"I've known her since she was knee-high to a grasshopper," he said, grinning. "Her daddy was a deacon, and her mama was a Sunday school teacher. And little Cammie here was always with them, learning about Jesus right alongside them. Then, she met our family and grew up with my own children. I baptized her myself. And all these years later, it feels like Cammie is part of the family. Like she's my own daughter. Like this gal is going to give birth to my grandchildren some day. Right, David?"

Oh, mercy.

David didn't even chance a glance over at Cammie, certain that she was blushing, remembering all that had gone on in the green room.

"So, you'll excuse me," Paul said, affecting great emotion here, "if I get a little choked up hearing about the great purposes of God.

Because He makes it personal, doesn't He? He calls us, He equips us, and He makes of us the workers He sends out into the field. And I'm proud." Here, he slapped David on the back again. "I'm so proud that my son is part of God's great work."

And with that, mercifully, Paul bowed his head to pray, saving them all from standing here any longer and playing the game.

Cammie

They had dinner with the family, where Charity and Hope talked over Charity's husband, John, their two children, and everyone in a five mile vicinity. Paul Connor had to keep checking his phone with updates from the other conventions and preparations for the big event, and Phoebe had to keep turning in her seat whenever yet another person would come by to discuss the ladies' events they had scheduled for the next day, hardly touching a single bite on her plate.

Cammie didn't notice half of what went on, though, as she nodded absently at the twins' ongoing dialogue, sitting quietly next to David, a fork in one hand and her other hand in his underneath the table. They exchanged no words, of course, but his fingers would slide through hers slowly and deliberately, his thumb would rub her palm comfortingly, and he'd squeeze her hand in his, barely refraining from lifting it into sight and up to his lips as he did so.

No words, but David had said plenty.

After dinner, they headed out to get ready for the big assembly and were intercepted by someone from the board not five steps outside of the ballroom. They were swept away again to go downstairs for another hour without a chance to say a private word to one another, to talk about what had happened, or to define much of anything.

Not that it needed to be defined. Cammie already knew what this was.

Love. Head over heels, happily ever after love.

"Let's get out of here," he whispered, just as soon as they were done with the board representative, and she'd hurried with him onto the elevator.

He didn't waste any time.

"So," he leaned down and whispered in her ear, just as soon as the doors shut. She burrowed in closer to him, her head tucked down enough on his chest to hide her smile. "How did I do?"

She thought of how he'd carried himself with his father during that awful speech Paul had made, how he'd been diplomatic with the board representative, how he'd said the right things, offering just enough insight without agreeing to anything, and being, above all, so Christ-like in everything he'd done.

She loved him even more for it.

"You did great," she said, looking up at him, delighted by the light in his eyes as he watched her. "You didn't go off on your father or anyone else for that matter, which is nothing short of a miracle. You did just what you should have done."

"I wasn't talking about that, Cammie," he said softly. "There's a whole lifetime of that ahead of me. Enough time to worry about that later."

"What were you talking about, then?," she asked.

"The kiss," he said, smiling at her, whispering this.

And again, she felt warmth flood her. Excitement, too, as she became acutely aware of his hands at her waist, his arms pulling her closer.

David Connor. Who knew?

"Kisses," she grinned back, whispering as well, even as she kissed his jawline softly. "Plural."

"Yeah. First time I've ever kissed anyone," he said, falling back into that familiar, amazing drawl, returning her kiss with one to her lips. "Wanted to make sure I did okay."

"You did great," she said, blushing, kissing him again and again. "Really great."

"And this," he said, looking at her. "You and me?"

"Wonderful," she said, staring up at him. "Exciting."

"Exciting," he said, a laugh in his voice... then silence. "You deserve exciting."

"I think everything about you is going to be exciting for a long, long while, David," she said. "I mean, if that's what you were.... well, intending..."

He hadn't made any promises. She was assuming too much. Too eager, Cammie, too ready for this to be it, forever and ever, a happily ever after.

He put his hand to her face, looking down at her. "I was intending forever."

Oh, the very thought. Amazing.

He was just as eager as she was. And just as certain.

"I'm going to be happy with you," she said softly, rising up on her toes to kiss him again. "Happier than I thought I could be."

"Mmm," he murmured, bringing her even closer, kissing her again.

Before things could get too involved, the door to the elevator opened.

And Hope, after a short moment of looking at the two of them, wrapped in one another's arms, stepped onto the elevator.

"Forgot my jacket in the room," she said. "You two going upstairs?"

"Not together," Cammie said, a little embarrassed to have been caught like this.

"I didn't think that," Hope said, pushing a button. She looked at her brother. "David Paul, you have lipstick everywhere." She glanced over at Cammie. "Just how much lipstick did you put on this afternoon?"

"A lot. Stage lights," Cammie murmured, blushing. "That's what they said to do."

"Did they tell you to blot it out on David's body? Like you obviously have been?" Hope pointed at several spots on his face, his chin, his neck...

Oh, good grief.

"Uh... I should probably get it cleaned off," David said softly, entirely missing the looks exchanged between the two women.

"Are you on the twelfth floor?," Hope asked him calmly, finally looking back to the numbered panel.

"Yeah."

"Not me, I'm on the fourteenth," she said. "How about you, Cammie?"

"Fourteenth as well," Cammie answered.

"Okay," Hope said, just as the elevator stopped. "Here you go, David. Twelfth floor. We'll meet you downstairs."

And David gave Cammie a helpless look as his sister held the doors open for him. She nodded to him encouragingly, and with a sad wave, David slipped out.

Once the doors were shut, Hope turned to Cammie.

She expected shock. Disgust. Irritation.

But Hope was, in fine Hope form, doling out the unexpected. Like always.

"Bless your heart, Cammie," she said, a detached look of nonchalance on her face. "How weird is all of this, right?"

Well, yes.

"Weird and wonderful," Cammie acknowledged.

"You were kissing my brother," Hope clarified. "And you were really enjoying it. A lot. I mean, it looked like that. Am I right?"

Cammie simply nodded, her hand to her lips, her cheeks blushed.

"Well, then." Hope nodded. "Weird."

"Yes."

"Very, very weird." She looked back at Cammie again. "But he's happy, huh?"

Cammie thought about David in Namibia, doing what he was called to do, where he was called to do it.

He was happy with who he was in Christ, even before her, even without her in the picture.

How much happier would he be now?

259

"Yes," she said softly. "He's happy."

Hope nodded. "That's got to be good for his work back in Namibia. Being happy like that. With you there, he probably has no reason to ever come back and let Dad talk him into anything."

Paul Connor talking him into anything... this was news. Sure, there'd been the talk about how Paul didn't want him on the mission field, as David had shared with the students, but what did Hope mean?

"Talk him into anything?," she asked. "What is he trying to talk him into?"

Hope shrugged. "New Life-Dallas. He offered David the student ministry position."

Cammie very nearly gasped at the thought. It was likely the most high profile job in his field, the biggest calling in his area of ministry... and David hadn't gone for it.

"Wow," she murmured.

"I, for one, am glad that David turned him down," Hope said. "I'd love it if he was back here, but something happens to him around Dad. He's just not the man I know he is. It's almost like he gets eclipsed by Paul Connor." She took a breath. "Like we all do," she muttered.

"Are you okay, Hope?," Camille asked, concern in her voice. Concern for David, concern for Hope, concern for them all.

"I will be," Hope managed dismissively. Then, looking Cammie into the eyes very sincerely, "And you and David... well, I'm glad for it. Because he needs someone who believes in him. Someone who thinks he can do anything." She stood silent for a long minute. "Do you think that about him?"

And Cammie thought of all that she'd seen Christ do through David, and she said, very simply, "I do."

Hope smiled. "Well, then. Good for David. And good for you, Cammie."

David

He'd gone back to the room and changed into a suit... after reluctantly wiping the rest of that lipstick off.

For all that wasn't right here in this place, things were all right indeed. Cammie, in his arms, talking about forever...

Once he was back downstairs, he made his way backstage, notes in hand and ready, hoping to find Cammie already there as well, waiting to sit with him before he was called to the pulpit.

That was when he ran into his father.

His father and a couple he didn't recognize.

"David," Paul said, grinning, clearly up to something. The very name *David* and his sudden appearance had the couple standing taller. They were his own parents' age. Convention people, likely. People he needed to impress for his father's benefit.

"Hey, Dad," he said, pasting on a smile, looking to his father for an introduction, counting down the minutes until he could stop playing this game...

"David, this is Daniel Boyd, Sara Boyd," he said. "I believe they're the missionaries you replaced."

And like that, Paul Connor changed the game.

David hadn't replaced anyone. Not like that. Or at least he hadn't thought so. He knew now that they'd been forced out, of course, but he hadn't known when he took the job.

Besides, they hadn't been forced out to create a spot for him. He'd just been another part of a plan. A plan he knew nothing about.

But what had they been told about it all since? Were they playing Paul Connor's game, too?

Everyone wanted something. Paul, Kait, the board, the convention... could David trust anyone anymore?

"Mr. Boyd, Mrs. Boyd," he said, a moment too late, holding his hand out to them as they studied him... him with intense scrutiny, her with tentative warmth.

"Hello, David," Daniel Boyd said. "We heard your presentation earlier. Buy a donkey. Always the big joke."

"Yeah," David said softly. "That was Piet's idea."

"You know Piet?," Sara said softly. "Is he well?"

"Uh, yeah," David murmured. "Just got married, actually."

"To Kait?," Daniel asked, frowning.

Well, their heartfelt sentiments on Kait matched up, at least.

"Of course, to Kait," Sara said. "We've been out of touch with Ana Marie for the past few weeks with her traveling, but we do keep up most of the time."

"She didn't tell us much about you, though," Daniel said. "Likely thought it would be..."

"Difficult," Sara finished for him. And from the looks on their faces, it was difficult.

He couldn't imagine.

"Thank you," Sara said, "for sending those Christmas ornaments to us."

"That was Cammie," he said. "But I'll let her know that you got them."

"Hey, David," Paul said, putting his hand on his shoulder, cutting through the chitchat, like usual, "just wanted you to hear from Daniel here what happened. What the board did. Because I don't think your friends let you know the whole story."

David prepared himself, even as Sara looked at him sympathetically and Daniel frowned further.

"We were forced out," he said. "The board was done with Namibia. We thought we were secure, but it changed. And it can change again."

It could. It very well could. David knew this. But his security wasn't in a place, was it? Or even his job, right?

Except it all seemed that way, given all that he'd just learned about why he'd been sent to begin with and what it meant for the rest of his life.

Always linked up to Paul Connor.

"Well, I appreciate the advice," David said, knowing that it hadn't really been advice. Just a warning.

"And we appreciate you," Sara said, genuinely. "Your stories about that church in Swakopmund, all those young people. It means something to us. If we can't be there ourselves... knowing that the work is still going on there means so much to us."

David nodded, wanting to say many other things to them, but Paul gave them their goodbyes and moved away before he could.

"So, I take it you were surprised to be brought out here," he said to his son as they walked away. "Quick trip to the States and all."

"You could say that," David told him. "But I don't guess you were surprised."

Paul shook his head, grinning. Of course, he hadn't been surprised. He likely had orchestrated the great majority of this whole fiasco himself.

"No, the election committee talked to me about it a long time ago. Kept it a surprise for your mother and sisters, though. I only told them last week, about the time you probably found out as well. Wanted you to be their belated Christmas gift."

"Yeah, well," David said, thinking of Kait and Piet, not telling him much of anything for three years. "We were all surprised then. Except for you."

"Wondered when you'd figure it out," Paul noted.

And David glanced at him warily, just as they stepped into the green room. "And by that you mean what?"

"They tricked you," Paul said, looking at his son straight on. "Tricked you into going there, not because of what you could do, but because of the publicity they could generate. I was irritated by it at first, but I was also impressed with their shrewdness, quite honestly. That's why I gave it my big thumbs up once I figured out what was going on."

David didn't miss this mention. Paul had known all along. Of course, he had. Was there anything he didn't know?

"That wasn't all of it, Dad," David said, aware that it was a whole lot of it. "It wasn't just you. That wasn't the whole reason they brought me out there. And it has nothing to do with what's happened since I've been there."

"Maybe not," Paul conceded. "And it didn't turn out all bad, did it?" He grinned knowingly. "Cammie Evans. Wish I had been behind that missionary appointment so I could get the credit for doing something very, very nice for you."

"Don't talk about Cammie," David said, clear warning in his voice.

"Didn't say anything bad," Paul laughed. "If I could've picked a girl for you, it would've been that girl. Would've tried to talk her into you myself, but you seemed to be able to handle that all on your own. Of course, if she can't handle being the first lady when you take on the pastorate at New Life, we can find a better --"

"Don't, Dad!," David finally yelled at him. Yelled. At the biggest man in the convention. At the man who'd led him to Christ. At the man who'd taught him everything he knew about God. At the man who'd laid all the spiritual foundations in his life.

What if Paul Connor had been wrong? He was wrong in what he was doing now. Could he have been wrong before, in vastly more important things?

David's faith was his own. It had always been his own. Even handed down and delivered by a man who didn't get it right, didn't always do it right... it was still truth. And David's faith was his own.

And it wouldn't be ripped apart tonight, not by Paul Connor. Not by colleagues half a world away. Not by New Life-Dallas.

David would survive this.

"Well, mercy, David Paul," his father sighed. "I didn't mean to upset you. Cammie is a closed subject. Got it."

"Everything is a closed subject now," David said. "I'm doing what's right for me. And you've got to stop trying to change my mind."

265

"You'd be so great at New Life-Dallas," Paul said again.

"Dad," he said to him, "you only want me to follow you there so that you can continue to control everything, even after you've moved on!"

"How would I be controlling anything?," Paul asked. "You'd be in charge. Your own ministry now. The whole church later. You'd be in charge."

"As in charge as I've been my whole life," David said. "I had to go all the way around the world to get out from under your thumb, and you tried to keep me from that. You're still trying to keep me from that."

"David, that's not how it is," Paul said, correcting him even now.

"It is," David swore. "My calling is not like yours, Dad, but it's still a calling. And my work doesn't look anything like yours, but that doesn't mean it isn't worth something."

"Worth plenty," Paul shrugged. "But you could do more."

His whole life had been like this. Hearing that he didn't measure up to what Paul Connor thought was enough. When he'd been a weird little kid without any idea who he was or where he was going, he'd been a disappointment to his father. Once he figured it out and began growing into who he was going to become, the places where he served weren't big enough. And when he left for the mission field, he'd been told his life would be a waste.

He was tired. So tired of living in this man's shadow and hearing, at every step on this road, that he wasn't enough.

"I'm just saying, David," Paul said.

He was just saying it. He'd been saying it forever.

David took a deep breath and prayed that there would be some understanding. Paul was sincere in his faith, so surely... surely, he could hear God's prompting in this, could be given some divine understanding, and could move past this. Surely he could be a voice of affirmation to David, as his father, as his spiritual mentor, and as his pastor, as he'd certainly been for all of David's life.

David prayed it so, even as he doubtfully raised his eyes.

"Dad," he said softly. "When is it going to be enough? When am I going to be enough? Doing what I'm doing? Living my life for Christ? I'm doing what you taught me to do, all those years, from the pulpit. I'm living for Him. When is it going to be enough? When is that going to be enough for you?"

Paul regarded him for only a moment before he answered him. "You were made for bigger things, David Paul. Bigger things than what you're settling for."

And it broke David just a little bit more, hearing this from his pastor, even as Paul Connor turned and walked away.

Cammie

Cammie had gotten away from Hope.

It had been tricky, but she'd done it.

She'd disappeared into her room, taking off that ridiculous dress in record time, slipping into a little black one in its place, zipping herself up, shaking her hair free, slipping on her heels, and hurrying back down the hall before Hope could even come knocking.

It wasn't that she didn't want to have a three hour long conversation with her old friend. It was that she was more interested in finding David before he went up to the pulpit. She made her way to green room, searching for her pass in her purse, grateful to find that the door was open anyway, with David in there by himself.

In there by himself and looking so broken.

Until he saw her.

"Well," he said, his eyes widening. "I like that dress much better than the last one."

"It wouldn't take much," she said, crossing the room towards him, even as he closed the distance between them.

"Oh, but I really, really like this dress," he said, his hands on it as soon as she was within reach, his lips on hers.

Only a few hours into this, and it already felt so natural, like it had been life for them all along.

"Are you ready?," she asked, breaking away from him and smoothing down his tie.

"As ready as I'm going to be," he said softly.

"I'm nervous for you," she said. "All those people."

"Tried to get them to have you up there as well," he said. "Told them you have more experience than I do --"

"I don't care," she said. "I've got nothing to prove to anyone. I know who I am."

At this, he smiled. "Wow. What happened to the fiery edicts on gender inequality in the convention? This is the place to air your grievances, Cammie. Make strides for women in ministry everywhere."

She grinned at him, thinking on how much things had changed. The importance of opinions on her accomplishments had fallen away in light of the work. The value of the perception of her gifting had diminished as she'd seen Christ work.

The need to be affirmed wasn't there like it had been, working alongside someone who valued what she did and told her, again and again, that God was honored through her life.

It was the best accountability and encouragement she'd ever known.

"It's all good, David," she said. "I'm glad to follow you as you follow Christ."

He let out a long breath. "Maybe you shouldn't follow me," he said.

What was this? More of the same, more of the insecurities? More Paul Connor?

"David," she said softly.

"I mean it," he said, running his hand across his face. "I feel like... David Connor, absolute joke."

"You aren't a joke," she said.

"I'm here because of Dad," he said. "Not because of anything I've done. Everything I do, everything that comes my way... all because of him."

She knew this better than he thought she did.

"Hope told me he tried to get you to take a position at New Life-Dallas," she said. "You turned it down."

And she thought about what it must have been like for him, being offered everything and saying no. Because he knew who he was and what he was meant to do.

He'd done the right thing, even though it hadn't been easy.

At this realization, there were tears in her eyes. "David, you turned it all down."

"You think I made a mistake," he said, sighing. "Logic screams that I did. Life would be a lot different for me now if I'd just taken it, like everyone in the world would have told me to."

"That's not it," she said, wiping at her eyes.

"Then, what is it?," he said softly. "Why are you crying?"

"Because you gave it all up," she said, thinking of all the men she'd known who had no real commitment to the mission field, who would have given up reaching the nations, who would hold back on God's clear call to them for all the acclaim and praise in the world.

It would have been his. All of it. The power, the prestige, all of it.

David had given away the world's best for God's calling on his life.

"David, you did the right thing."

"But what does it matter now?," he asked, shrugging. "I'm still just Dad's pawn. Still just part of the bargaining chips at New Life-Dallas. That's who I am."

"No, you're David Connor," she said to him fiercely, wiping away the last of her tears. "And that's enough. Enough for Christ. Enough for what's ahead." She took a breath. "Enough for me."

And she bowed her head and prayed for him, asking God to make him believe.

He was due onstage any minute now.

Cammie was a nervous wreck, remembering his face as she'd kissed him goodbye one last time, murmuring prayers in her heart as she'd turned and had to leave him.

Phoebe looked to be nervous as well, farther down the row, sitting next to Paul, who was chatting up several convention leaders who'd come to talk to him.

And Cammie, the unofficial Connor, was sitting between the twins.

They were talking. Like always.

Charity leaned over to Cammie.

"Does David have a girlfriend out there? You know, in Africa?," she hissed.

Hope looked pointedly at her sister.

"Like you're not wondering," she said. "I swear, Cammie, I wonder if he's even straight. Because there hasn't been anyone here, and --"

"What do you think, Cammie?," Hope asked, switching her gaze to her friend. "Is David turned on by women? Or one woman in particular?"

"Um," Cammie swallowed nervously. "Well, he --"

"Good night, Hope, don't put it in those terms," Charity interrupted, making a face at her sister and putting her hands on her pregnant bump protectively, as if to keep this conversation from reaching her baby's ears.

"In what terms?," Hope asked, flipping through the program.

"Turned on," Charity gagged. "This is David Paul we're talking about!"

"You just asked if he was gay, so I figured we were free to say anything --"

"I would love him either way, of course," Charity said, putting her hand on Cammie's knee. "Honest. Gay, straight, still my brother. But I think he's into girls, right? Hope, do you remember the way he looked at Cammie back when we were teenagers? And that time he got in trouble for spying on us when she was in our room changing clothes, and --"

"You two knew about that?!," Cammie sputtered. "Why didn't you tell me?!"

"Didn't find out until later," Hope murmured. "Didn't want to gross you out when there wasn't anything you could do about it anyway. And I mean, I *thought*, at least, that the very idea of David *ever* seeing you like that would have made you sick." She narrowed her eyes at Cammie. "I mean, David, wanting you like that, touching you, kissing you --"

"My word, Hope, I think I'm gonna barf," Charity interrupted. "And it's not morning sickness. It's the thought of Cammie and David together. Ugh."

"Kinda makes you physically ill," Hope murmured.

"Uh, yeah!," Charity exclaimed, snatching up Hope's program and fanning herself with it. "But there's a girl out there, Cammie." She raised her eyebrows at this.

"Out where?," Cammie asked.

"In Africa," Hope said dismissively, grabbing the program back from her sister. "I don't think he's into her, Charity."

"Well, maybe Cammie has better intel than you!," Charity shot back. Then, with a smile at Cammie, "Her name is Kait. We know that much. She worked for the board. Talked David into going there three years ago. I mean, she called him ALL. THE. TIME. So, you know..."

"Know what?," Cammie asked.

"Maybe they've got a little somethin' somethin' going on? Missionary love and all, huh?"

Cammie thought of Kait, how David had regarded her right before they left.

"Yeah, I don't think so," she said.

"Me neither," Hope sighed, closing her program with some finality. "Because I think David, assuming he's straight, would be into... oh, I don't know, someone more familiar, more like home... someone like Cammie, maybe."

Charity looked at their friend appraisingly. "Nah, that would just be too weird," she concluded.

"Weird," Hope agreed.

"Weird," Cammie murmured, just as the door opened to the stage, and David walked in right behind the leaders of the convention.

David

This is what it came down to.

David Connor. On the platform. Before the convention. A Bible in his hands.

Of all the places and situations he never would have imagined ending up, this was at the top of the list. It had never been his ambition to be here, never been his dream to stand where he was standing, and never been his goal to do this.

But life was like this sometimes, ending up somewhere you didn't plan, being given to a task that didn't seem to rightfully be yours.

Still good. There was still good in this. Because God was still good, and no matter what had been shaken today, the truth of who He was remained.

David looked down at the Bible on his lap, even as the convention man made introductions. He thought about his own faith, about how he'd found his significance in Christ and what He'd done. No matter what happened here or in Namibia, that truth remained. Even if his own father rejected him as he had done again and again, he still had significance in what Jesus had claimed and owned by His blood on the cross.

He was in Christ. And if he had nothing else ever in all the world, he had it all still, because he belonged to Jesus.

This was the truth.

This was who he was.

And it was enough.

As every eye in the room turned to him as he stood and took his place behind the pulpit, David Connor sent up a thankful prayer for this, even as he opened his Bible and opened his mouth to preach.

Cammie

He did so well.

Cammie watched from the front row as David spoke as eloquently as his father ever had, all those years that she had sat under his teaching, his leadership, and his ministry. Paul Connor had never been at a loss for words all those years, and his presence had always demanded attentiveness and responsiveness from his listeners.

David was different. Even here, as he walked through part of the book of Romans, he authoritatively spoke of the unyielding, unchanging supremacy of Christ, while still sharing the tender, faithful mercy of Jesus. He was certain and sure with his words, personable with the stories he told, and above all, sincere. So sincere as his voice caught and he swore to them all that God would use every last hardship and difficulty to display His power and His grace to even the least of these.

She knew it. Cammie knew the truth of it, but she felt it more profoundly as he spoke the words of Scripture that were written on his heart.

Cammie glanced over at his family once, the family she had known so well back in her youth, and saw that they watched him as intently as she did. His mother, wiping away tears. His sisters, smiling broadly. His father... with his fake smile in place, a thoughtful nod or two.

Paul Connor. There was so much she had never known.

She looked back to David and resolved that no one else mattered as much right now as he did. And she rightly concluded that of all the great things God could do through her and of all the great roles she could play for His purposes...

... well, all she really wanted was to help David through this.

David

It all concluded rather quickly after he left the pulpit.

There were handshakes and conversations, pictures to be taken, compliments to accept, criticisms to forget, opinions to give, plans to make, and time... time to put it behind him and go back to what he knew.

He'd done it all with Cammie right by his side.

There had only been a brief awkward moment when she came into the press room with his family, where he was already making statements and discussing issues with the convention people gathered there. His eyes had found hers, and she'd not hesitated for one second in going to him, pulling his face down to hers softly, and kissing him.

Charity exclaimed, "Oh, my stars!," and his mother gasped a bit. But it was only for a moment before Paul Connor stepped up to the men gathered there and stole the spotlight.

David was glad to let him have it, moving through the crowds with Cammie from then on, surviving the rest of this night with her.

They said their goodbyes, confirmed their early morning flight, and went out onto the terrace above the ballroom where they were finally alone again.

Neither of them said a word as they walked to the railing, hand in hand, and looked over the city, with lights stretching out as far as they could see.

Quiet and still. Even though they could hear the music and laughter going on inside, celebrating the imminent election of Paul Connor to the presidency of the convention, there was peace out there for them both.

"I loved what you said."

David closed his eyes at this, thinking of how tired he was, how spent he felt, and how he couldn't even remember half of what he'd said up there.

"Which part?"

He heard her sigh. "I liked it all," she said. "But I especially loved the part about the love of a father. The kind of love that nothing can separate us from. Ever."

David thought about it. Death, life, angels, rulers, things present, things to come, powers, height, depth, nothing in all of creation... nothing could separate him from the love of God.

"You weren't talking about earthly fathers, obviously," Cammie murmured. "Especially not yours."

He smiled and looked at her, only to find her smiling up at him.

"Obviously," he said, taking her hand and tenderly pulling her into an embrace. "I don't think anyone thought I was talking about him. Least of all him."

She put her arms around his waist and looked up at him. "It won't be fixed tonight," she said. "What he's done to you today."

He put his lips to her forehead. "Likely not."

"But I've got to believe," she said, "that one day, God is going to bring your dad around so that he sees things a little more clearly. And you're going to forgive him. Just like you're going to forgive Piet and Kait."

David raised an eyebrow at her, doubting this very much.

"Oh?," he said. "Why do you believe that?"

"Because Jesus can do miracles," she said and shrugged. "True story. I grew up hearing Paul Connor talk about it. And if we can't trust the future president of the convention, who can we trust, David?"

He smiled outright at this. "You make a compelling argument."

"See?," she said. "You're already on the road to forgiving him now, thinking of all that he taught you, all that he taught us both. He can't be entirely evil if he did that, can he?"

David pretended to think on this for a moment.

"David," she chided.

"Maybe not," he conceded. "But that's all I'm willing to say tonight."

"It's a start," she said, kissing him.

"And speaking of starts," he said.

"Yes?"

"Me, you... Namibia... what's this going to look like now?"

He knew just exactly what he wanted it to look like. Together. Always. Every day, better than the one before, heading towards a covenant, heading towards forever --

She smiled. "It's going to be just like it was."

Oh. No different than the way it had been. For a moment, his heart plummeted, until she amended --

"But different, you know."

"Different," he nodded, relief in the word.

"Because I love you, David."

She said it. Just like that. With her eyes dancing, her smile for him alone, and sincerity in every breath.

"And I love you," he breathed, leaning down to kiss her again. "Now what happens?"

"Now," she said, wrapping her arms around him, "we just go back to Namibia and live happily ever after."

... the story continues in June 2015 with Hope Connor's story, "Perfectly Pretend"...

ABOUT THE AUTHOR

Jenn Faulk is a full time mom and pastor's wife in Pasadena, Texas. She has a BA in English-Creative Writing from the University of Houston and an MA in Missiology from Southwestern Baptist Theological Seminary. She loves talking about Jesus, running marathons, listening to her daughters' stories, and serving alongside her husband in ministry. You can contact her through her blog www.jennfaulk.com

19202315R00167

Made in the USA
Middletown, DE
09 April 2015